Scattered Leaves: The Legend of Ghostkiller

Lynny Prince

Scattered Leaves
The Legend of Ghostkiller
1st in The Ghostkiller Trilogy
by Lynny Prince
www.lynnyprince.com

Copyright ©2016 Lynny Prince ALL RIGHTS RESERVED

NO PART OF THIS BOOK MAY BE REPRODUCED IN ANY FORM, BY PHOTOCOPYING OR BY ANY ELECTRONIC OR MECHANICAL MEANS, INCLUDING INFORMATION STORAGE OR RETRIEVAL SYSTEMS, WITHOUT PERMISSION IN WRITING FROM THE AUTHOR.

Due to Ms. Prince's environmental concerns, this publication does not follow the traditional protocol of chapters starting on the right-hand page to avoid paper waste.

Disclaimer: This book is a work of fiction. Certain characters, names, places, and incidents, while real, are used fictitiously utilizing the author's imagination.

Cover art by Craig Martin & Lynny Prince
Cover photo of Matthew Black Eagle Man by Marshall Photography

Revised Edition – April 2016

ISBN: 1532728085
ISBN-13: 978-1532728082

This book is dedicated to the Dakota Oyate.

ACKNOWLEDGEMENTS

For those who made this book possible:

Caske, Killing Ghost, Wabasha, John Other Day,
Mankato, Lightning Blanket, Spotted Eagle,
Big Eagle, Little Crow, Medicine Bottle, Sakope (6th Born Son)

The 38:

Caske *(His Thunder)*	Tunkasitku Ikiyena Nazin *(One Who Stands Close To His Grandfather)*	Maka Akan Inazin *(One Who Stands On The Earth)*
Tipi Hdo'Ni Ca *(Forbids His Dwelling)*	Tunka Siku Icahda Mani *(Walks with His Grandfather)*	Wakute Wiyaya Mani *(One Who Walks Prepared to Shoot)*
Ptan Duta *(Red Otter)*	Ite Duta *(Red Face)*	Tate Hmi YanYan *(Rounding Wind)*
Taoyate *(His People)*	Ka Mdeca *(Broken to Pieces)*	Wasicu *(Mixed-Blood, A Frenchman)*
Hinhanska Koyagmani *(Walks Clothed in an Owl's Tail)*	Hepi Da *(3rd Born Son)*	Hotan Inku *(Voice That Appears Coming)*
Maza Bodu *(Iron Blower)*	Mahpiya Akan Inazin *(One Who Stands On a Cloud)*	Cetan Hunku *(Elder Hawk)*
Wahpe Duta *(Red Leaf)*	Henry Milord Hanke Dakota *(Baptiste Campbell)*	Canka Hda *(Near the Woods)*
Sdodye Sni *(Meaning Unknown)*	Tate Ka Ga *(Wind Maker)*	Hda Hin Hde *(Sudden Rattle)*
Hda Ya Mani *(Tinkling Walker)*	He Inkpa *(Tip of the Horn)*	Oyate Aku *(He Brings the People)*
Hda Inyanka *(Rattling Runner)*	Nape Sni *(Fearless, One Who Does Not Flee)*	Mahuwehs *(He Comes for Me)*
Dowan Sa *(The Singer)*	Wakan Tanka *(Great Mystery)*	Little Thunder *(Wakinyan Cistinna)*
HePan *(2nd Born Son)*		Tate Hhdihoni *(Wind Comes Home)*
Sunka Ska *(White Dog)*		
Aicage *(To Grow Upon)*		

Foreword

The bright moon did little to light the black leaves as they danced their dead dance in the brisk wind. Howling as it was, their faint murmurs could still be heard:

Skittle, skittle scratch! Skittle, skittle scratch!

A lone streetlight, the single beacon of life along the dark and deserted road, blew out as the leaves scampered past. It was as if the leaves needed a shroud of darkness for their mission; and though they could do little about the moon, the street light was but a nuisance.

The Great Sioux Uprising of 1862, which took place in Mankato, Minnesota during the months of August and September, provided me the basis for this story.

On December 26th of that year, thirty-eight Dakota Sioux warriors were hanged for crimes against white settlers. The crimes were in retaliation for corrupt and questionable acts on the part of the United States government after the Dakota signed over their land. They were promised payment and provisions, both of which were more often than not late or absent altogether.

After a spring of failed crops due to bad weather conditions and their latest annuity payments from the Government several months late, the Dakota were starving to death despite bulging government food stores. Crooked traders, guilty of overcharging the Dakota, refused to issue them credit. One of the traders, Andrew Myrick, was documented as saying, "So far as I am concerned, if they are hungry let them eat grass or their own dung."

By the summer of 1862, the Dakota had had enough, and they went on a rampage that lasted forty days. The victims were not chosen at random, rather they were focused on those traders who had cheated them and their families. In the end, four hundred people died, including settlers, troops, and Dakota. (The number of dead varies according to different sources). Andrew Myrick was found dead - grass stuffed in his mouth.

The worst offenders fled to Canada leaving the remaining Dakota to bear the brunt of the punishment. Many of these Dakota actually tried to save their white friends from being killed by hiding them out from the marauding offenders.

My Ghostkiller character is based on one such man. His name was Wakinyatawa Chaske or *His Thunder*. Chaske (means *First Born Son*) saved a woman named Sarah Wakefield and her children from certain death. Despite her testimony on his behalf and a presidential pardon, Chaske lost his life.

It was reported in the Saint Paul Minnesota Press that a priest named Steven Riggs actually urged Mrs. Wakefield to say she was raped, but she refused to lie. In the basement where the thirty-eight were kept, Riggs and several others in the military knew who Chaske was, and knew he'd been pardoned, but said nothing. Riggs later sent a reply letter to an outraged Sarah Wakefield telling her there had been a "mistake" made at the last moment. She never believed that.

Chaske was hanged at the largest mass execution in United States history after he and over four hundred other Dakota reported to *Camp Release* which the government disguised as a place for peace talks.

While this story is based on historical facts, it adds a paranormal twist by telling the story of what could have been had someone stepped in to change the deadly events soon to occur. This comes in the form of a descendant of Chaske who inherits the ability to time travel.

Many amazing and unexplained things happened to me while writing this book. The spirits have sent many signs to show their approval and sent those among the living to aid me in writing this story. I am honored beyond measure to have endorsements from the descendants of Baptiste Campbell, Rattling Leaf, Medicine Bottle, Alexander Eastman, Kit Fox Society Warriors, Shirt Wearers and many others from the Dakota Oyate who fully support this book. They all feel, as I do, that the other side of the story concerning the Uprising needed to be told.

It is my hope that this book --and subsequent movie -- helps these ancestors by creating a different reality for them in the spirit world.

Perhaps one day we'll all know for certain that it did.

~Lynny Prince

Lynny Prince

1

Father Wilson O'Rourke was locking the doors to St. Paul's Catholic Church when he heard the familiar sound that had haunted him for so many years. The blustery winds of the impending fall season hummed around his ears sending a chill down his spine. *Skittle, skittle, scratch!*

Dusk was falling. He had to hurry!

He knew this fall brought the promise of another season of hell – a hell he had survived in the past by nothing else but sheer will, and of course, his faith. He wasn't entirely certain of what role the leaves played, he only knew he dreaded seeing them regardless of what time of the year it was. However, tonight was different; it was a signal, an omen, and it frightened him because he knew what it meant. IN his mind, to hear the leaves meant certain death.

As if a switch is turned on, he thought forlornly, *the leaves begin their restless search for victims!*

Clutching car keys in one hand and his Bible in the other, he hurried down the church steps and rushed to his car. The howling winds blew the hat off his head as he fumbled with the keys. The sound grew louder, closer!

Skittle, skittle, scratch, skittle, skittle, scratch!

Knowing he would not make it before they arrived, he turned back, catching his hat as it blew past his feet, and ran to the steps, scrambling up as fast as his elderly legs would carry him. Once safely inside he slammed the doors shut, dropping the Bible in his haste. He quickly slid the door lock in place, knowing deep down it would do little good if *they* decided to come in. But they wouldn't. They couldn't. The walls of the church had always provided safe refuge, but that didn't stop the fear that threatened to send him into a panic. Out of breath, he leaned his back heavily against the door.

The curse will prevail for all of eternity, a little voice said, *unless HE comes back!*

"Please," the priest whispered in desperation, "please come back!"

He leaned over to retrieve the Bible that lay open on the floor, and a line from The Acts of the Apostles almost screamed at him from the open page:

Suddenly there came a sound from Heaven as of a rushing, mighty wind, and it filled all the house where they were sitting...

He stared at the words and thought about the correlation between scripture, what he had seen in Indian ceremonies. He could go back hundred and fifty-three years and see similarities, yet the church always frowned upon anything that did not resonate with the doctrine. Father O'Rourke snatched up the Bible as thunder rumbled the rafters of the church. This *thing* outside, was this the wrath of God?

Of course not, a little voice told him, *this is of the devil!*

The old church groaned in protest as Indian summer winds roared outside, and Father O'Rourke wondered if the old part of the building might finally sacrifice itself to the weather it had survived for over two hundred years. In 1862, the basement housed prisoners before they were executed, and Father O'Rourke always felt uneasy when in the sanctuary alone. Tonight was no exception.

Rushing to a window, he looked out anxiously and glimpsed a cluster of leaves swirling under a street light. He felt his heart catch in his throat as he watched the leaves dance, thinking how odd it was to see a dust devil at night, but then considered maybe he had just never noticed before. Swallowing hard, he realized there must be dust devils at night, just as he knew the devil himself was lurking in the leaves that blew around.

He gave pause to contemplate his nemesis: These were the same leaves children played in, the same leaves countless homeowners tried to contain with rakes or the mundane drone of a leaf blower. The unfortunate ones were taken by garbage bags to the landfill, but those that survived were free to wage their war of hell on the unsuspecting.

They go along with the effort of the humans, then gleefully go out and kill the neighbors while we all sleep, he thought.

At that moment, he imagined they were individual, living entities who enjoyed their role, and he could almost hear the laughter of the wicked dead things as he watched them swirling under the street light.

Their beautiful colors and earthy smells are a front, he thought, *a cruel joke from God!*

In his momentary lapse of reason, he could almost hear the leafy veins exhaling a macabre sigh as the dust devil released them and they drifted to the ground.

The facts of Father O'Rourke's self-described hell went against everything he believed in and, in fact, reeked of nothing but wickedness. The circumstances dealt with the supernatural, things that were evil and foreign to his beliefs. He struggled with it every day, that maddening knowledge of what it meant to hear the *skittle scratch* sound on the pavement, knowing the leaves were on the move again. He'd tried for years to make sense of how and why they were involved, but the only thing that did make sense was something he was not prepared to accept – the Ghostkiller family legend. Despite all he knew about it, he couldn't believe it had anything to do with what he had experienced over the past fifty years since moving here. The belief that an ordinary Indian boy was the town's only salvation to annihilate a curse was just too farfetched. For one thing, only priests of the highest order were trained in the Catholic rituals that called upon the Holy Spirit, and the church did not teach its parishioners how to call on the spirits themselves. So how could an ordinary Indian boy have the same power if it weren't rooted in some sort of evil?

But ye shall receive power, after that the Holy Ghost has come upon you...

He shook the scripture from his mind, but as he stood at the window watching dusk slip away into the black of night, he tried once again to reason it out in his mind.

He had heard the legend and every variation under the sun over the years, but still there was no easy explanation. Every one of the Indians who lived here believed this boy could save them and there was no changing that; nor could the facts of the gruesome murders be changed, either. There was something evil involved, but how to get rid of it was another question. An exorcism, perhaps?

The Indians won't go for that, a little voice said. *They have their own way of dealing with these things.*

"That's right," he mumbled aloud, "they have their ceremonies."

They had a ceremony for everything – even a ceremony to start ceremonies – and Father O'Rourke had been to every one of them at least once. The first time he'd attended a healing ceremony he just *knew* someone was hiding in the dark making noises and flashing lights. However, the ceremony held in the church last year could not have been rigged, because he was the one who prepared everything for it. What kind of spirits were the Indians conjuring up? Seeing large shadows in the ceremonies had reminded him of the angels who were cast out of heaven. Some claimed they were tied in with the Nephilim or giants who married human women, and the more he learned about the ceremonies, the more scripture he found that seemed eerily similar.

He thought about these things so often in made his head literally spin. He had no answer, but his gut told him it was evil. It always had. Some of the occurrences in those ceremonies defied explanation, after all, how does one explain flapping wings from unseen birds, horses galloping, buffalo snorting, and tiny lights darting around the room? They all defied explanation and scared him half to death. It didn't matter how many times he saw those things, he still felt the same way. *They were probably performed by the devil himself!*

"Evil!" he whispered hoarsely. "Pure, unadulterated evil!"

And there appeared unto them cloven tongues like as of fire, and it sat upon each of them….

What is a cloven tongue of fire…a tiny light? He shook his head, refusing to accept the parallel. No amount of scripture could change his mind. Period.

It was true, he had been privy to the Indians' ceremonies and had seen many things he could not explain, but he still refused to accept any sort of connection to scripture. Besides, this boy, the town's only supposed salvation, was an Indian, and *that* was what really made all the difference. Whether the good father wanted to admit it or not, it was the true reason he could not accept the boy's alleged powers or destined path. He scoffed at his murmur of a few moments ago begging the boy's return. He had always been taught Indians were savages, and that label still held true even in this day and age to some extent, especially when their ideas of worship came into play. It was evil through and through! *How do you know their ways are evil?* The little voice asked.

Father O'Rourke watched his breath fog the glass. He thought briefly it might obstruct the leaves' view, but he realized it didn't matter – they couldn't come into his church, his haven.

He anxiously scoured the streets but saw no signs of life. The leaves were gone, the town was dark, and the people who lived there had already turned in for the night.

They roll the sidewalks up pretty early around here, he heard a voice say. It was James Ghostkiller's voice. Father O'Rourke remembered the proud Dakota Chief who had died a little over five years ago at the ripe old age of ninety-nine. James was a spiritual man, a medicine man among his people, and was highly respected in town and throughout the reservation. He was one of but a handful of elders that hadn't drunk himself to death; he had simply died quietly in his sleep of old age. It was he who had first told O'Rourke about the curse, for it was one of James's ancestors who had been hanged after the Great Sioux Uprising and had prophesied from the gallows. James had been adamant in his storytelling, but Father O'Rourke refused to believe any of it, despite having seen the healing miracles that were the result of their ceremonies.

All was quiet except for the tree branches lining the darkened streets which moved silently against a hushed breeze. From the stillness inside the church, O'Rourke could hear them groaning softly, and the sound reminded him of an old man's arthritic bones. *My own old bones*, he thought. For the moment, there were no other sounds, no *skittle scratch*, nothing out of the ordinary. The father began to breathe a little easier. *Perhaps this year would be different*, he thought as he looked up towards the heavens. *Maybe it's not THAT year.* He saw a million stars shining down at him through the leaves, pleading for his silent prayer to project towards the heavens and make a difference.

Suddenly seeing headlights, his momentary reprieve was met with dreaded reality. He saw four silhouettes in a darkened Chrysler and could hear the loud thumping of the stereo as they cruised past the church. He was instantly afraid for the people inside the car; a faction of dead leaves was coming at them from the opposite direction. He gasped and watched in horror as the leaves scattered and crunched under the passing tires, then came together and followed the car down the road.

Father Wilson O'Rourke slumped to the floor.

2

Yellow police tape stretched around the car and most of the area surrounding Rock Road and Highway 13, known to the town as "Devil's Corner." Despite the fact the car was nose-first in a ditch, it was obvious the victims' injuries were not caused by the crash. That was the first thing Chase Riley realized once he had regained some semblance of composure.

A call for a routine traffic accident had come in shortly after 6 a.m. just after Chase started his shift. The dispatcher was no help when Chase asked him why he was sent alone to the crash site. He wasn't too keen on going onto reservation land with his boss, mostly because he couldn't get any answers from the Indians there; they didn't like outsiders, much less white outsiders. He figured it was probably just another drunk driver, so he wasn't too concerned about fishing for details from the locals. He sure as hell wasn't expecting what he found. A detective from L.A. with ten years' experience with homicide should be used to looking at death. Even *he* thought he had seen it all. The horrible murder scenes that played havoc with his mind were what prompted him to take the job in the small community of Moccasin Flats— he'd wanted to get away from all the carnage in the big city and move to a small town with little crime. No such luck.

"Who the hell did this?" Crimson was splattered across the inside of the vehicle, making the windows opaque. With his gloved hand, Chase popped the door handle and peered inside. There were four teenagers — two couples —whose throats had been cut. The cuts were jagged with erratic borders, instantly reminding Chase of a smile carved into a jack-o-lantern. He put a gloved hand over his mouth as bile rose into his throat. All the victims were smiling.

The sun was just beginning to poke its head over the horizon when Chase realized he was standing beside his car. He felt as if he had just woken from a dream and had to shake his head to loosen the cobwebs. Images of the crash site came rushing back. He turned towards the Chrysler and the crowd that had begun to form nearby. As Chase watched the sightseers and obligatory siren chasers, he wondered how long he had been standing there. The radio in the cruiser garbled that a team from the Minneapolis police department would arrive any minute. He realized then no one else had been allowed to approach the vehicle. No one had yet looked at the carnage inside. He felt apprehension crawl down his spine anew. The kids in the Chrysler were mutilated, and the most horrific thing were those smiles — hideous smiles, something out of a nightmare.

Leaning against his cruiser, he reached into his shirt pocket, extracted a pack of Marlboro reds and lit one with nervous fingers. Taking a deep drag, he raked a hand through his blond hair. *Where the hell is Mason?* He thought, forcefully blowing out the smoke. He was getting aggravated that his boss still had not arrived. Reaching into the cruiser, Chase grabbed the mic and called the station. The dispatcher assured him again Mason was on his way.

He hollered into the mic, "Well, doesn't he have his fuckin' radio on?"

"He'll be there, *detective*," Sam Thinnergan answered.

Chase gritted his teeth and hurled the mic back into the car with enough force to knock his box of powdered donuts to the floorboard.

"Perfect!" He jerked opened the door and sat sideways in the driver's seat, stretching his long legs out in front of him. "Might as well take a freakin' nap," he said sarcastically. At 6'4, he kept the seat adjusted as far back as possible — not conducive to sitting sideways in it. Frustrated, he stood again and leaned against the Crown Victoria instead.

Chase was a good looking man in his mid-thirties, with blue-grey eyes and a smooth complexion. He was muscular and worked out as often as he could, which was a lot more frequently since moving here to *Hicksville*, as he called it. He tanned easily and had always loved the sunshine in L.A. It was the only thing he missed about the place, however.

This is typical Mason, he thought as he took another drag off the cigarette. *Lonesome Dove meets Tonto!*

Mason was the kind of Police Chief who didn't always play by the book, but that was one of the reasons Chase liked him. Working with Mason was like a breath of fresh air, especially after having been subjected to the assholes in L.A. That, and the fact the job itself was so laid back, at least until this morning. He wondered if Mason had seen any other cases like this. Surely, he would have mentioned something this gruesome? He told Chase he had been involved in the Wounded Knee uprising on Pine Ridge in the early seventies, and during that time murders occurred almost every day. Chase remembered how Mason soured when recalling those days, and especially about the corruption within the BIA and FBI out there. It was common knowledge even back then and Chase had been privy to that information as his career grew, as well. He also knew that was why Mason didn't trust most white men, or *wasichu*, as Mason called them, but especially ones who wore FBI badges. Chase didn't blame him. Working in L.A. had taught him that lesson, too.

This job was wrought with drunken disorderly calls, but not much else. Mason always handled the cases involving Indians, which made up the majority, with what Chase called the *Patience of Job*. He knew it was because of the time Mason had spent at "the Knee," as he called it. It seemed being drunk was as much a part of being Indian as bloodlines, at least by Mason's description. He was sympathetic and always said a drunken Indian was better than a sober *wasichu* any day of the week. Chase took it as a joke, but he knew Mason was serious and even agreed with him to a point. Chase had seen some pretty corrupt cops and FBI agents in his day, but the whole mess of dealing with drunks was a bitter pill for him to swallow. Chase had very little patience for drunks. He was of a mind that if you didn't want to drink, you just didn't. Mason knew better. He'd said, "It's in the DNA" more times than Chase could count, whatever that meant. One night they'd picked up an old man on the side of the road who was staggering and dropped him off at what he said was his house Chase. As they drove away, Chase watched as the old guy walked out the front door and headed back towards town.

"Why don't you just throw the bastard in jail, Mason? He's only gonna go right back to that bar!"

"Because " Mason had explained, "if that's the only joy he gets out of life, I'm not takin' it away from him. Besides, *wasichus* get drunk all the time and cops let them go. I can't tell you the number of politicians I've seen drive drunk. They are escorted home with no more than a slap on the wrist and my people deserve the same. One of them *wasitchus* killed a 'skin while driving drunk and is free as a bird, barking orders from some high-ranking office in DC now. *Wasichu* bastard!"

Chase knew he wasn't going to get anywhere arguing with Mason, so instead he'd asked Mason what *wasichu* meant. He already knew the reference to "skin" Mason used meant a redskin or Native person. He had guessed *wasichu* meant white people, but Mason informed him it more specifically meant "men who take of the fat," and said so with side-splitting laughter, breaking the tension.

"Riley, you mean to tell me after all this time you never knew what it meant?" Chase didn't find it amusing, and that had made Mason laugh even harder. They had an easy friendship, kindred by their understanding of the brotherhood of police work. Their current positions placed them in a town where not much went on, so they had time to nurture their friendship. The only thing they really ever fought about was Sam Thinnergan, the dispatcher. Sam drank on the job and Mason overlooked it far too often.

Chase lit another cigarette. He was sure Mason had a good reason, but it wasn't like him to drag ass like this. Of course, he didn't know what was really going on, either. Most of the calls they got for traffic accidents ended up being drunken driving violations or someone hitting a runaway garbage can.

I sure wish he'd hurry his ass up this time, Chase thought. Just then, a familiar dark blue Ford LTD pulled into view. Squinting his eyes from the morning sun, Chase recognized his boss and Sioux Tribal Police Chief Thorn Rivers inside. The car slid to a dusty stop beside the cruiser.

Mason emerged first, planting his signature black Stetson securely on his head as he stepped from the vehicle. He wore his long, black hair in a braid that fell down his back, and Chase often joked he never took the hat off because the braid was attached to it. Once, while at a town meeting, Mason took the hat off giving Chase and the amused crowd an exaggerated bow. The braid was real.

Mason was tall and lean, in his early forties, with dark brown eyes and a scar above his left eyebrow that looked like a lightning bolt. He had told Chase he'd gotten it in a bar fight back in his drinking days. Mason had been on the wagon now for twenty years.

Thorn stood taller than Mason by a few inches. He was a cousin of Mason's, younger by a few years, and often joked he was the better looking of the two. He was lean and muscular and had a walk that reminded Chase of a panther. Thorn's family ties went back to Chief Touch the Clouds, who was a cousin of Crazy Horse. He and Mason both referred to themselves as *skins,* a term the full bloods used, but Mason had told Chase once that his great-grandmother had been white, not that it mattered. Chase noticed that Thorn's hair, usually worn long, was cut short and he remembered Mason told him the Sioux traditionally cut their hair when a relative died as a symbol of mourning.

"Whadda we got, Riley?" Mason asked as he and Thorn approached.

Chase balked. "Whadda we got Riley? Is that all you can say?" Chase ground out his cigarette with the toe of his boot and shook Thorn's hand.

"What do you want me to say?" Mason asked, slightly irritated.

"Well, you can start by telling me why it took you so goddamn long to get here."

Mason looked around quickly. "Excuse me," he said, patting himself down. "When did I die and leave you in charge?" Feigning panic he thrust his wrist out towards Thorn. "Quick take my pulse — I must be dead!"

Thorn took a step back and held up his hands in surrender, stifling a chuckle. "It's all you, Chief, I ain't touchin' no corpse."

"Ha, ha, very funny," Chase said.

"Look, we got held up, okay?" Mason said. "Now just cool your jets and tell me what's going on."

Mason had to lighten up the situation somehow because he knew damn well what was in that car sitting in the ditch. Chase took a deep breath, willing himself to stay calm.

"I've never seen anything like this before, Mason!" Chase lit another cigarette, taking a deep drag and blowing the smoke out nervously.

"There are four kids in that car down there with their throats hacked up like a fuckin' jack-o-lantern," Chase exclaimed, "and I can about garun-damn-tee you that crash you see didn't cause their injuries!" Chase was no rookie, but Mason wasn't taken back by his reaction — he knew what awaited him down there.

"Those kids are smiling, Mason!" Chase continued. Mason remained silent. "They have fuckin' smiles on their faces!"

Mason glanced at Thorn, pushed the Stetson back on his head and studied Chase thoughtfully. Since they'd first met, Mason's gut told him there was much more to Chase Riley than what was on the surface. *This must be why I felt it,* he thought. *Riley was gonna be the first on the scene this time.*

The timing of Chase's arrival in Moccasin Flats seemed eerily coincidental, but Mason had dismissed any notion of it having to do with the prophecy. Now, Chase had arrived on the scene first, Mason was inexplicably tardy, and today was the twentieth anniversary of the last murder. A hot-cold flash of reality washed over him in waves. Twenty years ago, a young couple named Mark and Charlene Bolton had been the victims, and their deaths could not be called an accident, either. No trace of evidence pointing to a killer had ever been uncovered, but Mason knew there was no killer *per se*. The couple had been mutilated, and Mason remembered their serrated smiles, too.

"Devil's Corner" and the surrounding area was notorious for being the site where several mysterious killings had occurred over the last one hundred and fifty years. It was also the hanging site where thirty-eight Dakota warriors had dropped to their death in 1862. A huge concrete buffalo marked the site and there were many stories of how it snorted at people as they walked past, among other ghost stories. Mason wasn't surprised to see the car in the ditch. He had seen that before. When the call had come over the radio, he was on his way to the reservation to pick up Thorn's citations for the month. The call hadn't fazed him at first; it was only after he realized what day it was that he began to get the jitters. Thorn had told Mason he'd go to town with him, but when they stopped at *McDonald's* for coffee first, they'd lingered over breakfast just to put off the inevitable. Neither of the men had brought up the legend, but both of them knew. It was the twenty-year anniversary of the last killing, and now only one more thing had to happen to know whether the prophecy was true or not. Mason half expected to see Kyle Ghostkiller at the murder site, and had been a bit disappointed when he wasn't. Mason shook the thoughts from his mind and turned his attention back to Chase, waiting for him to continue, but Chase was standing silently, staring off in the direction of the Chrysler.

"They're smiling," Chase said finally. "It's fucking sickening."

Mason and Thorn exchanged knowing glances. Chase's hand was shaking as he took the last draw off his cigarette, threw it down and ground it out.

"It looks like a... a sacrifice or something!"

"You shouldn't smoke," Thorn told Chase. Chase rolled his eyes.

"Have you called the coroner?" Thorn asked.

"Yes," Chase answered with a sneer.

"All righty then," Mason sighed half-heartedly, "let's go have a look. Thorn, can you help out with the lookie-loos?"

"That I can do." Thorn answered.

The crowd that had gathered just outside the perimeter of the yellow tape labeled "crime scene," had been growing as the morning wore on, and the reservation police officers were struggling to keep people away from the scene.

Blowing out a sigh, Mason walked down the small embankment to the Chrysler, pulling latex gloves out of his pocket as he went. Chase remained with the cruiser. He had no desire to look at the corpses again.

The first sign familiar to Mason was the blood-covered windows. They almost looked as if they had been smeared deliberately. *Just like last time,* he thought. He paused, pulled on the gloves and hesitated again before opening the passenger door. He held his breath and opened it slowly.

"Jesus!" he exclaimed, jumping back as an arm flopped out and dangled from one of the bodies. He stood there for several seconds and watched as blood trailed down and dripped off the fingertips.

"Holy…" he whispered. The teen in the passenger seat still had her seatbelt on. Her head lay back against the headrest, her throat slit in a jagged pattern, just as Chase had said. And those smiles — gruesome and distorted. There was no look of horror, no expression of fear or trepidation on their faces — just blood smeared smiles. *They honestly look happy.* Mason was sickened at the sight and almost slammed the door on the limp arm. He turned away instead, leaving the door swinging open.

Swallowing bile that rose in his throat, he rounded the bumper and made his way to the other side of the Chrysler. Before he could grab the handle, the driver's side door swung open on its own. Mason instinctively reached for his gun. He half expected something to come bounding out of the car, but he only saw a few dead leaves fall out onto the ground. *Must be the door Riley opened*, he thought to himself. The wind stirred slightly and he heard what sounded like a whisper that seemed to be coming from under the car.

"Crow Walker," he heard the voices say. He swung back around and watched the leaves get caught up in the breeze and scamper down the hill.

"Shit, I must be losin' it," he mumbled as he turned back to the grisly scene.

Mason shuddered at the hideous expressions of happiness. He didn't want to believe it was happening again, but there was no denying it. He tried to comprehend what this might mean in regards to the Ghostkiller legend, but in the past nothing about the victims, not race, ages, or genders, had mattered. The curse, it seemed, did not discriminate. He glanced back and saw Chase waiting anxiously by the cruiser, pacing and craning his neck to see.

"Looks like two boys and two girls!" Mason shouted. He had to say *something*.

Chase started towards the Chrysler but stopped short when the coroner's wagon pulled up. Whitey Smiley and Dan Tarkington climbed out of the vehicle. The two young men were big as mountains, and both from the "big city" as Mason often sarcastically referred to Minneapolis. Whitey was an albino, true to his name. Dan was tall and lanky with brown hair and a thin mustache. Dressed in white jumpsuits and already donning gloves, the men reminded him of the *Ghostbusters*.

Mason threw Chase a wry look. He and Chase had only worked with them on two other cases. Two women had died on the reservation last summer of what Dan and Whitey had reported as "natural causes." Mason, though, questioned that verdict. He knew that many deaths on Indian reservations were covered up. The FBI had the coroner's office in its back pocket, making it easy for them to lie about the facts. He tried hard not to let his memories of his time at "the 'Knee" cloud his objective here at home, but it did. He wasn't at all impressed with the two *wasichu* coroners who had just stepped out of the ambulance, either. How they'd ever gotten their jobs sure beat the hell out of him.

"What do we have here?" Dan called as he made his way towards the car. He immediately began snapping pictures and looking over the outside of it like he was about to buy the thing. Whitey looked at Mason's bloody gloves with an expression of what Mason could only construe as delight. *What a frickin' sicko.* Mason knew they hadn't been with the coroner's office long enough to know anything about the murders twenty years ago, and they sure as hell wouldn't be prepared for what they were about to see. He hadn't been prepared for it, and he'd known what was coming.

Dan smiled to Whitey. "A bloodbath."

"It's a murder scene," Chase told them as he approached, "so treat it as such."

Mason raised an eyebrow. He liked Chase's style.

"That's right," he chimed in. "No chance of labeling this exposure, eh boys?"

Dan ignored Mason's sarcasm and continued to smile at Whitey, clearly loving the fact that they had a "real bloody murder" to work on. Taking his cue, Whitey cleared his throat in authority and bellowed, "We'll take it from here, Mason."

"Fine by me," Mason said. He and Chase walked the

few short steps back to the cruiser before Chase spoke.

"What do you make of that?"

Mason chuckled, busying himself with removing his bloody gloves. "You mean the two Ghostbusters down there?" He knew that wasn't what Chase was asking.

"Hell if I know," he answered quickly, "looks like a damned animal got a hold of 'em."

Hearing Dan retch from a distance, Mason glanced up and smirked. *Serves you right, you weird ass,* he thought.

Chase followed Mason to the back of the LTD

"You can't be serious?"

The CB radio inside the cruiser blared the news the FBI would arrive any moment. *Great,* Mason thought, *the media is next!*

"Welcome to the circus," he mumbled. Stuffing the gloves in an evidence bag, he stuffed the gloves into it, threw it into the trunk and slammed the lid shut. "I need a drink!"

3

The sun shone brightly through a stained glass window projecting an image of Jesus on the wall of the church. The limbs of a nearby tree gave it life and the image seemed to dance with its arms outstretched, swaying to and fro. Caught up in the figure's graceful waltz, Father O'Rourke held his arms up, reaching for the shadowy form as it willed him to stand.

The priest awoke to screaming sirens and the sun streaming in on his face. Lying in a pew he sat up, realizing he had been dreaming. As the siren faded, he glanced up at the wall, saw the shadows moving, and prayed silently the night before had been a dream, as well. The sudden shrillness of a second siren told him it was not. He closed his eyes, willing the siren to be in the advancement of a fire truck gathering donations for the Moccasin Flats Children's Fund or Lower Sioux Home of the Innocents. He just knew if he prayed hard enough, he could make it so. He fully expected to look outside and see the firefighters collecting from each business as they always did this time of year with those big, yellow boots. It was with this hope he chided himself optimistically; *you won't find out sitting in this pew all day!* He smiled, shook the sleep from his head, and stood, stretching the kinks from his back. Briskly, he shuffled his old frame to the door and stopped short when he saw the door was locked, knowing the doors were never locked unless the alarms went off in his head. His optimism died instantly. *You knew this was coming!* Tears filled his eyes as trepidation began to take over. He hurriedly unfastened the latch and threw open the doors, stepping out onto the stoop. A chill ran through him as he felt the frosty morning air curl around him like the fingers of a cold, dead hand. The streets of Moccasin Flats were abuzz with activity – dogs barked, townspeople scurried about, and haphazardly-parked police cars dotted the roadside. Sirens screamed as a police car whizzed past. It didn't look right for a town that resembled a western movie set to have all this twentieth-century bustle going on. Moccasin Flats was a quiet little town, the only town within a sixty-mile radius of the Lower Sioux Reservation. It was a town trapped in a time warp, and that's why tourists loved it so much. They had not a clue as to the secrets the town had hidden away. But he did.

  Father O'Rourke came from a long line of priests – or *black robes*, as the Indians called them. From the beginning of westward expansion, black robes had forced Catholic teachings down the throats of Indians from the east coast to the west coast, denying them their way of life, beliefs, and religious ceremonies. In an effort to civilize them, mission schools were put into place specifically designed to brainwash the Indian out of the children. Taken from their parents and shipped hundreds of miles away, the nuns cut their hair, made them wear uniforms, and beat them if they spoke their own language.

  The good father struggled with this knowledge. He understood the act of taking away their livelihood, their languages and ceremonies, had given birth to a generation of Indians far removed from the strong, independent Sioux of the nineteenth century. The Native Americans of today, at least by his observation, were governmental dependents who lived with poverty, joblessness and alcoholism. Today's reservations were overrun with gangs and drugs. He often wondered if the past had anything to do with the present if the life force that had been so prevalent in the Indian of long ago would someday extract its revenge for past atrocities. He had seen things since he had been in Moccasin Flats he couldn't explain, things that would confirm his suspicions. The murders being but one. However, his loyalty to the church forced him to turn a blind eye to what he knew deep down in his soul to be the truth.

Indeed, Father O'Rourke had awakened to this very horror twice since he'd moved to Moccasin Flats some forty-odd years ago. He knew despite all the efforts of law enforcement officials that now converged upon the town, no killer would be found amongst the dark woods or lonely prairie that made up this area. *No indeed*, a little voice said, *the killer is as elusive as a shadow in the darkness.* That reality alone prompted his next thought: he would call the Monsignor today to announce he was leaving in the morning to visit his sister in Montana. He hadn't taken a vacation in years and a few weeks away from this place was just what he needed. That decision made, he turned to go back inside when he heard someone call out to him.

"Father! Father! Over here!"

The father looked to see a young Indian man making his way across the street. He was well over six feet tall, with dusky skin and long, black hair that blew lightly in the chilly morning breeze. He was dressed in jeans and cowboy boots, and as he drew closer, the father could see a black t-shirt under his sheepskin coat with "My Heroes Have Always Killed Cowboys" brazenly written across the front of it.

Father O'Rourke stood frozen, but it wasn't the young man's intimidating size or even the shameless t-shirt he wore that made him stand out. It was who he was. With the look of determination on his face, it was easy to see he was a force to be reckoned with. It really didn't surprise the clergyman he had thought of the boy just last night. It was the fact he was actually here. The legend he'd been told long ago came rushing back; Kyle Ghostkiller had come home, and the run-of-the-mill Indian boy was about to live out a prophecy through the beliefs of his people.

The priest noted Kyle had ridden in on the same horse his grandfather had ridden for many years, a massive brown and white paint stallion. The horse stood tied to its regular spot, a hitching post across the street in front of the general store. He wondered how much longer the animal could possibly live. He couldn't count the number of times Kyle's grandfather had tied the horse to that very spot and strolled across the street for a visit. It seemed like a lifetime ago, and he could have easily mistaken the scene for an apparition, history elaborately painted on a canvas from the past — the Indian, the horse, and the traffic, had all played out before. He stood holding a collective breath as the big Indian maneuvered through traffic and made his way up the church steps.

"Good to see you, Father," Kyle said as the two men embraced.

Father O'Rourke stepped back. "Kyle. You're a sight for sore eyes, my son."

In the early morning light, Father O'Rourke began to think more clearly and that gripping fear seemed to abate as he looked at the grown up Kyle Ghostkiller. He thought of how ridiculous it really was to believe that a curse could cause all of this chaos. He had his beliefs to contend with, and he didn't want to damn himself by making it sound as if he believed that Kyle actually had some sort of magical powers that could annihilate this so-called curse. He also knew, however, that in speaking to Kyle he had to choose his words carefully. Anything else would leave him in an unfavorable position for saving the boy's soul from eternal damnation.

With what they could see from the church steps, it would have been easy to imagine the worst. The streets were crowded with police cars, townsfolk scurried toward the scene of the crash, and kids on bikes, with yapping dogs at their heels, all strained to have a look at what was causing the commotion. Kyle looked anxiously at the priest.

"Father —"

"Let's talk inside," Father O'Rourke interrupted, taking Kyle's arm and guiding him inside the church. He had to talk sense into the boy somehow and couldn't very well do it in the middle of the street.

"Father, you know why I'm here," Kyle said as they sat down in a pew near the doors. "I tried to get back before this happened, but it seemed everything that could go wrong did!" Kyle had a look of anguish on his face. The priest looked at him thoughtfully.

"You may not have been able to prevent it anyway, Kyle," he said, holding his breath, hoping Kyle wouldn't start in about the curse. He certainly couldn't allow it to be discussed in the church. What would happen then? Fire and brimstone?

Kyle frowned. "What?"

"It is wonderful to see you. Your grandfather would be proud of the man I see before me now, but you simply must put this idea of a curse out of your head! That's not the solution to this problem!" Kyle was shocked.

"How can you say that when you know the prophecy as well as I do? My grandfather told you of this long ago, Father, even before I was born!" O'Rourke fought the urge to clasp his hands over his ears.

"Yes, I know the story, Kyle!" the father spat out. James Ghostkiller had told him a countless number of times that only one person could deal with the entity responsible: the seventh generation first son born son of Ghostkiller, a Kit Fox Warrior Society member. James had raised Kyle after his parents died and had told the stories to him all of his life. *Filling his head with legends and hogwash*, the priest thought.

"The old ones spoke of this," James used to say. "It is Kyle's place to end it." He had drummed it into Father O'Rourke's head for the past forty years, ever since their first meeting at the funeral of three young children who'd died in what was called a mountain lion attack back in 1942. It had been his first year in Moccasin Flats, and the first of many funerals O'Rourke would officiate over. James had patiently explained the legend to him time and again over the years, and they had had many heated discussions about it. The priest had a hard time believing anything about a curse, even after the next murder happened twenty years later. O'Rourke had always maintained his religious position on the matter, and even on James's deathbed, he had upheld his stance in a last ditch effort to save the poor old man from the fires of hell and damnation.

"You must understand my position on this, James," O'Rourke had said to the old man for the umpteenth time. "These things are not looked favorably upon by the church."

"You believe in a god who says all you need is the faith of a mustard seed," James weakly argued, "and whether you believe in our ways or not, it doesn't change the fact that it lies with my grandson to end this." When O'Rourke didn't answer, Ghostkiller had looked at the clergyman with the black eyes of a wise old warrior and patted his hand. "Have a little faith, Father."

Kyle watched as the priest turned all of this over in his mind, remaining silent until he found the perfect place to break into his thoughts.

"My grandfather spoke to me on his deathbed too," Kyle spoke softly, "Have a little faith, Father."

4

Grady's Bar was just the place to have a stiff drink, and that's exactly what Mason intended to have after the events of the morning. Who cared that it was barely 9:00 a.m.? Hell, he deserved this drink. The morning had brought the promise of things to come, prophecies were unfolding, and Mason knew *all* about them. He had grown up with them, had planned and prepared himself for them — but God help him, he wasn't prepared to go toe to toe with Chase.

Grady's was the local hang out, and only eight blocks from Devil's Corner. It was the closest place, and the only place in town, to get a drink. The other bars had closed after an ordinance passed restricting liquor sales near the reservation. Though New Ulm was closer to the reservation than Moccasin Flats, they did not have such an ordinance, and New Ulm did over a million dollars in liquor sales annually. White people also ran the town. Mason knew Moccasin Flats was targeted because Indians owned the bars there and the powers that be didn't want Indians making any money at anything.

"What'll ya have?" the bartender asked Mason as he and Chase took a seat.

"Jack and Coke," Mason answered, studying the interior of the bar and the people inside — anything to avoid Chase's quizzical gaze. How was he going to explain a 9:00

a.m. drink? Pressure from the killer curse? He almost laughed aloud. The bartender looked at Chase for his order, but Chase waved him off. "Just coffee."

Mason watched the man as he moved away to fill their order. Old Tony Chases His Horse had owned the place forever, it seemed, and Mason felt as if he had known Tony just as long. He was a tall, plump full-blood who wore two long gray braids that fell down past his knees, with deep lines in his face that looked more like well-worn leather. When Mason had been a regular customer, he'd often joked to Tony that he must be as old as Methuselah. Tony always smiled with a gleam in his dark, piercing eyes. A missionary school survivor, he knew exactly who Methuselah was, and got a good belly laugh out of Mason's reference to the Bible character.

It was cool inside the building and smelled of cigarettes, stale beer and something else — Sweetgrass maybe? Mason glanced around and saw a braid of it smoldering in an ashtray nearby. How odd to see the sacred herb smoking the place up. *It's probably doing the bar a world of good*, Mason thought ruefully. A handful of Indians were sitting at the opposite end of the bar nursing drinks and gossiping in rapid Dakota. Moccasin Flats was a diverse town full of mixed bloods and full bloods, most of whose roots hailed from the Great Sioux Nation. The difference in the language was just dialect, which was minimal and made little difference when speaking it to each other.

Mason recognized a few of the men sitting at a corner table playing cards: old men nursing beer mugs and shrouded in cigarette smoke, full-blood relatives of some of the most famous and powerful chiefs ever to hit the history books: Big Eagle, Little Crow, Lightning Blanket & Shakpe to name a few. They were dressed in polyester pants, ripped jeans, and old flannel shirts, all from the five-dollar-a-bag special that the neighborhood Goodwill store offered. Most of the men didn't even have their real teeth – or any teeth, for that matter. They were elders, who in another time might have been the spiritual leaders of their tribe. As Mason watched them, he suddenly felt the clash of two world's right smack in his face: Firewater and Indians were never meant to go together. Nevertheless, the *wasichu* had seen to it the reservation Indians stayed drunk, *especially while they signed the treaties,* he thought bitterly.

"What do you make of those kids down there?" Chase was asking.

Mason didn't answer right away. He was busying himself with a bowl of peanuts on the bar. *Thank God we drove here separately,* he thought. *But I should have just kept driving. I can't stand a bunch of damn hammering right now!*

Thorn had gotten a ride back to the reservation with one of the tribal police officers, so Mason at least had a few minutes to try to grasp what was happening on the short drive to Grady's. But how he could explain it to Chase, was another story, not to mention how he himself fit into it all. He couldn't shake the incident with the leaves, either.

"Look," Chase said, exasperated. "I know you, Mason. You have some idea of what's going on around here and I need to know it, too!"

Tony returned at that moment and placed their drinks in front of them. As Mason's eyes followed the old man's retreating back, he caught sight of something out in the street. Peering through the nicotine-stained window, he watched the back of a big Indian galloping out of town on a huge paint horse, his blue-black hair whipping in the wind. A very familiar sight, indeed.

Well, I'll be damned.

"Well?" Chase asked. "I'm waiting!"

"All right, all right!" Mason exclaimed, throwing back the glass and swallowing the golden liquid in one gulp. This isn't gonna be easy! If that Indian on the horse was who Mason thought he was, he either needed to get up and chase him down or stay and explain the whole story to Chase. He had to tell Chase *something* if only to get him off his back. Mason chose the latter, and using a line made famous by his favorite old T.V. show, he said, "I guess it's about time you knew the facts, Riley."

5

Nina Bolton had dreamed about this day for the past seven years. Kyle had always told her that his twenty-fifth birthday held a special significance, but because of what it meant for their relationship, she had often refused to listen to anything he had to say about it. To her, it just meant he would be going away and giving up his relationship with her until that birthdate, all in the name of some legend. And he had. She hadn't heard from him since he'd left seven years ago.

"Kyle." She said his name aloud as she nervously brushed her hair away from her face. Just the sound of his name sent shivers down her spine. Memories came flooding back of the countless nights they had spent as teenagers down by the creek – their special place— in a tangled web of arms and legs. She forced the images from her mind.

"He left you," she reminded her reflection in the mirror. "You're over him."

He had been a significant part of her life, however, and forgetting him had been much easier said than done. Truth be told, she had never been successful at it.

Kyle had been the first to make friends with her when she'd come to live on the reservation after her parents' death. His Aunt Rosie had adopted her, and as they grew up, they became inseparable. They'd spent countless summers running around on the reservation, riding horses, shooting up imaginary enemies. They spent most of their days down by the creek where Kyle told stories he'd heard from his grandfather. Most were stories of bravery and honor, battles, and skirmishes, many of which revolved around an old cave near Yellow Medicine River where the Indians had hidden out to avoid the army years ago. The "Cave of the Old Ones" was well known among the locals, and stories about it were filled with the spirits and ghosts of past relatives. The first time Kyle told her about the cave she begged to go, and it quickly became a favorite place. They spent many an afternoon playing hide and seek with other children from the reservation there, and later it because a private place for them to be alone.

Ever the tomboy as a kid, she'd had no problem keeping up with Kyle. He taught her how to track, ride a horse, and shoot a bow "like a real warrior" he always said and he'd brag that he was going to be the best warrior of all someday. Nina aspired to be like him while growing up. She always wished that her skin wasn't so white, but he had always brushed away her fears, saying it didn't matter what her skin color was; his people had adopted her and she was one of them, regardless of what others' said.

Life had been good in Aunt Rosie's house and Nina adjusted well. Her parents had known the Stillwind family for years, both socially and professionally. Nina's parents were social workers on the reservation, as was Rosie, so the families got together often. Their deaths were a blow to the entire community, not just those who sought help from them. After they died, six-year-old Nina naturally went to live with Rosie so the transition was as easy as it could be considering the circumstances. However, shortly after she moved in, Nina began having nightmares about her parents' death. They were killed in a car crash, but she was never told the details.

Obviously, the adults in her life did not see the need for it, and she never asked about it as she got older, either. She hadn't been in the car, but the crash replayed in her dreams as if she had been right there when it had happened. The nightmares became so severe that she would wake up screaming, often running out of the house in a blind panic, going missing for hours at a time. Aunt Rosie had panicked the first time Nina disappeared, but Kyle had always known where to find her. Their favorite place was tucked into a stand of weeping willows down by the creek, and that was the spot Nina always ended up. It became somewhat of a ritual after that first night Kyle found her there; he would hold her until she quieted down, wipe away her tears and rock her until she fell asleep. He would then carry her home and put her to bed, the family relieved he'd once again found *Sungska Cikala*, or 'Little White Horse,' as they called her, safe and sound.

 Over time, she got past the nightmares, but as they grew older they would still meet at that same spot, only for a different reason.

 Their love was born out of truly understanding one another and it was as passionate as it was volatile. And they had their fair share of passionate close calls. As they grew into their teenage years, it seemed like the most natural thing in the world for them to get married, and no one doubted one day they would. However, Kyle was the first-born son of Leonard Ghostkiller and everyone on the reservation knew what that meant, including Nina: He was going to have to leave. That's why she somewhat understood when he didn't elaborate on marriage plans; she knew he had things to take care of first, but she lived with the trust and knowledge it would happen one day. Or at least, that's what she thought.

 Nina knew Kyle's destiny had been laid out years before. She had grown up with that knowledge, and would never dare argue about it. But just because she knew what he was supposed to do, it hadn't made it any easier when it was time for him to do it. When Kyle turned sixteen, he went to Pine Ridge for the winter to be with his grandmother's people, the Oglala. Grandfather James said it was important for Kyle to continue his education with other traditional elders of the family, those who would understand the medicine he was inheriting. Nina understood why he had to go, but it was the most miserable winter she'd ever spent. When he returned to Moccasin Flats, he was different. He was happy to see her, and things seemed to be the same between them on the surface, but the light in his eyes was gone, replaced by the grown up fire of a man. He was often somber and serious, always burning with the desire to get older. Grandpa James died two years later telling Kyle on his deathbed he needed to go back to Pine Ridge until his twenty-fifth birthday. When Kyle told Nina what his grandfather had said, she was devastated.

"I have a job to do, Nina! I have to do this!"

"I'm so sick of hearing about your job!" Nina shrieked, "It's all you've talked about your whole life! I don't care about some stupid curse! What about me and you?"

"This is not just some fairy tale, Nina," Kyle told her. "People are dying!"

"I don't care!" she screamed back at him.

"Well," he answered coldly, "If you were a real Indian you wouldn't be so damned SELFISH!" And with that, he stormed out. That was the last time they spoke.

As dramatic as teenage love was, she remembered how she had fallen apart at that moment, knowing he had said the worst thing he could've possibly said to her.

Shaking the memories from her head, she looked at herself in the mirror, turning this way and that, happy with the result. She was purposefully dressed as the infamous "Indian Barbie" and was determined in her effort. She and Kyle used to poke fun at the girls at the powwows who dressed this way, and that was precisely the point. *He'll think I've converted,* she laughed to herself. *Little does he know that while he was off chasing ghosts, I managed to get a law degree!*

Smiling smugly, she gave herself the once over twice. She had brushed her long, blonde hair until it shined; her little black skirt hugged her rounded hips nicely; her breasts swelled beneath her blue peasant blouse and her knee-high moccasin boots fit like a second skin. She hardly looked like the valedictorian of her law class in this getup, but she didn't care. *A little makeup and I'll be ready to go,* she thought.

"Just wait 'til you see me now, Mr. Kyle Ghostkiller," she said aloud, grabbing a tube of red lipstick. "Little White Horse is all grown up and *you're* in for the surprise of your life."

6

Chase slammed his coffee mug down on the bar
"You actually expect me to believe this cock-n-bull story about a legend?" He spat out. He had spent the last forty-five minutes listening to what he thought was going to be some insight into that horrible murder scene he'd discovered earlier, and was none too happy with what Mason offered as an explanation. It also pissed him off that Mason was slamming back whiskey like it was going out of style. It was completely out of character, but Chase knew he was only doing it to avoid the issue.

"Believe what you want, Riley." Mason shrugged. "I'm just telling you the facts as I know them."

"Facts, huh?" Chase almost laughed. "Okay, let me get this straight: A bunch of Indians were strung up by order of President Abraham Lincoln no less, and with his dying breath one of them cursed the town and all the people in it to a terrible death?"

Mason sighed, rolling his eyes. "No, he didn't curse the town. He prophesied that a curse would befall the town," he explained again, twirling the ice in his now empty glass, "and you left out the part about the killings that have occurred every twenty years *as predicted*."

"Oh yeah," Chase said slowly, dramatically rubbing his chin, "I almost forgot that sordid detail." He quickly scoffed, "Now tell me the real deal, Mason cuz I'm not about to fall for this hokey pokey bullshit!"

Mason massaged his throbbing temples, fighting the urge to throw his glass. He sighed heavily and waved Tony over for a refill.

"I know it sounds crazy to you, but like I said, believe what you want, Riley; I'm just telling you what I know. I've lived here all my life and I've seen this happen before."

Tony returned and placed a glass of ice water in front of Mason. "Slow down, Koda," He said before moving back down the bar.

"Then tell me what you know!" Chase shouted impatiently. He was getting damned impatient with this whole conversation and the Indians in the bar could tell it, too. Mason glanced around and saw them all looking in their direction. Tony took it all in, too, as he absentmindedly wiped a glass at the other end of the bar. A black and white TV hanging above his head blared news of the murders.

Mason grasped the water glass slowly, watching as tiny lights sparked and jumped around the rim of the glass. He knew he was the only one seeing it, knew why they were there. He picked it up and took a long drink, feeling the cold, crisp water hit his empty gut like a rock and then bathe him with a sense of relief. Prayers answered. He closed his eyes and allowed it to happen, knowing he needed to pace himself because he had to explain things just right. But at the same time, he needed to get Chase out of the bar before he got his ass kicked. Placing his glass gently on the bar, he turned to Chase and looked him straight in the eye.

"I've already told you what I know," his voice was dangerously low. "It's not my fault if you don't believe me, but if you don't keep your voice down you're gonna have a shitload of Indians up your ass, you got me?"

"Mason," Chase said in a hushed tone, his eyes darting around the room, "a shitload of Indians up my ass is the least of my concerns! I came here from Los Angeles, you know, a modern-day, real-life city, not a backward, Hicksville town where bad things are blamed on legends, okay? I deal in facts, not myths, not curses or mystical bullshit! I am not about to believe some ghost or spirit is responsible for what happened out there!"

That's the problem with you wasichus: no faith, Mason thought.

"We have four kids lying on a slab who've had their throats carved out like a goddamned jack-o-lantern — that's the facts, THAT is real! *Somebody* killed those kids, not a spook, not a specter and it sure as hell wasn't Santa Claus!"

Mason knew he could waste no more time trying to convince a non-believer. He wasn't Dakota. He just didn't get it. The Indians in the bar all believed it, however. It wouldn't take much more for them to react to what he was saying. Four old men at a corner stopped their card game and were staring at them. Glancing down the bar, Mason saw others were watching just as intently. It sure wouldn't do to have them all come down on this white boy's head for challenging their beliefs, or worse, have them believe that he himself was questioning the realities of the legend. He had to get Chase out of there in a hurry, so he did the only thing he could think to do.

Mason threw a few dollars down on the bar and abruptly stood. "C'mon. There's someone you need to meet."

7

Kyle sat astride the big paint stallion and gazed out over the Yellow Medicine River. He had always been told the horse's name was derived from the huge mastodons that used to roam the earth thousands of years ago. Macedone. His name fit. The stallion was huge, measuring well over seventeen hands high with well-defined muscles and a long, silvery white mane and tail. He was white with brown patches that resembled various states on a modern day map.

Macedone had belonged to Kyle's grandfather and the old man had always told Kyle the horse had been in the family for generations. Growing up being told those things made them easy to believe. Kyle hadn't been surprised to see Macedone waiting for him outside the small airport in New Ulm when he landed. The horse always knew when and where Kyle would be. Of all the things he had seen in his lifetime, it was completely believable that Macedone had special powers bestowed upon him, including the gift of eternal life. It was these same gifts from the Creator that had brought Kyle to this junction in his life — a destiny that would soon be fulfilled.

He wasn't exactly sure how he'd ended up at the river. He'd felt restless after leaving the church, and instead of going straight to Aunt Rosie's, he'd given Macedone his head when they'd left town and somehow ended up here. The Yellow Medicine River was his favorite place in the whole world, and if there was any one place he could possibly find some breathing room, it was there. *My twenty-fifth birthday.*

He wasn't sure how to take Father O'Rourke's reaction to his return. At first, the father seemed ready to help, but a moment later, he was throwing up the damning-of-your-soul stuff to him. It didn't make any sense. O'Rourke knew that 'Creator' was just another name for God. There were even passages in the Bible that referred to the sanctity of ceremony, and other similarities that were indisputable. The priest also knew the entire history of the legend and the steps Kyle had to take to remedy the curse, yet he continued to argue about it. It was confusing because the old man knew these things even before Kyle was born. But Kyle hadn't forgotten the way O'Rourke had argued with his grandpa, either. It seemed he was just as confused as Kyle was. *No matter. The spirits will guide the way.*

Kyle blew out a sigh as he shook the thoughts from his head and took in the beauty around him. A few wispy clouds enshrouded with brilliant tangerine reds of the late morning sun played their shadows over the water creating shapes that looked like animals – a horse rearing, an otter with a flat tail, a huge bird with outstretched wings. The clouds' colors, he knew, were beautiful warnings like that.

"Red in the morning, sailors take warning," he remembered his Aunt Rosie saying. That meant rain, and he recalled the days when he and Nina had wanted to go to the river on 'red' mornings and she had forbid it. She was right every time about the rain. Rosie was right about a lot of things, especially when it came to Nina. Rosie had told him that Nina would be alright after he left for Pine Ridge. It didn't make it hurt any less, however. He had heard she was doing well over the years. She'd gone to school, got a degree, but he never heard whether or not she'd gotten married. He hoped she hadn't.

He sighed wistfully. Nina. Just her name, but it brought with it the memories he couldn't erase. The taste of her, the smell of her, that gorgeous face, all of the things he had tried to forget. It was hard to wipe a lifetime out of his memory.

His Aunt Rosie was his mother's sister, and she and her husband Joe had taken in more children than Kyle could remember over the years, providing a stable, loving home that the kids otherwise would never have had. Kyle's own mother had died shortly after his father was killed, and he went to live with James soon afterward. The houses were right next door to each other, so he and Nina had been together constantly. Nina. Learning, playing, growing up together, and sharing the first taste of innocent love once they had gotten older. He smiled at the thought. The happiest days of his life had been spent here at the river with her. Those days were filled with the love they'd found in each other. A young Nina, with her blonde curls and indigo eyes looking up at him wide-eyed as he told her stories of the old days, overnight excursions to the Cave of the Old Ones, riding together, learning to track and shoot with Uncle Mason. She was his best friend and one didn't do anything without the other.

As they'd gotten older, he began to look at Nina in a different way – as a beautiful girl with skin as soft and unblemished as a first fallen snow, lips the color of a pale rose and soulful eyes of cobalt blue. He'd fallen hard for her and had spent many years building that love. It had been innocent, never consummated, because they had promised themselves to each other only after they were married. He had loved her totally; so completely, in fact, that he never had eyes for another woman. He still loved her despite the way they had left things. He had been shocked and hurt at her reaction when he had to leave Moccasin Flats all those years ago. Her little regard for the people who were dead was disappointing. If she'd only known the truth, it would have made things so much easier. He hadn't even had a chance to ask anyone about her in all the confusion of the day. He knew he'd do better if he got her out of his mind and concentrated on the reason he came back. But how could he forget her, especially being here?

He had tried to get back to Moccasin Flats before the eighteenth, but a bomb threat at the last minute forced everyone off his plane and he had to wait for a later flight. Getting through airport security had been hell. He barely had time to think of anything but getting to town before the next killing, much less think of Nina. But he had time to think about her now, here where his memories lived. He never asked about her and Rosie never offered when they spoke. Hell, Nina probably wouldn't even want to see him after the way he had left things. She was most likely married by now, maybe with a few kids. He clenched his jaw as thoughts of her with another man crept into his mind: her lips kissing someone else, her silky blonde hair spread out on pillows as another man hovered above her. He wasn't fooling himself. He had to find her! No matter what else he did, he had to find Nina, had to try to convince her all this had been for her, too. He could make her listen if he told her what the driving force behind his preparations had been. Even if she was married, he just had to put things right before he left again. Somehow, he had to make her understand. Macedone stamped restlessly as if sensing his thoughts.

"You always could read me couldn't ya, fella?" he said, patting the horse's neck.

Turning the stallion back towards the reservation, they sped off towards Aunt Rosie's.

8

Hot grease sizzled in the fry pan as Rosie Stillwind lovingly created her family's favorite treat. A group of kids from the local church were having a cookout tonight and she had promised to send over Indian tacos, made with her famous fry bread. She was always doing something for the young people on the reservation. Usually, it gave her great joy to be involved, but a feeling of doom had gripped her as soon as her feet hit the floor that morning and it was still gnawing at the back of her mind now. She knew better than to think it was anything more than what it was: Today was Kyle's twenty-fifth birthday, and it was only a matter of time before she heard something about the legend. A knock on the front door roused her from the kitchen. She hollered up the stairs at Nina just as she was coming down.

"Would you see who that is?" she called. "I need to finish this fry bread or it'll never be done by tonight!"

Nina sighed, not wanting the interruption from her mission of finding Kyle.

"Auntie…" Nina began to whine as she entered the kitchen, watching Rosie add a piece of flattened dough to the hot grease.

"Look at you!" Rosie commented, raising her eyebrows

at Nina's outfit. "Where are you off to?" Before she could answer, the knock came again, saving Nina from having to lie instead of revealing her plan.

"Here, see to this fry bread and I'll get the door! Hurry on!" said Rosie, shooing Nina towards the stove and handing her *the pinchers,* as she called them.

"Auntie…" Nina whined again.

"Be glad I'm not using them on you!" Rosie scolded her, "and change your clothes!" She smiled as she made her way to the front door, wiping her hands on her apron before reaching for the knob. Her smile quickly faded when she opened it.

"Mornin' Rosie." Mason tipped his hat before leaning in to kiss her cheek. "I'd like you to meet Chase Riley."

She looked from one man to the other, eyeing Chase suspiciously. She noticed his police badge pinned to his shirt pocket and recoiled a bit. She was always thrilled to see her nephew Mason, but he never brought anyone out here, much less a *wasichu* cop. She'd seen the other man around town but had never talked to him before. She supposed it was par for the course that he was here considering what day it was. Her eyes settled back on Mason.

"What's wrong?" she asked, ignoring the introduction.

"Nothing," Mason assured her, "we just need to talk to you for a minute. Do you mind if we come in?"

She awoke this morning knowing Kyle was due back today, but if he hadn't made it back in time, the chance that the curse had struck again was a real possibility. Just then, Nina popped her head over her aunt's shoulder, startling her.

"Oh!" Rosie clutched her chest.

"Sorry, Auntie. Hi, Uncle Mason," Nina smiled. "What's going on?"

Mason knew the Stillwinds didn't have a TV and he

didn't hear the radio playing. There was a good chance they would have no idea about the murders. At least Nina wouldn't know, anyway. Rosie, on the other hand, had a way of knowing what he was going to say before he ever opened his mouth.

"What's up, cupcake?" Mason smiled at Nina and then leaned down to whisper into Rosie's ear.

"Please, Rosie," he said softly, "Chase needs to hear what you have to say about the Ghostkiller's."

Rosie stood back eyeing Mason, noting the smell of liquor on his breath. Her guard was officially up. He had been sober now for twenty years and she knew that something drastic would have had to happen for him to pick up a drink. Immediately understanding what was going on, she opened the door wide. "Do come in."

"What's going on, Auntie?" Nina persisted, backing away to allow the two men to enter.

"Now never you mind," Rosie turned to her. "Just sit tight a minute and don't ask any questions," she said in a hushed voice.

Nina did as she was told and stood patiently beside her aunt. As a small child, she'd figured out you learned more by observing; it was the perfect way to find out the minutest details and was, in fact, the traditional way, although Nina never thought of it like that. She just knew a strategically taken seat in the corner could glean all kinds of information for someone who would just be patient and listen. In fact, she had gotten quite good at picking out details that might otherwise be missed by the casual observer, like the fact that Chase Riley not only wore a police badge, but he was just as skeptical as that priest Father O'Rourke. *Why in the world would Uncle Mason bring him here?*

Rosie took Chase's elbow, guiding him towards a

cream-colored sofa decorated with horse pillows. The men's heavy, booted steps echoed loudly across the hardwood floor.

"It's nice to meet you, Mr. Riley," Rosie said. "Let's all sit down. This is my daughter, Nina."

"Nice to meet you, Nina," said Chase. He couldn't help but notice those long legs that disappeared at the hem of her short skirt, and made no bones about showing his approval.

"Likewise," Nina answered, hiding the smile that crossed her lips. *If he raises his brows any higher his eyeballs might fall out,* she laughed to herself. Mason elbowed Chase. "Close your mouth," he chided quietly before moving to take a seat in a recliner.

Taking Mason's cue, Rosie said, "Nina, go tend to that fry bread while I talk to the policemen."

Nina didn't argue and was actually relieved to be able to leave the room. She knew what they were going to talk about and had no desire to hear it. The whole idea of the legend was a sore subject. Making fry bread was just what she needed to bide her time until she could leave to go find him. She wanted to catch him before he made his way to the house, so she could give him the what-for he deserved out of earshot of Aunt Rosie. She smiled at Mason before excusing herself to the kitchen.

Chase watched Nina's nicely rounded behind exit the room as he took a seat on the couch. *Why had Rosie referred to the girl as her daughter?* Chase thought. Rosie was obviously a full-blood, with copper-colored skin and a long black salt and pepper braid that brushed the backs of her knees. Nina was as white as the driven snow with pretty blue eyes, a full mouth, and long blonde hair. She looked like she'd just stepped off the cover of Cosmopolitan Magazine. Indeed, Chase couldn't wait to hear the reason why, but for now, he would see what the older woman had to say. He'd consider it an exercise in patience, one he had learned to do well since he'd started working in Moccasin Flats and dealing with the Indians. None of them liked him, at least the traditional ones. He was an outsider, and outsiders weren't welcome. Period.

As Rosie and Mason chatted, Chase took the opportunity to check out the room. It looked like a nice enough place though he couldn't imagine himself living on a reservation. Most of the houses out this way were no more than shacks, some not even equipped with indoor heat or plumbing. They had junk strewn in the yards, mattresses, old appliances, and rusty cars by the dozens. It looked as though Rosie Stillwind's house was an exception, however. Not only was the yard free of junk and rusty cars, the house was immaculately clean.

There was a recliner and an overstuffed chair that matched the sofa, each of which sat in opposite corners of the room. A few small end tables sat on either side of the couch. Frilly, tan curtains with a leaf print in the colors of autumn hung at the windows. A coffee table sat in front of the sofa. The walls were painted a cream color and sported the same leaf border as the curtains. A buck stove stood on the far wall and an old cedar chest sat near the front door. Chase noticed there was no T.V.

"Are you boy's hungry?" Rosie asked.

"No, no Auntie, thanks," Mason answered. "Chase here just needs to be brought up to speed on some things. He found the prize this morning." The room grew quiet. Chase's eyes rested on Rosie Stillwind's face and as she spoke, he could almost feel the room start to spin.

"I'm going to tell you what I know," she told him, her gaze intent. "You can take it for what it is or not, but my advice is to listen carefully so you don't miss anything."

There was something about the way she spoke that

made Chase realize this woman was on to him and it wasn't a comfortable feeling. He felt as though she could see right into his soul with those piercing black eyes of hers. He wasn't one to be intimidated and that wasn't *quite* what he felt. It was something else he couldn't put his finger on.

As the next hour passed, Chase found himself drawn into the story of the Indians who were hanged in town. He knew from somewhere deep down the story of the hanging was true. He seemed to remember reading about it in a history book or on the Internet. *The Great Sioux Uprising* she said it was called, but the details he'd read and the ones Rosie gave were altogether different.

Chief Little Crow was the leader of the Indian bands at that time. According to Rosie, the treacherous dealings on the part of the government were what had caused the uprising in the first place. Treaty money was stolen by corrupt Indian agents, and the Indians were left to starve because annuity payments were often late or never came at all. Any type of food given on credit was later charged astronomical amounts of money and the Indians ended up on the bad end of the deal.

Ghostkiller had been hanged by mistake when he was rounded up with the rest of the Dakota at a place called Camp Release. He had not been involved in the fighting but had hidden a white woman and her children from the marauders. The Army accused him of having an affair with her, which was not true. He was hanged despite her testimony on his behalf.

"My nephew Kyle will play a very important role in righting the wrongs done to our people, as Ghostkiller had made it very clear who was to be in charge of intervening." Kyle had some key elements to work with, one of the most important being a medicine bundle that had been passed down by Ghostkiller's grandson, He Runs With Thunder. This bundle was put together specifically for Kyle. Ordinarily, Chase would have immediately wondered what was in the bundle, but as Rosie continued to speak, he found himself entranced; her black eyes seemed to draw him into another world, and he was pulled into the past where he began to see the images she was speaking to him about. Any question he might have had fell silent on his lips.

"He Runs with Thunder said Kyle will travel a great distance to help our people," she leaned towards Chase for emphasis, "which will be necessary to change the course of history."

Mason watched from beneath the Stetson lowered over his eyes. If Chase still doubted the story after this he'd better prepare himself because once Kyle arrived, all this 'hokey pokey bullshit' was going jump up and bite him in the ass.

Chase's mind screamed with questions as he sat there listening to what Rosie was saying. *Travel great distances? Change the course of history?* The words swam in his head as if written on paper scraps. Suddenly, the letters melted off the paper and they spun into an inky, black mass that swirled around the gallows. His jaws ached and he began salivating. He couldn't speak, couldn't force any words out. He closed his eyes, trying to bring himself back from wherever it was Rosie's story had taken him. His mind screamed. *Why can't I speak?* Something deep inside him told him to gather his inner strength and focus it on coming back. *Project the energy out!*

"Change the course of history," he heard Rosie repeat. The rest of what she said turned into static noise like a T.V. that had signed off for the night. He could even see the snow with his mind's eye. Rosie patted his hand. "Anything else you want to know?"

Her touch brought him back; immediately his eyes flew

open. He shook his head and leaned back against the sofa, forcing himself to focus. *Get hold of yourself, man*! His thoughts raced and he felt the clash of reality hit his waking mind like a semi-truck hitting a stone wall. Of course Rosie would spew all this Indian crap, too! Mason was related to these people somehow, and Chase already knew Mason believed the legend. *They're all family!* Of course, that was it! He couldn't allow himself to get suckered into their Indian voodoo. *They are all in it together.* The entire town seemed to believe this legend nonsense, but for all Chase knew Kyle was the killer. It wouldn't be too farfetched to imagine the whole town protecting their 'golden boy.' After all, he was their savior! As quickly as it had come, he dismissed what had just happened to him and the magic of it faded from his mind.

Chase looked up at Mason, surprised at how laid back he seemed to be. He was sitting in the recliner, hat pulled low over his eyes, legs lazily crossed at the ankles, and obviously very comfortable in Rosie's house. *He sure as hell isn't spilling all he knows*, Chase thought. If all he could do was bring him here to listen to more about 'the legend of Ghostkiller,' then Chase decided he would just have to solve the murders on his own. He had more experience than some tiny town Chief of Police anyway. The first thing he had to do was find out more about Kyle.

"So where is this Kyle Ghostkiller?" Chase asked, finally finding his tongue.

"He'll be along," Rosie said, rising from the sofa. "Would you like some fry bread?"

"I'd love some!" Mason sat up then, adjusting his hat. His head was a bit light after the drinks from that morning and he knew he needed something on his gut besides alcohol. He regretted drinking, but falling off the wagon was the least of his concerns right now. He would deal with that later. His mouth began to water for the taste of Rosie's fry bread. He rose from the chair, motioning Chase to get up, too.

"I'd like some, too, Mrs. Stillwind," Chase replied. "Thank you."

"Please, call me Rosie," she said. Crossing the room towards the kitchen doorway she called out to Nina, "Is that fry bread done yet?"

Nina almost knocked her down as she came around the corner at the same time. "Almost!"

Both women laughed as they retreated to the kitchen. Chase smiled as they left the room, watching Nina's nicely rounded behind walk away in that tiny skirt was becoming most enjoyable. Mason, the ever-protective uncle, noticed his wandering eye.

"Down, boy," he drawled. Chase chuckled and turned his attention toward a grouping of photos hanging on the wall above the sofa.

Mason could tell he wasn't buying the story. *He had damn well better buy it,* Mason thought. His white-assed life depended on it, and maybe that's what he needed to have reiterated to him. Otherwise, he'd find himself dead with his own throat slit and it'd be the locals who got him.

"Is Stillwind Rosie's married name?" Chase asked, interrupting Mason's thoughts.

"Yes."

"Her husband still alive?"

"No."

"Nina's white," Chase stated bluntly.

"She was adopted by Rosie and Joe when her parents were killed," Mason paused, and then added, "Nina's last name is Bolton."

"Mason, I just have to ask you —" Chase was interrupted by the shrill whinny of a horse. In quick succession, heavy footsteps bounded up the porch steps and the front door burst open as Kyle Ghostkiller's tall frame filled the doorway of Rosie's house.

"Well, I'll be," Mason spoke slowly. "This can't be that snot-nosed nephew of mine all grown up!"

"Mason!" Kyle exclaimed as the two men embraced, clapping each other on the back. "Great to see you, Uncle!"

"You're sure a sight for sore eyes," Mason told him softly.

Kyle stepped back and nodding his head toward Chase, he smiled, waiting for an introduction.

Taking the obvious cue, Mason said, "Kyle Ghostkiller, meet Chase Riley, the newest edition to our never-growing police force."

Kyle extended his hand and Chase hesitantly shook it. Kyle noticed Chase's reserve but didn't say anything.

"I suppose you've heard by now…" Kyle's voice trailed off, his eyes riveted on Chase.

"Oh hell, yeah. Chase here is the lucky guy first at the scene," Mason said, clapping Chase on the shoulder.

Chase stood there returning Kyle's gaze, sizing him up. He had waist-length black hair, stood well over six feet tall, was muscular — the kind of build that could easily overpower a young teen, Chase thought. He didn't much care for the t-shirt he wore, either. 'My Heroes Have Always Killed Cowboys' was a redneck slogan if ever he saw one.

"When did you get into town?" Chase asked.

"What's all the commotion out here? Kyle!" Rosie almost dropped the plate of fry bread she was carrying when she saw her nephew.

"Ah, Aunt Rosie," Kyle closed the short distance between them, ignoring Chase's question.

He took the plate from her hand and scooped her up in

a one-armed bear hug.

"You look twenty years younger!" he exclaimed, kissing her cheek playfully.

"Oh stop that!" Rosie mused as Kyle placed her gently on the floor. She adjusted her skirts as he handed her plate back.

Nina stopped just outside the doorway of the living room listening, her heart pounding.

"Well, we've gotta be going, Rosie," Mason said, grabbing a couple of pieces of fry bread and kissing her cheek in the process.

"Great to see you again, Kyle!" Mason told him, meaning it. "I'll be in touch."

"You too, Mason, and I look forward to it," Kyle said as the two men embraced and clapped each other's backs once more. Mason whispered "I'll be back" in Kyle's ear.

Turning to Chase, Kyle said, "And nice to meet *you*, Mr. Riley." He knew Chase was sizing him up, but he didn't care.

"*Detective* Riley," Chase answered, shaking Kyle's hand and gauging the size of it for later reference.

"Sure thing," Kyle drawled.

"Oh Mason, do come back soon, will you?" Rosie asked, giving Mason's hand a squeeze. Mason sensed the urgency in her voice, but it was lost on Chase. "And I hope I've helped you in some way to understand all this, Mr. Riley."

Chase smiled at her but didn't reply. He did take a few pieces of the fry bread she offered, though.

"Oh, I will," Mason assured her, "and you have. We'll let ourselves out, Rosie."

"Bye Nina!" he yelled as the two men headed through the front door, closing it behind them.

"Nina! Kyle's here!" Rosie called out as she herded

Kyle over to the sofa. "It's so good to see you!"

Nina stood frozen. *He's here? He can't be here!* Her plan was to go out and find him, not face him here on her own turf! *Well, what are you afraid of?* A little voice said. *Here he is, so get in there and tell him off like you've wanted for the past seven years!*

For several seconds, Nina fought the urge to run out the back door. How was she going to face him? Why shouldn't she? Ever so slowly, she rounded the corner, silently praying her auntie's chatter hid the sound of her footsteps.

"Do you want some fry bread?" Rosie was asking. "When did you get into town?"

"Nina's here?" Kyle asked, ignoring his aunt's questions. Seeing someone from the corner of his eye, he turned his head.

There she stood, not only as beautiful as remembered but even more so. Her hair was longer, and she was a bit taller, with legs that seemed to go on forever. His body reacted immediately to her, and his heart pounded in his chest.

"Nina?" Kyle rose and walked towards her slowly. "My God, look at you," he whispered, taking her into his arms. She didn't reciprocate and kept her arms at her sides.

"Kyle," She acknowledged curtly, backing away from him. *God, he looks good*, Nina thought, hating herself for it.

Kyle gawked at her like some love struck teenager, and Nina reveled in it, building up to the tongue-lashing of a lifetime.

9

The ride back to town was uncomfortably silent. Mason stared straight ahead, eating his fry bread slowly while he drove making it last as long as possible so he wouldn't have to talk. The miles passed quickly, in part due to the fact that Mason was driving about a hundred miles an hour. He was planning how to ditch Chase so he could drive back out to the reservation and talk to Kyle alone. It wouldn't be easy, though, he was sure of that. But he couldn't risk Chase following him; he simply had to talk to Kyle first, alone. Kyle had all the answers right now and could shed some light on the whole situation.

Chase stared out the window, absentmindedly chewing his own fry bread as he replayed Rosie's words in his mind: "In December 1862, President Lincoln ordered the hanging of thirty-eight Dakota Indians for various crimes against white settlers. One Indian was hanged by mistake and it is this one, Kyle's third great grandfather, Ghostkiller, who said the seventh generation would make things right." Kyle is a seventh generation Kit Fox Warrior who has the remedy to break the murderous curse. But how was he supposed to do that? Changing the past was something out of science fiction movies or fantasy novels, not real life. And what does it mean to "make things right"? Blow up Mount Rushmore? *It is pretty shitty that the Black Hills have the faces of four white guys blasted into them as if showing the Indians that the government overtook that sacred place, too,* Chase thought. Well, he was a detective and if he was going to make any sense of any of this, he was going to have to look at the facts. Maybe then he could put something together.

The part about the hangings was plausible enough. He would have to look it up again for the details, but he remembered reading about the Great Sioux Uprising somewhere and knew that it had really happened. The crap about a curse was another story. It having to do with the murders was just nuts. What was worse was the whole family seemed to believe it, and could possibly be involved. Hell, the whole reservation could be in on it. Why do all these people believe in this crap?

"Mason," Chase looked at his boss, swallowing the last bite of his fry bread. "Do you honestly believe in this curse?"

Mason glanced over at him. It was the way he'd asked that took Mason back. It was the first time today that Chase had actually asked something with a twinge of sincerity in his voice. "Yes, I do," Mason answered, looking him straight in the eye.

Mason wanted to say: *It would be far better to have you believe it, too, and help me, then to have to hide the fact that Kyle Ghostkiller's medicine is the only way to end the killings!* But he didn't.

"What about this Kyle Ghostkiller?" Chase asked. "How does he really fit into all this?"

Mason hesitated, surprised that Chase seemed to have read his thoughts. It seemed Chase might actually be coming around.

"Like Rosie explained, Kyle is the descendant of

Ghostkiller and is the one who can make things right."

Silence followed as Chase absorbed the information again. All these generations and confusing metaphors about some secret society boggled his mind. He was frustrated at the thought of even discussing it at all. Despite his innermost feelings that there was something more to this curse, this was modern-day not 1862. Maybe someone was murdering just for the sheer fun of it?

"But this is just crazy!" Chase burst out. "How do you know Kyle isn't the killer? To have him showing up all of a sudden after these murders sure looks fishy. Maybe we should be bringing him in for questioning?!"

Mason had hoped that Chase's silence indicated he was beginning to believe him, but those hopes faded with that outburst. He clenched his hands around the steering wheel, determined not to lose his temper. As angry as Chase was making him, he had to keep it together. He'd never accomplish anything if he was full of anger, and he knew it.

He turned the car into a parking spot in front of Grady's, thankful that the ride was over.

"Look, Riley, I know how hard this is for you to believe. If I were a white-assed guy like you, I wouldn't believe it either, but twenty years ago I found a couple murdered just like those four kids up there at Devil's Corner, okay? The same scene, the same spot, everything. Go look up the Bolton file for yourself if you need facts." He threw the car in park and turned to look at Chase. "I'm not about to sit here and argue with you about whether or not Kyle is the killer. I know how those kids died and I'll do what has to be done for this shit to be over! Now get outta the car!"

Chase stared at Mason for a long moment, almost as if seeing him for the first time. He had been drinking, which he never did, and that fact alone shook Chase to the bone. Mason had worked hard on it and was proud of his sobriety. For him to fall off the wagon said a lot to Chase about this case and a lot more about his boss. He actually believed this ridiculous farce. For the first time, Chase saw Mason the Indian and knew Mason was more Indian than he'd ever guessed. To argue with him at this point was futile. Sorry to say, but he would have to go about it alone. Mason was simply too close to it to be objective.

"All right," Chase said at last, "you go chase your ghosts and I'll go look up the Bolton file." He hesitated, "And maybe I'll bring Kyle in myself…for the facts." With that, he got out of the LTD and slammed the door shut.

10

"Nina?" Kyle said her name apprehensively, but he could tell by the look on her face she wasn't going to listen to him no matter what he said. If looks could kill, he'd be dead where he stood. He searched her face and noted the changes: she looked matured, certainly wiser; the hurt that had haunted those eyes seven years ago was gone, and in its place was a look of defiance and loathing. He noticed she wasn't wearing a wedding ring, and despite the shock of the moment, he was happy about that. She was strikingly beautiful, more so than he remembered. Since she was here at Rosie's, he could only hope it was because she still lived at home and wasn't married.

Look at him drool, Nina thought with a smirk. This was just the reaction she had wanted to see for so long! Little White Horse is all grown up and now Kyle wants to talk, huh? *Well, too damn bad!* She allowed the years to melt away, the anger of long ago to fuse through her body like boiling lava. *How dare he come back here after all this time and try to take me into his arms! The gall of him to think that I would just forgive and forget after leaving me like he did!* As she stood there looking at him, all her resolve to make him squirm with her looks went out the window. Suddenly, she felt as she did on the day he left. All the pent up emotions of the past seven years came rushing back. She spoke before she realized what she was saying.

"Back to save the day?" she asked sarcastically. "After all, how will we ever be able to survive the curse unless *you* come back and save us all?"

A deafening silence followed and the very air seemed to crackle with electricity as the words she spoke hung in the air. Rosie's gasp broke the silence.

"Nina! I will not hear you speak so disrespectfully about this to Kyle!"

Nina stopped, interrupted by the sound of Rosie's voice. Suddenly back in the present, she could have bitten off her tongue. Horrified by what she had let slip in front of Rosie, she immediately apologized.

"Sorry momma," she whispered as tears welled up in her eyes. She looked defiantly at Kyle, holding her chin high. She was sorry, but not for saying what she'd wanted to him. She could easily say so much more, but out of respect for Rosie, she wouldn't.

She stared at him for a long moment, then turned and fled through the front door, slamming it hard behind her. Kyle started after her but Rosie touched his arm.

"No, *Thunder Boy*, you don't have time to run after her now. She'll be all right and you two will have plenty of time to make amends later."

Rosie saying his sacred name stopped him in his tracks. She was right. He had to get his mind focused on his preparations. A childhood love affair was the last thing he needed to worry about. He thought Nina might still be angry and upset with him, but the extent of her anger had surprised him. The hurt was obviously still fresh. Was it because she still had feelings for him? That possibility alone was enough to make him smile.

Rosie squeezed his hand. "C'mon. I have something for

you," she said as she moved towards the cedar chest.

Lifting the lid, Kyle recognized the bundle inside, tied securely with sinew. He walked over slowly as Rosie reached inside, carefully lifting it out. The red cloth was a bit faded, but otherwise in pristine condition. He knew his grandfather had always taken the utmost care of it.

"Your grandfather left this for you," she told him, "but I couldn't give it to you until now."

"Grandfather," Kyle whispered as she handed it to him.

"You have everything you need in here." Rosie said, "I'll have some food packed for you in no time." She smiled at him, and then scurried off towards the kitchen.

Kyle sat down on the sofa with the medicine bundle in his lap. He could feel the spirit of his grandfather surrounding him, could sense the power of the ancient objects inside and was humbled by it. He remembered all at once the many things his grandfather had taught him, the numerous healings he had performed and the lives he had touched with this bundle. He often said sometimes people had to see the power of God so they would not have any doubts, that doubting was a human trait that was no one's fault, it was just a lack of faith.

He had proven this at a Sundance when Kyle was little. James had handed him a bucket of water and a ladle, instructing him to stand on one side of the arbor with it. James had then walked to the center of the arbor with a hollow buffalo horn in his hand, and announced this was not a dog and pony show, but sometimes people needed to see things so they would believe in the powers that surround us all. He held the horn out towards Kyle and motioned for him to ladle pour out some water as if he were filling the horn. Kyle did as he was told, and a second later Ghostkiller turned the horn upside down and the water Kyle had poured from a distance came spilling out of it.

On Kyle's sixteenth birthday, James had called for a sweat lodge ceremony to be held in his honor. As everyone sat around the fire outside, James placed something from the bundle in Kyle's hands and clasped his own hands around them.

"It is not my power, *cinks*," James said, "it is the Creator's power and it can be taken away just as quickly as it is gifted." The object in their hands began to glow blue. "Always handle this medicine with great care. Be thankful. Be humble. Never forget where you came from."

Kyle smiled sadly at the memory. Turning his attention to the medicine bundle, he unfolded layers of red cloth revealing its contents; colorfully painted sticks, a horse fetish, among other recognizable items that flooded him with memories

A wooden box painted with an image of a paint horse sat beneath an eagle fan. *Looks like Macedone.* He curiously lifted the lid and gently explored its contents; a perfectly round stone, a set of talons from a large bird, and a fragile, yellowed envelope with faded markings were among the items there. He removed the letter from the envelope and unfolded it carefully. The official letterhead of the White House in Washington D.C. dated December 26, 1862, glared up at him — it was the order from President Abraham Lincoln, pardoning his ancestor Ghostkiller from execution. The ink had faded over the years to the point where the document was blank. Under that envelope lay a medicine bag. It was doe-skin white and decorated with red porcupine quills. He recognized it as the bag holding the blue medicine James said would allow him to time travel. Tears welled up in Kyle's eyes. *Here it is,* he thought. He could hear the words his grandfather James had spoken so many times reverberate through his mind. *Never forget where you came from.* He knew however he was supposed to handle this curse that advice would carry him through. He also knew anything else that seemed pressing or important to him at this moment would have to wait, including the blonde-haired beauty that had just run out the front door of Aunt Rosie's house.

11

Father O'Rourke sat staring out the window of his office. The trees in the yard of the church rocked back and forth in the cool, fall breeze. The late afternoon sun peeked through the colorful leaves and its rays danced with shadows on the ground. Lost in thought, he hardly noticed the leaves that fluttered down. In the light of day, they were not the ominous entities that haunted his nights. In the light of day, everything seemed as right as rain.

His office was furnished with a brown leather couch, two matching high-back chairs, a huge mahogany desk and a fireplace that kept the place toasty warm during the bitter cold days of Minnesota winters. *A far cry from the shacks out on the reservation.* Three walls held floor-to-ceiling bookshelves crammed with every religious doctrine imaginable, and dark red carpet that made every footstep fall silent covered the floor. The shade had always reminded the clergyman of blood. *The blood of Christ shed for you.*

After gathering some of his things from the room he kept at the church, he had stopped by the office thinking he might pick up some reading material to take on the train, but he found he had no desire to spare a glance at anything on the bookshelf. He couldn't concentrate, couldn't bear to even think about filling his head with any sort of religious drone. He felt mentally frozen and simply could not shake the feeling of impending doom. In his mind, he pictured it encircling his head like a teenager's orthodontic apparatus.

A high-pitched screech from outside the window roused him from his thoughts. Children running through a nearby yard made his frown deepen. It reminded him of yet another time in some innocent, distant past. *The Dakota's lives would have turned out so differently if they had been left alone*, he thought. Their ceremonies and way of life would have remained intact, and perhaps eventually they would have given up their nomadic ways and settled down in one place on their own. They could have continued to hunt and fend for themselves, although he imagined they would have eventually taken up farming. Some of them actually had. *If they had lived as intended, this curse would not be an issue now.* He shook the thoughts from his head. Why think about that? Things were the way they were, and there was no changing it. *No point in rearranging deck chairs on the Titanic*, he thought ruefully. Or was there? His bags were waiting by the door and he glanced at them, wondering if he was doing the right thing. He had fought inner battles before, but none like the one he faced now. The curse continually plagued him and Kyle coming back into town just made it worse.

Kyle. The Father considered him for a moment. His grandfather James had given a good argument for his cause, that was for sure, and he seemed to have an answer for every question O'Rourke asked, too. What if everything he said about the legend was true? What if Kyle could right the wrongs in history somehow?

His mind batted the complexities of the situation, trying to reason it out in his mind. If there really were a curse and dark entities lurking about, O'Rourke certainly could be of assistance with that. He couldn't shake the feeling he was damning himself by leaving and not doing all he could to help. However, would he damn himself if he stayed? To stay would mean he believed in Kyle and everything James had told him, and that was the true problem. *Beware false prophets!*

"There is such a thing as the gift of discernment," James had told him. "Jesus Christ had that gift. We call upon our brother, *Wanakia,* Jesus, in our ceremonies. Surely you can't find fault in that, Father?" However, he could and did, but why? *You speak of a God who says all you need is the faith of a mustard seed.* James had said that to him many years ago, and here he was, running like a scared jackrabbit away from this town, away from his church. He dropped his head in his hands.

"Have I lost my faith?" He cried aloud, "Is that why I can't stay?"

Maybe he was too old. His seventy-fifth birthday was tomorrow, and maybe he just needed a break. Surely, God could understand that? Maybe he just didn't want to deal with it anymore? One thing was for certain, if he didn't stop badgering himself, he would never get on that train.

He rose from the chair and walked towards the doorway, pausing to look at the crucifix that hung over the mantle.

An altar of earth thou shalt make unto me.

He thought of the earthen mounds he had seen the Indians lay their sacred pipes on during ceremonies and stood for several minutes looking at the image of Christ on the ivory cross as he contemplated his decision. At last, he took a step back.

"We wrestle not against flesh and blood, but against spiritual wickedness in high places." He sighed as a lone tear trickled down his cheek. Turning towards the doorway, he clutched his Bible to his chest, lifted his suitcase and turned out the light.

The thick walls of the church and the expensive, stained glassed windows muffled the sounds from outside, the very sounds the Father needed to hear. As the wind whispered through the trees, a bird sang, a dog barked and the laughter of children playing nearby drifted away on the breeze – all answers to his prayers, and all lost in the massive spans of brick and mortar that made up St. Paul's Catholic Church.

12

Mason pressed hard on the accelerator hoping he would make it back to Rosie's before Kyle left. He knew once she gave Kyle the old man's medicine bundle, he would waste no time in getting to Redwood Falls. He noted the late afternoon sun and wondered briefly if Kyle might wait until daybreak to go, but then dismissed the thought. Kyle would be all too ready to leave as soon as he got the bundle. Truth be told, Mason was just as anxious as Kyle to be done with this whole curse business once and for all. These killings had been hanging over his head for as long as he could remember, and the sooner it was resolved, the better.

He secretly hoped Nina would confront Kyle, keeping him there for a while. If he knew Nina, she wouldn't let him leave without telling him exactly what she thought of him. She had been none too happy when he'd left her seven years ago, and she'd had plenty of time for that anger to fester.

It must have been hard on Kyle, he thought, living with the curse his whole life and knowing he was the one responsible for destroying it. To know that something so immense rested on his shoulders couldn't have been easy. No one would have blamed him if he had decided not to come back today. Nevertheless, of all the families Mason knew, the Ghostkiller's were fearless warriors who didn't let anything stand in their way of a fight, even if it involved evil spirits.

But, there was much more to it for Kyle. He knew how Nina's parents had died, as did they all; however, no one had ever told Nina. It was pointless for a child her age to deal with something like that, and as she grew up there had been no good reason to share the details with her. Becoming a surrogate uncle to her, Mason had grown to love her like his own, and it had been hard for him to watch her pine for Kyle all these years and still keep the truth from her. It must have torture for Kyle as well, being as in love with her as he was. *Still is.* Mason smiled. He was sure of that. If any two people deserved to be together, it was those two. Mason had only been in love once, and he remembered the joy of it every time he saw Nina look at Kyle and vice versa. *Well, they'll have all the time in the world to fix the mess their love life is in if all goes well,* he thought. The main thing right now was to get back to the reservation as soon as possible. He had to tell Kyle about Riley and figure out a few other things, too, like how Kyle was going to travel back into the past without anyone interfering. *Ha! Time travel? This day just gets better and better.*

"What a mess," Mason said aloud as he slammed the accelerator down, hating the fact the reservation was another half hour away.

13

Well, it's all here, Chase thought, *and every detail the same.* He sighed as he re-read the Bolton file.

Mark and Charlene Bolton were a young, white middle-class couple driving home one night and, Chase guessed, at the wrong place at the wrong time. Devil's Corner was the wrong place all the time, apparently. The obituary said they left a little six-year-old girl behind. *That must be Nina,* Chase thought, reading on. There was no evidence that pointed to a killer, and the couple was found in the same condition as the four kids last night, right down to the smiles on their faces. Mason was right about one thing – the murders were identical. He read the toxicology report and there was no drugs or alcohol in their bloodstreams. Reading further, he noted they had no prior warrants or arrests, not even a traffic ticket.

Chase yawned and stretched his arms overhead. It felt as if he had been reading for hours, although it hadn't been that long since Mason had dropped him off; or rather, had ordered him out of the car. He had been shocked at the way Mason had acted but figured the alcohol had something to do with it. He had seen it many times before with the Indians on the reservation, but Chase never knew Mason to drink. He was in recovery; maybe the murder just really shook him up. He had said he had been the first on the scene when the

Bolton's were killed. That was probably it. Well, either that or his mind was so wrapped up in the curse theory that he failed to see how ridiculous he was acting.

Shaking the thoughts from his mind, Chase stood and walked over to the window. The sun was beginning to set and he watched fiery fingers of golds and pinks reach far into the horizon.

God, he was tired. He had a mind to go back out to Rosie's and interview Kyle; but hell, he probably wouldn't get anything out of Kyle anyway except a bunch more mumbo jumbo crap.

Suddenly feeling ravenous, he decided some dinner and a bit of research were what he really needed to concentrate on. This wasn't L.A., and he didn't have any other cases pending, though this would take precedence if he did. He had the particulars, but this whole curse theory needed investigating, too. Not that he believed any of it, but if he had details about the hangings maybe he could find something tangible that would help. If all went well, he might even be able to talk some sense into Mason, get him to drop the whole curse theory and actually investigate. It would sure help in finding the real killer.

He had ordered a new Dell computer a few weeks ago and it arrived yesterday. He decided to order take out and spend the evening looking things up on the Internet. Maybe he could even find some information about the Ghostkiller or Stillwind names. He thought briefly of Nina, wondering how she fit into the whole story. She sure was a beautiful girl. *But she's young enough to be your daughter!*

"Touché!" Laughing at himself, he grabbed his jacket and headed towards the door. A thick, juicy steak would have to satisfy his manly cravings for now.

14

Nina tried with all her might to slow Macedone down, but he didn't stop until he was damn good and ready. She was terrified as he loped to just inside the edge of Crooked Gulch and slid to a stop two feet from it. She was out of breath, but Macedone was hardly fazed, blowing out a snort and stomping his foot restlessly. Thank God she was a better-than-average rider! Macedone was a huge stallion, and any weekend rider would have fallen off five miles back; but the sense of satisfaction she felt by taking the horse would have been worth a fall, she thought. It was a grand way of getting under Kyle's skin.

She sat there for several minutes, taking in the sunset with its crimson reds and lavenders mixed with the dark blues of dusk. Wispy clouds shrouded in lilac and pink hues hung in the sky as a cool breeze picked up the scent of wild sage. She only wished she could actually enjoy this beautiful Indian summer weather.

Thoughts of what had happened earlier plagued her mind, ruining the beauty around her. How dare Kyle come back and try to take her into his arms? It was his fault she would dare say what she did in front of Rosie. He was to blame, and it served him right to be stuck at her house for a while. It suddenly occurred to Nina that in coming back on his twenty-fifth birthday, Kyle had done exactly what he'd said he was going to do. "That's the only thing he made good on," she spat aloud.

For him to have expected her to wait for him all these years was his mistake. And he had thought that. She saw it in his eyes. On the other hand, waiting for Kyle is just what she had done, too, and she hated herself for it. Although she had managed to go to college and get a law degree during their separation, it had been hard, but she'd quickly learned that throwing herself into her studies was the easiest way to get Kyle out of her mind. She'd studied hard, and had kept such long hours that she was too exhausted to even think about him most days. She was due to go back for her Ph.D. in the spring and then planned to open her own law office assisting American Indians with their legal needs. Her career was on track, and she had spent the past seven years turning down dates while working her ass off in school, all the while quietly pining away for someone who had been too busy elsewhere to care.

"All in the name of some stupid legend," she scoffed. Macedone stomped his foot and snorted.

She wondered how many women he had dated while they had been apart. For a man with Kyle's good looks, there were probably too many to even count. The thought of Kyle's lips kissing someone else made her sick to her stomach. She remembered the girls that used to show up at the powwows to watch him dance. She and Kyle called them *Indian Barbies* and used laughed at how ridiculous those girls looked with their short buckskin skirts, or short-shorts, cowboy boots and skimpy, fringed halter tops. She smiled, but the smile quickly faded when she realized she had actually let herself dress like one today. *And he saw you like that!*

"Great!" she groaned aloud, rolling her eyes.

As darkness began to fall slowly around her, Nina

decided she had better get started back. There was a chill in the air and she wasn't dressed for night riding. She was thankful at least that she had changed into a pair of dirty jeans left in the barn before she left. Her blouse, however, was little more than a wisp of material. She looked around suddenly realizing how foolish it had been for her to go out so late in the evening half-dressed and without a weapon. Wild animals roamed the dark and Macedone might be a wonder horse, but a mountain lion or black bear could still easily bring him down. Turning the horse back towards the reservation, she silently prayed he wouldn't fall into a ground hog hole along the way.

15

"Macedone's gone!" Rosie heard Kyle yell from the living room.

"Gone? What do you mean he's gone?" Rosie exclaimed running from the kitchen to find Kyle standing at the front door.

Kyle's mind raced. The consequences of her taking Macedone were not good. He had to go to Redwood Falls and he had to ride Macedone there — it was part of the preparation. Nina was going to make sure he didn't go. It seems she fought him at every turn.

"That fool girl," Rosie said with a look of desperation. "It's getting dark, Kyle; it's not safe…" Her voice trailed off.

"Macedone won't let anything happen to her," Kyle soothed, giving Rosie a hug, hoping the horse would protect Nina.

Oh hell, he thought, *Macedone knows her! Of course, he would look out for Nina!*

The sound of skidding gravel brought them both out onto the front porch. Mason jumped out of the LTD and bounded up the steps.

"I'm glad you're still here, Kyle," Mason said, "I've got to talk to you about tonight."

"I won't be going tonight," Kyle told him. "Nina has taken Macedone."

Mason saw the look on both of their faces, and it immediately sunk in. "Took Macedone... oh Lord." Mason sighed. "What was that girl thinking?"

"She's thinking she's hurt and I'm to blame."

"But Christ, Kyle, she knows —"

"Nina is young and only knows her heart," Rosie interrupted. "She does not see the seriousness of what Kyle has to do." Then, looking up at her nephew, she said, "Nina has her reasons."

Kyle gave Rosie a grave look. He didn't realize that leaving Nina the way he had could result in something like this, but apparently Rosie had.

Mason was adamant. "Whatever the reason, Rosie, we've got to find her!"

"There's nothing we can do, Mason," Kyle said. "Macedone has probably just taken her on a joy ride and is already on his way back by now." He looked out over the vast prairie. "We just have to wait."

He didn't want to say aloud what he feared most — Macedone might just take his head and go to Redwood Falls, regardless of who was riding him. He had a meeting with destiny, and knowing the horse the way he did, the vastness behind his spirit, Kyle feared the worst. *Surely, he would come back for me?* He thought.

Mason and Rosie both picked up on Kyle's thoughts at once.

"Holy mackerel," Mason said.

"Sweet mother, no," said Rosie at the same time.

"Now don't both of you start!" Kyle said, nervously pacing the porch. "Macedone knows just as well as we all do that I have to go to Redwood Falls, too!"

"But does he think he has to take you there himself, or just go there at a particular time?" Mason asked.

Rosie looked at Kyle with fearful eyes. "Oh nephew, surely he wouldn't go with Nina, would he?"

"How long have they been gone?" Mason asked abruptly.

"An hour," Rosie answered, "maybe a little less."

"Let's go, Kyle." Mason was heading down the steps. "They could be half way there by now!"

Kyle knew that to wait and see if they returned would only put Nina in greater danger. If Macedone decided he was going to Redwood Falls, she could do nothing to stop him. If the horse did bring her back here, Rosie could tie him up in the barn until they got back. Kyle hesitated for just an instant. "All right," he said, turning to go back into the house, "but let me get something first."

"C'mon, man…" Mason began but stopped short when he saw Kyle emerging with Ghostkiller's medicine bundle.

16

Chase hooked up his computer after a dinner of steak and fried potatoes, courtesy of the Roadkill Restaurant, and then sat down to the task of compiling information. A quick search or two and he'd probably have enough to go on -- little did he know his search would turn up hundreds of pages of information.

After sifting through the fluff, he found about twenty pages which deemed worthy of a read. They were history sites with sources. He decided he'd tackle them one at a time and print out the ones that were the most relevant. However, even after narrowing it down, he still found himself with a stack of papers a mile high. When he printed the last one out, he sighed and picked up the one on top entitled, "The Minnesota Sioux Conflict."

> *After being driven off of their land, and months of fraudulent dealings on the part of agents of the government, war broke out between the Sioux and whites in Minnesota, after a white bootlegger named Robinson beheaded an Indian he caught hunting on his land. Abraham Lincoln appointed General John Pope to head the military forces in the area. The war had ended in early October, and over 1,000 Indians were held as prisoners (Nichols 1978, 94). General Henry Sibley, a former Minnesota governor who had been involved in highly questionable trade and claims deals with the Indians,*

subjected the Sioux to hasty military trials and, one month later, Lincoln was notified by General Pope that death sentences were to be carried out on 303 of the convicted Santee. Pope expressed his view that Lincoln was certain to approve the convictions and thus permit the executions: "The Sioux prisoners will be executed unless the President forbids it, which I am sure he will not do. (Brown 1970, 58)." Lincoln, however, telegraphed Pope requesting him to mail "the full and complete record of these convictions" in order to be evaluated before the executions were to take place (Basler V, 1953, 493).

Finally, on December 6, Lincoln wrote Sibley ordering that 39 of the 303 condemned Santee be executed (V, 1953, 542-43). One of the remaining 39 was pardoned, and on December 26, 1862, thirty-eight Sioux Indians were hung (VI, 1953, 7). At least one Sioux, named Ghostkiller, who had not been approved for execution by Lincoln, was hanged, apparently being included by mistake. Nichols notes that the hanging of the Sioux was "the largest official mass execution in American history in which guilt of the executed cannot be positively determined. (1978, 117)."

"So, Rosie was right," Chase said. "That one Sioux hanged by mistake was Ghostkiller!"

He quickly typed the name in the search box and a page popped up. This one talked about Ghostkiller and the curse itself, and claimed to be from eyewitness testimony:

Those present at the hanging said the Sioux danced and sang death songs all the way to the gallows; some even tried to hold hands that were bound by ropes. Once they reached the platform, they each called out their names as if introducing themselves, then thirty-eight nooses went around thirty-eight necks. When asked if they had any last words, one savage warned that a curse would haunt the town after his death. Once the interpreter finished translating, the rope holding the platform was quickly cut, and thirty-eight Indians were left swinging in the air. They were then taken and buried in a mass grave...

An update on the page stated the following:

It appears the mistake of hanging Ghostkiller was a grave one for the town of Moccasin Flats. Records show since 1862 there have been deaths near the site of the hangings. A white buffalo statue memorializes the site at Rock Road and Highway 13, otherwise known as Devil's Corner

Chase was suddenly wide-awake after reading that last bit of information. The next thing he printed out were obituaries he had found by doing a search on Google. A newspaper archives section from The Moccasin Flats Daily had popped up, and after entering a few keywords, he hit the jackpot. It didn't take long to sift through and see a pattern. The earlier obituaries were full of details:

September 19th, 1882
Man Killed While Hunting Bear Near Hanging Site
The curse of Ghostkiller may have rung true when Joseph Sidebottom was found dead yesterday morning. His wife Millie informed the Sherriff he had left before dawn to go bear hunting. When he did not return by supper, she and concerned neighbors struck out looking for him. They found him late in the evening at the old hanging site with his throat torn out. The searchers determined the bear had gotten the better of Joseph, but Millie insists the curse of Ghostkiller had

come true. Ghostkiller was among the thirty-eight Sioux Indians hanged twenty years ago for the crimes of murder and rape against white settlers. Millie's mother, Mary, had been one of the witnesses at the Indians' trial.

September 21st, 1902
Couple Found Dead at Lover's Leap
David Montgomery and Tabitha Holland were found murdered at Lover's Leap near Moccasin Flats. Tabitha's parents, Mr. and Mrs. Burchey Holland, said the young couple had left three days earlier to go on a picnic and never returned. Despite a desperate search by family and friends, the couple seemed to have vanished.

Two hunters discovered their bodies yesterday near Devil's Corner, apparent victims of a mountain lion attack. It is unclear how the bodies came to be in town. Sheriff Brady is warning one and all to stay close to home until the mountain lion is caught or killed.

So, the name Devil's Corner stuck through the years, too. Chase read on:

September 20th, 1922
Man Found Dead -Victim of Mountain Lion Attack
Thirty-eight-year-old Jesse Goff was found dead yesterday near Devil's Corner. Doc Connelly said he was the victim of a mountain lion attack.

September 19th, 1942
Three Children Killed near Redwood Falls
Three children, whose ages ranged from two to seven years old, were found yesterday evening in the back yard of their Redwood Falls home. Sarah, Mary

and Iceipheny Hayes, the children of Charlie and Nettie Hayes, were found with their throats torn out in an apparent attack from a mountain lion. Funeral arrangements are pending.

Eagle Lake home? He thought. *How far is Eagle Lake from Devil's Corner?* Another quick search brought up a map and he saw the two locations were within a mile of each other. Okay, so at this point the people of Moccasin Flats were associating the deaths with mountain lion attacks instead of the dreaded curse.

Reading through the rest of the obituaries, a thought struck Chase. *Maybe the total number of victims added up to thirty-eight? Yeah, thirty-eight victims to compensate for the thirty-eight Indians who were hanged?* Hell, if he was going to work on the facts of a curse, he might as well be as thorough as possible.

He counted until he reached the four who were killed the night before. "That only makes thirty-five," he said aloud. If the curse could be broken after Kyle's twenty-fifth birthday, why aren't there now thirty-eight victims?

Well, that blew his theory out of the water. *Of course it does*, Chase thought. *Because there is no such thing as a curse.* What there was, however, was a string of unsolved murders, over half of which were being blamed on a mountain lion. That would make sense, except that there were no mountain lions within fifty miles of Moccasin Flats now, much less ones that would politely close the door of a car before fleeing the scene.

"Uggg!" Chase blew out a sigh of frustration. "Thirty-five deaths including the one's last night," he whispered thoughtfully, lounging back in his chair and locking his fingers behind his head.

Besides the details he'd just read, the later obituaries gave few particulars about the deaths. One said 'hunting accident,' others said 'pending investigation,' and one even blamed Bigfoot; but they all fell around the same time in September. He could do a deeper search to see if there were any follow-up articles, but he probably wouldn't get the real story anyway. The mountain lion theory had most likely changed later with the fear of attacks so close to town. The curse story didn't show up anymore either, but that didn't surprise him. The town was small enough as it was. The newspaper wouldn't report rumors of a murderous mountain lion or an Indian curse that would scare potential business owners or tourists away.

He lit a cigarette and took a deep drag, contemplating his next move. Picking up the newspaper he had bought earlier, he skimmed through the pages, stopping when he came upon an article about Father O'Rourke that said he was celebrating his birthday tomorrow. It gave a few details about the priest, one in particular that caught his attention: he had lived in town for over forty years and had been the priest at St. Paul's Catholic Church since he'd arrived.

Chase decided he would talk to Father O'Rourke. If he'd lived here that long, he'd know about at least three previous murders, and maybe he could even shed some religious light on the curse. As skeptical as he was, Chase had to be thorough. For now, he was calling it a night. He didn't bother to look at the clock. His body was screaming for sleep, and he intended to give it what it wanted.

Grinding his cigarette into an ashtray, he arose from his chair, stretched the kinks out of his back and walked into the bathroom. He turned on the tap, splashed some cold water on his face and wiped his face and hands with a hand towel.

Looking at himself in the mirror, he mused, "Looks like

you're chasing a ghost after all, Riley."

17

It was well past dark when Kyle and Mason reached Redwood Falls, and despite their desperate search along the way, there had been no sign of Nina or Macedone.

"They're probably back at Rosie's by now." Mason offered as he and Kyle exited the vehicle.

"I hope so," Kyle said softly. Looking out over the river he watched as moonlight danced on the water like wet diamonds.

"I need to stay here," he said suddenly. "I have a feeling something is here that I need to wait around for." He then added, "I don't know if it's Nina or not, but this is too strong for me to ignore."

Mason understood. He had a weird feeling, too; something in the air felt almost tangible.

"Okay," he answered. "I'll go back to Rosie's and see if they've come back. If they have, do you want me to come back for you?"

"No," Kyle said, looking up at him for the first time. "I'll be back later." Mason took a step back when he saw Kyle's eyes. They were glowing like two black, shiny crystals, and tiny white lights were swarming all around his head. A blue glow began to rise up from the ground behind him and seemed to move towards where Kyle stood.

"I'll leave you to it, then," Mason said, respecting the

fact that he was witness to something otherworldly and not sure if he should stick around for it.

    Kyle leaned into the car, retrieved the medicine bundle, and walked towards the falls. The wind picked up brown and yellow leaves, which began to dance around the blue glow and follow the path Kyle took. Mason stole a glance at the water tumbling over the rocks in the nearby river seemed to surge faster as if responding to Kyle's approach. The pull to stay was so strong that Mason had to force himself to get in the car and drive away. He knew he had to let Kyle do whatever it was he had to do and dismissed his strong urge to stay as just a part of his own DNA working within him. As he pulled out, he noticed a blue mist had begun to roll in off the river, and when he checked his rear view mirror again, Kyle was out of sight.

18

Nina had finally given up on reining in Macedone. She had tried with all her might to turn the horse back towards Rosie's, but the stallion obviously had other plans, because there was just no stopping him. She had burn marks on her hands, a feeling of dread in her heart, and no idea where she was going. Macedone was running at full speed and seemed to be floating over the prairie, but that did little to make her ride any less uncomfortable. She thought she would die from the constant rub of the saddle and was kicking herself for taking him in the first place.

Doesn't this horse ever get tired? She screamed to herself.

The scenery had started looking familiar until the full dark of night closed completely around them. She prayed that Macedone wouldn't fall into any holes or trip over an unseen rock. Just then, the headlights of a car came into view and Macedone started to slow down. Nina waved a hand in the air, desperately trying to get the attention of the driver, but she couldn't let go of the saddle horn long enough to make any difference. Her legs were too weak from the physical demands of the ride to allow her to let go and wave with both hands. She watched hopelessly as the car drove out of sight. The full moon was playing dodge ball with the clouds, and she doubted the driver could see them anyway. Finally, she recognized what looked like the crest before Redwood Falls.

Maybe Macedone would be drawn to the water for a drink at least? Rounding a wall of boulders just before the floodwall, she saw a fog rolling in and it caught her off guard. It was an eerie light shade of blue that sent a shiver down her spine. *Now what?* Macedone slowed down to a trot and Nina thought she was finally going to gain control of him when she caught a glimpse of something in the distance. *Is that a man? Oh God!* What would happen to her if she ran into some deranged killer? Panic engulfed her and she tried once more to turn Macedone around, but he jerked his head forward and sped up again. He was running right towards the man!

"Oh God!" she cried.

Macedone lit out at a dead run and the man just stood there, as if he didn't see them. It was definitely a man, but she could see a strange, blue light surrounding him.

"What is *that*?" Nina cried out in a panic.

She tried once more to turn the horse. She could feel the reins getting slippery in her hands, and knew she was bleeding. It was no use. They ran closer and closer until Macedone was almost on top of the man

"Look out!" she shrieked, squeezing her eyes shut for the impact. All at once, the horse came to a dead stop, and Nina went sailing over his head. Time stood still as she waited for the crushing pain the ground was sure to deliver. Good Lord, at this speed she could break her neck. In one moment, she felt herself tumbling through the air; in the next, she was landing. Momentarily stunned, she lay motionless for several minutes, almost afraid to see where she was. Slowly opening her eyes, she looked up and found herself staring into the face of Kyle Ghostkiller. His face looked angelic, surrounded by a blue list and tiny white lights. She realized she was laying in his arms.

"Kyle?" she whispered. He smiled down at her and

that's when Nina noticed it was bright outside, not the dark of night as it should be, and there was a blue glow, almost like a shimmering mirror, engulfing them. Nina was mesmerized for several minutes and watched in awe. Was she dead? Had the aurora borealis come down from the heavens to get her? God, it was beautiful! It was then she'd remembered the stories she'd heard as a child about how the aurora borealis would come to you if you whistled to it. She found herself whistling involuntarily, a tune she recognized as a pipe-filling song she'd heard countless times as a child.

Turning her attention back to Kyle, her eyes widened as his face began to change. His eyes were the color of onyx, glowing with pinpoints of multicolored prisms around the pupil. The soft blue glow ascended around his face. Her heart began to hammer in her chest when she realized she wasn't dead at all and was looking at someone who just might not be Kyle Ghostkiller after all. She knew the stories of how ghosts and spirits could manifest themselves into things people wanted to see. She didn't know where she was exactly but knew she didn't like it. She had to get away, and fast!

In the distance, she heard a thunderous roar that sounded like a freight train coming straight for them. It reminded her of what people said tornados sounded like if they were lucky enough to live through one. The sound grew louder, the air pressure suddenly dropped, and it felt as if the air itself was being sucked out from around them. A cluster of dead leaves leaped up from the ground and began to swirl around them. Terror engulfed her as the leaves spun round and round, faster and faster. She started to scream and the man holding her shouted something in Dakota and took off running with her in his arms. Panic rose up in her and she kicked and screamed, struggling to break free. She had to get away! Suddenly she felt a crushing pain in her head and she felt herself falling, falling, and then everything faded to black.

Nina awoke to the sound of a crackling fire and a slight headache. The air was filled with the smell of wood smoke mingled with sweet grass, and she took in a deep breath of the familiar fragrances. She sat up slowly, trying to see if she hurt anywhere else, and that's when she felt the throb pulse through her hands. She looked down to see them wrapped in bandages. Traces of dried blood showed through the white material, and it was then she remembered her wild ride on Macedone. *Not a wonder why they feel like raw meat,* she thought. Someone had treated her wounds, but who?

Taking in her environs, she found herself sitting in a clearing surrounded by huge boulders. It was still dark and she couldn't see much from the glow of the fire, save the boulders and a few sprigs of sagebrush. She didn't see anyone either, not even Macedone. She tried to stand but her legs wouldn't cooperate, and in her frustration she dragged herself closer to one of the rocks, intending to use it to pull herself up; only her hands hurt too badly to even try. All at once, she heard muffled footsteps coming towards her. She looked around frantically for a weapon of any kind and saw nothing – not even a stick. She backed up against the rock, still warm from the afternoon sun, and waited, holding her breath. Suddenly, a large shadow of a tree person moved over the rocks towards her, and then Kyle emerged from around one of the boulders carrying an armload of firewood. Nina let out a yelp.

"Oh!" she cried, looking at him warily for any sign of the man with the glowing eyes. Finding none, she breathed a sigh of relief. "You scared me to death!"

"You scared me pretty bad, too," he smiled, dropping the armload of wood near the fire. "How do you feel?"

"Like I've been hit by a truck," she told him, rubbing

the back of her neck gingerly. "And my hands....what happened out there?"

"Well," Kyle walked over and sat down beside her. "Macedone and I had a date, so-to-speak," he checked the bandages on her hands, "and you caught the brunt end of that."

"A date? Kyle, what was going on out there? All those eerie lights, and that roaring sound – and where did you come from"?

Kyle thought for a moment about not telling her the truth, but what good would that do? It's not as if she'd never heard about any of this. Maybe if he told her everything, she might realize what he had worked so hard towards all his life had a lot to do with her, and she would forgive him for the past.

"Well, like I said, Macedone and I had someplace to go, but when you took him it messed things up a bit. He was still determined to get there, but he had the wrong person on his back. Once he saw me, he stopped before going through the, uh..." Kyle hesitated a moment before continuing, "...the veil."

"Veil?" she asked hesitantly.

"A gate to another time, a doorway to the past."

Nina wasn't sure she wanted to hear any more. She knew she had seen something other-worldly tonight, but she didn't want to believe it. Not after all she'd been through most of her life because of it. This whole thing about his *job* was the last thing she wanted to face right now.

"This is about the curse, isn't it?" It was more a statement than a question.

"Nina, it's real," Kyle began. "I've been trying to tell you, you need to understand this—"

"No!" she yelled, covering her ears, ignoring the pain

in her hands. Now she was sure she didn't want to hear any more. "How can you even feel right about telling me this after everything that's happened?"

"Nina, you have to hear this! You saw the veil yourself! You have to understand!"

"Understand what, exactly?" Nina fumed. It seemed she was right back in the living room at Rosie's and was about to explode all over again. The only difference was now she could say whatever she wanted without having to consider Rosie's feelings. "Why you left me seven years to go off to Pine Ridge for...whatever...to do *this*? You never even called! I didn't even see you at Grandpa James' funeral!" Nina said hotly. "My God, Kyle, I was so in love with you I didn't even know my own name!"

"Are you still?" his sudden bluntness caught her off guard. His eyes searched her face as he tried to gauge her reaction. The look of shock and then resolution on her face said more than any words could have. He remembered all of her then: the smell of her, the taste of her kisses, the way he had dreamed of making love to her. He had never forgotten any of it, regardless of how much time had passed. He couldn't count the number of sleepless nights he had spent thinking about Nina, fantasizing, imagining them together in a tangled web of arms and legs and soft sheets. All thoughts of where he was supposed to be and what he was supposed to be doing left him then. She was the only woman he had ever loved and it killed him not to be able to touch her now.

"What?" she spat out, scrambling to her feet. The anger that washed through her gave her legs strength they didn't have a moment ago. Tears welled up in her eyes.

"How can you ask me such a thing after all you've put me through?" She was not going to cry, dammit! But, it was too late. The tears came fast as she looked at him through tortured eyes. Kyle was on his feet in an instant, his tall frame towering over her, frustration oozing through his pores.

"What I put *you* through? You're the one who never tried to understand! What do you want an apology?" His face started to cloud over and Nina remembered his anger the last day they were together. She had no desire to repeat that argument. She didn't say a word, but simply brushed past him and walked towards an opening in between the boulders, not knowing where she was going except it was away from him.

Kyle was on her in an instant. He grabbed her shoulders and roughly turned her around to face him, gritting his teeth as he repeated the question, "What do you want from me? I won't apologize for trying to save my people!"

Nina looked up at him and suddenly burst into fresh tears, wrenching herself away from his grip. She knew he was right, knew she had been selfish to think of it any other way. It wasn't personal. Of course, he had done this for his people. Hadn't she researched enough to know what the Indians had been through? Hadn't they suffered long enough? She didn't want to admit just how selfish she had been.

"They're not just your people!" she choked, turning to run, but he caught hold of her around the waist, pulling her back. She cried out and let the tears flow, leaning into his arms as he held her to keep her from crumbling to the ground. She knew he was right, knew he'd had to do what was not only expected of him but what his heart had led him to do. It still didn't make it any easier to love him.

"No, baby, no," he soothed her, pulling her back against his chest. "Please don't cry." He turned her around and gathered her into his arms.

"Please Kyle, don't." She whispered, putting her hands against his chest. She intended to push him away, but couldn't deny the need to be near him. It was overpowering, and not wanting to fight it any longer, she went to him willingly, sobbing against his chest.

"Oh, baby," he soothed, stroking her hair.

Nina cried harder and Kyle held her tighter, trying to will the hurt from her heart. He felt torn between his love for her and the fact he had to deal with the curse, for that meant he would have to leave her again.

He held her shivering body for several minutes, trying to warm her with his own body heat, but it wasn't working. It was getting late and growing colder; he could see the mist of their breath in the chilly night air. Looking down at her clothes, he knew she was hardly dressed for the dropping temperatures. He held her for several minutes as her body racked intermittently with sobs and cold shivers. Finally, he scooped her up and carried her back to the fire. In one fluid motion, he sat down cross-legged in front of the blazing fire and tucked her tighter into his arms, rocking her back and forth until her sobs eased at last. He felt like he had indeed gone through the veil and they were back in the past. He could feel their remorse for the way they had left things. It was unspoken but he felt it as strong as his own feelings of love for her. And oh, how he loved her! That love sent desire shooting through him that burned hotter than ever before. How odd he would find himself aroused at such a time as this, but it was Nina, and his craving for her was still as fresh as it was when he was sixteen.

When her breathing finally became normal, he loosened his hold on her and drew back to look at her face. He pulled a bandana out of his back pocket and wiped her eyes, handing it to her so she could blow her nose.

Quietly he spoke her Indian name. "Sungska Cikala, I never meant to hurt you."

She looked at him then. His black, smoldering eyes burned into hers, sending shivers through her body that weren't caused by the cold. He loved her, wanted her, it was as plain as if he'd said it out loud. She couldn't tear her eyes from his, felt dizzy with the awareness and longing she saw there. How handsome he was. She reached up, softly tracing a line around his mouth with a gentle fingertip, and then dropped her hand back to her lap. What if she gave in to this feeling?

They stared at each other for long moments; time seemed to have no meaning for either of them. She called out his name in her mind and he heard her, the silent magic between them slowly coming to life. He lowered his head until his lips were scant inches from hers.

"What do you want?" Kyle whispered as he searched her face. She was so beautiful. Her eyes, dark pools of indigo that showed her every thought, looked up at him longingly. He looked at the full, pouty lips that demanded to be kissed and he intended to do just that.

"Answer me," he softly urged her.

"You," Nina answered, "just you." And with that, he claimed her lips slowly, giving her plenty of time to refuse. He didn't have to wait long for a positive reaction.

Her arms snaked around his neck and he pulled her closer. They both responded with all the pent up passion and frustration of the past seven years. Their mouths were hot and one hungrily searched the other for the taste of tongue and breath. This was a kiss like none Nina could remember, but she yielded to him, not caring the circumstances that brought them together went against all she thought was rational, giving in to the moment. She had waited so long. Kyle responded in turn, no other thought in his mind but Nina and all the love he had been waiting to give her.

They came together like two eagles fighting in midair, beautiful to behold, but violent at the same time. Their hands restlessly caressed each other, each of them feeling the heat that threatened to spiral out of control. Nina moaned into his mouth, running her tongue over his lips, driving him wild. He wasted no more time and her clothing seemed to magically disappear without so much as a snap being undone.

He lowered her down gently to the still warm earth, marveling at her body in the firelight. Her skin was so soft it felt like silk beneath his fingers. He ran his hands over her slowly, drinking in the vision before him. Her breasts were full, her belly and hips softly rounded. She wore her waist-length, flaxen hair parted in the middle and often kept it in braids, but he always loved to see it free and wild like it was now, spread out on the darkened earth like billows of silken clouds. Her eyes smoldered as she looked up into his face, her lips moist and slightly parted. She was no longer shaking, and the tears from a few minutes before were forgotten as she pulled his mouth down to hers once again.

He stretched out beside her, his face so close she could feel his breath fanning her face. His tongue traced slow circles around her mouth as his arm snaked around her waist. He quickly drew her on top of him, crushing her body to his. His arousal was evident and Nina pulled him to her.

She caressed his chest, taking in the hard muscles that tensed under her touch, the broadness of his shoulders and back, his forearms that felt like warm steel beneath her fingertips.

Kyle rolled over with her and hovered above her, taking in her beautiful flushed face and her lips swollen from his kisses. *Don't let this go on,* a little voice told him, *not yet, not like this!*

Desire burned in her eyes as she circled her arms

around his waist, pulling him to her. He hesitated, willing the voice to go away as he allowed his hand to explore her most intimate areas. Nina gasped and writhed beneath him. His body ached for her so desperately that for a moment he felt as if he might lose his breath if he didn't get control of it.

"Don't let this happen!" the little voice warned again, louder this time.

With a deep breath, he stopped what he was doing and looked down at her. He knew they had to stop.

"Nina," he groaned as he rolled off her and onto his back.

"What?" she gasped. "What's wrong?"

"God help me, I can't. As bad as I want you, I can't, not now, not like this."

Nina lay beside him breathing hard. At first, she was angry, but as her desire subsided, she quickly realized what almost happened would've been a mistake. She had fallen right back into his arms, just as she'd swore she would never do. As badly as she wanted him a moment ago, she wasn't about to lose her head over someone who would up and leave her again.

"I'm sorry," he said, gathering her into his arms.

"No, it's okay."

She laid her head on his chest, willing herself to close her eyes.

He would leave again. She just knew it.

19

The town was dark except for the glow from a few lamplights lining the street. The fact no one was out and about was actually a blessing to Mason.

When he had arrived back at Rosie's house earlier, he'd told her Nina had shown up at Redwood Falls and was there with Kyle and Macedone. He didn't know how he'd known, but he had and had gotten the message while driving back to Rosie's from the river. Even though Rosie had offered him the couch, he decided to come back to town. Despite her worries about him driving back so late, he assured her he would be all right and would return early in the morning. Indians often disappeared on the reservation at night, and he knew that had been Rosie's real concern. She had nothing to worry about. He packed a loaded 9mm everywhere he went and always wore extra ammunition in two clips he carried on his belt. There would be no hesitation if he were to come across undesirables, even if it meant shooting one of the FBI agents. They certainly had no qualms about shooting Indians. No, he would have no problem shooting them at all.

He parked in front of Grady's, thinking he would go in and talk to Tony, but something urged him to walk across the street to the police station first. He had radioed dispatch when he'd left the reservation and became alarmed when he didn't get an answer. *It would be just like Sam to be sleepin' off another drunk behind the desk,* Mason thought irritably. He hoped that's all it was, but he didn't like the feeling in his gut.

The night air was cool, yet thick with electricity, and so oppressive it almost felt as if the oxygen was being sucked from it. Mason felt it as soon as he stepped from the LTD. Lightning storms felt this way, but that would be unusual for this time of year. Now that he was here in town, he wished he had stayed out at Rosie's place. An eerie feeling hung in the air; something wasn't right, and the closer he got to the police station, the deeper the feeling sank in, right down to his bones.

As he walked slowly towards the police station, he thought about the mountain of paperwork he had waiting for him, but he really had no desire to tackle that tonight. He knew the FBI would rifle through his files and try to dig up whatever they could to pin the murders on an Indian. In his experience on Pine Ridge, they pinned everything on Indians, even if there was no crime committed. Wounded Knee taught him that.

Might just put that paper shredder to good use tonight, he laughed to himself.

He stood in front of the police station for several minutes facing the door. Taking in the sound of silence, a cold chill ran down his spine. He turned and looked up and down the street, but there wasn't another soul in sight. He suddenly felt as if he were the only person in the world.

All at once, the wind started to pick up. A newspaper carelessly left on a nearby bench fluttered behind him, and he turned quickly to watch its pages scatter and go dancing wildly down the street. He could hear the limbs of the huge cottonwood trees that lined the road groaning in protest. He could smell the grease from the Roadkill restaurant mingled with dust kicked up by the breeze. A dog barked far off in the distance. It was then he heard something else – a familiar sound, yet one he hadn't heard in a long time. *Skittle, skittle scratch, skittle, skittle scratch!* He looked to his left and saw a dust devil carrying a pile of leaves swirling towards him. It seemed odd to see this on the sidewalk. *Don't they need circular air to form and move?* Mason shrugged mentally as he watched the whirlwind bring the leaves closer. The sound they made was familiar enough, but then it turned into something else. He strained his ears to listen. It was almost a whisper, and he was suddenly reminded of the leaves under the Chrysler.

All at once they were upon him, the leaves spinning around him in a cloud of dust. He began to choke and cough, flapping his arms as the dirt stung his eyes and nose. Then he heard soft voices begin to call his Indian name.

"Crow Walker, Crow Walker," they cried softly, "save Ghostkiller, save Ghostkiller."

"Wh — what?" he called out, but the dust devil swirled noisily around him, faster and faster. It seemed urgent that it get its point across. He spun around and lunged for the door of the police station, but the door wouldn't open. Crouching down, he pressed his shirt sleeve over his face as the dust continued to assail his eyes and nostrils. The leaves called out to him again.

"Crow Walker, hear us!" they whispered. "You and the *wasitchu* must help save Ghostkiller!"

It was over as quickly as it had begun, leaving Mason coughing and gasping for breath as he turned and slid down the doorjamb. He sat there for several minutes, trying to get his bearings, hearing the *skittle scratch* sound make its way down the street.

"What the hell was that?" he gasped aloud.

Trying the knob again, he found it opened easily this time. Still dazed and out of breath, he managed to crawl inside, slamming the door shut behind him. Leaning heavily against it, he tried to grasp what that message meant.

What is going on? 'The wasichu'…who, Riley?

He took off his hat, dusting it against his knee. The leaves had left little doubt that they wanted him to do something, but what exactly was he supposed to do, and why the big production?

Now all he had to do was figure out what it meant. *'The wasichu has to be Riley*, he thought. *Save Kyle? Is that what they meant by Ghostkiller?* Kyle had been glowing like a neon sign out at Redwood Falls. Was Mason supposed to go back there? Was Kyle in trouble? No, that couldn't be it. Kyle was the savior in this whole mess, and he had the protection of the old man's medicine bundle, not to mention Macedone. No, this was something else, something that was meant for him alone. He thought briefly about going back out to Rosie's; she would know what to do.

He sat for a moment listening to his thoughts and suddenly realized there was not a sound inside the police station, not even the garble of the radio. He called out to Sam but got no answer. Surely the man had heard the door slam?

Irritated, he decided if he didn't find Sam here, he was most likely across the street at Grady's bar. The time had come to bust his chops once and for all. Sam had always denied he drank on the job, but Mason knew better. He couldn't count the number of times he had come in and caught him sleeping off a drunk during his shift. He knew he was going to have to do something about Sam or he'd never hear the end of it from Chase. Rising to his feet, he walked over to the front desk a few feet away. The eerie stillness in the room crept up his spine and made the hair on the back of his neck stand on end.

"I swear if he's not here…" Mason muttered irritably, trying to convince himself that everything was normal rather than face the feeling of dread creeping back into his chest.

He looked behind the front desk, half expecting to see Sam asleep on the floor, but he wasn't there.

"Sam?" He called again, but still got no answer. Mason rounded the corner and started down the hall towards the office he shared with Chase. He stopped short when he noticed the door to the bathroom was ajar. As he drew near, he saw that a shoe was wedged in it — a man's shoe.

Drawing his pistol from beneath his jacket, he crept to the door and slowly pushed it open. To his horror, he saw a man's body on the floor in a pool of blood. *So much blood!* Enough to paint the whole room. He walked through the door, mindful of where he stepped, and upon closer examination knew it was pointless to check for a pulse. The man's neck had the same jagged wound that had become so familiar, like a jack-o-lantern's smile – matching the one on his face. A cold chill ran down his spine.

"Jesus, have mercy," he whispered.

This was impossible. Mason simply could not comprehend what he was seeing, yet as he stood there staring at it, his mind slowly registered the fact that his friend, Sam Thinnergan, was the dead man lying on the floor.

20

Chase was running in slow motion. He didn't know where he was or how he had gotten there, but remembered reading somewhere you could wake yourself up from a nightmare by blinking repeatedly. It didn't work. Instead of waking, his blinking eyes brought the walls of a cave slowly into focus and he could finally see where he was. He was thankful for that, at least.

His legs felt like lead and he slipped a few times on the wet cave floor but continued on, running while dodging and ducking to avoid the stalactites that hung overhead. He didn't know why he was running, but the urgency to escape was all too real. Suddenly his steps came in real time, and he was no longer running in slow motion. At the same time, he heard the sound of horses' hooves clattering in the distance, echoing off the walls of the cave as they closed in. Then he heard another sound, difficult to discern until it dawned on him they were war cries – the whoops and howls of his pursuers. He was being chased! *Chase is being chased!* A little voice laughed. He was so out of breath he thought he would drop, but he knew he couldn't stop as if the terror that engulfed him would have allowed such a thing anyway.

Who is chasing Chase? The little voice whispered. There was a fork in the passageway up ahead and he saw a dim, blue light glowing out of the one to the left. *Go that way!*

He cut to the left quickly, following the voice's advice, and scurried down the corridor hoping he had found a way out. He ran on and on, slipping and stumbling all along the way until at last he found the end of the tunnel – but it was a dead end.

You're in a cavern that you can't escape from! The little voice cooed.

He searched desperately for an outlet — a doorway, a crack in the rocks, anything —to no avail. He was trapped, and knowing there was nowhere left to run, he stood stock still listening as the horses' hooves, the whoops, and hollers, drew closer. Breathing heavily, he swung around to face his pursuers, determined not to show fear, no matter what.

Die like a man!

As the sounds closed in, he felt the cold hand of death clutch at his heart. The hooves took on a different sound, almost like the rhythmic beating of a drum, as they clamored towards him from the dark recesses of the corridor.

Suddenly, all was quiet and he waited, almost afraid to breathe. Peering wide-eyed through the dim light of the room, he saw the shape of something beginning to form in the shadows near the opening he had just come through. A glowing, eerie blue mist surrounded the form, and as it grew brighter, the figure slowly materialized before Chase's eyes.

It was a Sioux warrior. Chase somehow knew it as soon as he saw him. He was sitting atop a huge paint horse, reminding Chase of the horse that had been tied in front of Rosie's when he had left her house earlier that day. The Indian's entire body was painted yellow. He wore leggings and a breechcloth that looked like it was made of animal fur. A full animal skin with its head still intact adorned the Indian's head in poncho fashion. The animal skin looked like a fox to Chase, but if it were, it was a young fox.

A kit fox, the little voice said, *very good.*

He was curious as to how the details of the Indian's costume were easy to see despite the lighting conditions, and almost as soon as he thought that, the blue light grew brighter. A few small pouches hung from the fox's nose and Chase recognized them as medicine bags; porcupine quills were embroidered on the fox's feet and ears, and strung to them were small bells. The Indian carried an S-shaped lance wrapped in fur; one end had a feather tied just below the point, and then three groupings of feathers adorned each of the crooks. Chase recognized the eagle feathers and knew the Indian had had to earn them before he could place them on the lance as he did.

The warrior had piercing black eyes, a straight nose, and a full, generous mouth. His copper-toned skin glowed in that unearthly blue light and his hair was long, straight, and shined blue-black. His jaw was clenched, showing the deliberateness of his cause. He was obviously very angry and Chase tried to back away from him, but his feet were frozen to the spot.

"Get out!" The warrior yelled in the Dakota language, waving the lance at Chase. Every movement made the bells on his poncho jingle.

"Get out!" He repeated louder, urging the horse to take a step closer. Chase may not have understood the words, but he got the Indian's meaning loud and clear.

"I...?" Chase began.

"You are not welcome!" The warrior yelled, and Chase heard him in English this time.

Chase tried to move, but his feet remained frozen to the ground. All at once, the warrior thrust the crooked end of the lance at him, hitting him in the shoulder. Chase's feet suddenly released and he stumbled backward, never taking his eyes off the Indian.

He knew somehow that the warrior meant it as a way of testing him, that this was a way of counting coup, to strike at an enemy without harming him. Chase instinctively reached for the lance, but the warrior withdrew it, staring at Chase with those piercing black eyes. Oddly enough, his face seemed to soften a bit.

Immersed in the cave's eerie blue light, Chase stared back at the warrior, jutting out his chin and thrusting out his chest, mentally saying he was not afraid, although he imagined he looked more like a deer caught in headlights. His heart was beating so loudly he felt sure the Indian could hear it. Suddenly a chill washed over him as more warriors appeared, all painted and dressed the same as the first. *Kit Fox Warriors!* His mind echoed what the little voice had said. He braced himself for death as they each drew back their lances in unison.

"*Hiya.*" The first warrior held up his hand. The others immediately dropped their lances. The warrior on the big, brown paint horse looked at Chase thoughtfully for several minutes, and then urged the horse forward. Chase stood fast and defiantly looked up at the warrior, petrified beyond belief, but determined not to show it. The horse stared at Chase, his soulful eyes sending a message telepathically saying, "Don't be afraid!"

The warrior pulled the huge paint stallion to a stop in front of Chase and looked down at him, his face a mixture of curiosity and admiration. Chase could smell the scent of horseflesh and damp earth. The glow of the eerie blue light illumined the warriors face, and Chase thought he recognized him, but couldn't quite put his finger on where he had seen him before. He could feel the sweat running down his back in anticipation of what would happen next. Suddenly the warrior leaned over and thrust the lance towards Chase.

Chase didn't understand a single word. *What do you want me to do?* He thought. As if the warrior had heard him, he leaned out further from the horse and thrust out the lance again. "Give this to my grandson."

Chase's heart was pounding like a runaway train. The warrior nodded and Chase cautiously took a step forward and reached out for it.

The loud ringing of the telephone snapped Chase awake. He sat bolt upright in bed, his heart racing as he struggled to come out of the fog of the dream. His face and body were bathed in sweat beneath the tangled covers. Heaving them aside he reached for the phone.

"Shit!" he muttered, finally grabbing the receiver. "Yeah?" he answered loudly.

"Riley?" It was Mason's voice. "Riley, you there?"

"Yeah, I'm here," Chase answered shakily.

Looking at the clock, Chase noted the time. "It's five o'clock in the freakin' morning, Mason…,"

"Get dressed," Mason ordered, "and meet me over at the Roadkill." Then, after a pause, he added, "Sam's dead."

Mason's words never even had a chance to register. The dial tone filled Chase's ear as he sat on the edge of the bed. His eyes fixed on an object that stood in a corner near the doorway; it was the lance from his dream.

21

It was daylight when Nina awoke to the smell of frying fish, and at first, she thought she was at home. When she opened her eyes, she saw the wall of boulders and turned her head to see Macedone dozing lazily in the morning sun. When she looked down, she noticed that she was wearing nothing but Kyle's shirt, and the events of the night before came rushing back. Examining her hands, they didn't hurt nearly as bad today. She sat up and hugged her knees to her chest as she remembered their lovemaking. She and Kyle hadn't gone all the way, but they had done enough to qualify. She was glad they'd stopped. She couldn't risk her heart again.

She spotted Kyle hovering near the other side of the fire pit, a stack of fried fish beside him on a tin plate. She watched him for several minutes, admiring the way his hair flowed gently down his back; it was such an inky-black color, it looked blue in the early morning sunlight. He had an eagle feather tucked into a hair knot that he'd tied behind his head. Lost in thought, she smiled as she watched him work. He was cooking the fish on a stick, and the tight cord of muscle in his forearm bulged as he turned it over, reminding her of how his arms had felt when he'd held her the night before – strong and sure, and yet gentle, treating her as if she might break. He wore nothing but a pair of Levis and his moccasins, and the sight of him aroused her tremendously. Nothing else was said last night, but she knew he hadn't slept any better than she had.

"Did ya go fishin'?" she teased. Kyle looked up at her, surprised that she was awake.

"Yep, and looky what else I have." He smiled at her as he reached for his knapsack and pulled out thick chunks of fry bread, courtesy of Aunt Rosie.

"That's gotta be auntie's fry bread!" Nina exclaimed, suddenly ravenous. The smell of the fried fish made her mouth water.

"Well, get your pretty ass outta bed and get over here," Kyle teased, as he plopped the last of the fish he was cooking onto the tin plate with the others.

Nina needed no further invitation as she scooted over to the fire and dug in, grabbing a piece of fish, then the fry bread, and biting into both.

"Someone's got a mean appetite this morning," Kyle mused as he sat beside her, joining in the breakfast he had cooked.

"I'm starving!" Nina smiled.

"Me, too," he smiled back, biting into the fish.

They ate quietly, each lost in their own thoughts. Last night had been magical, something neither of them would ever forget, but the question that remained in both of their minds was still unanswered. The light of day brought thoughts of the future, and that was something they really needed to talk about; but first, Kyle had to ask the question that had been burning in his mind all night. He wiped his hands on his jeans, then turned to face her.

"So, you got your law degree?"

"Yes," she answered, licking crumbs off her fingers, I was valedictorian of my class, too."

"Impressive," he pulled a leaf from her hair.

She pulled back a little. She really didn't want to get into all of this now. All she really wanted to do was go home. She was still too raw emotionally.

"We need to get home," she said suddenly, "Rosie must be worried sick!"

"Nina, we really need to talk about last night."

"Later," Nina said, "Can we just go?"

Kyle didn't understand why she was acting this way, but he knew it was best to get her home. He was already behind schedule.

"No problem."

They both scrambled to their feet to get dressed.

22

The Roadkill Restaurant was half a block from Grady's Bar and was owned and operated by Dakota Indians, just like most all of the other businesses in town. It was the only safe place to talk this morning, which is why Mason had asked Chase to meet him there. The FBI had converged on Grady's so he stopped by to check on Tony. He should've known that getting out of there wouldn't be as easy as he thought. After getting stuck in an interview with an Agent Ryan regarding the details of Sam's demise, Mason rose from his chair as another 'stuffed-shirt,' as he called them, approached.

"Agent Lee Tarkington," the man flipped out his badge and waved it in front of Mason's face. Mason rolled his eyes.

Oh, this is just great. He was already well acquainted with the man; he knew Tarkington from his Wounded Knee years out on Pine Ridge during the seventies. He was one of the agents who'd shot up the church during the takeover when Joe Stunz was killed. Of course, it was never proven they did it. After the Wounded Knee standoff, Tarkington had made it his life's mission to hassle full bloods. From housing issues to possession of eagle feathers, and everything in between, he was there making trouble. Tarkington had even once charged Mason with possession of a migratory bird, but the charges had been dropped, much to the lawman's chagrin.

Tarkington was an older man in his mid-fifties, tall,

with steely blue eyes, thin lips and dark hair graying at the temples. His potbelly hung over slacks that looked at least one size too small; the buttons on his shirt bulged, threatening to pop off any minute.

"I'm well aware of who you are," Mason drawled. "Any relation to Dan Tarkington?" he smiled sarcastically.

"My son," the agent answered, tight-lipped.

So that's how Dan got his job, Mason thought, *Daddy is the FBI!*

"Ah, I see," Mason said as he started past him.

"I need yesterday's report before you go," Agent Tarkington stepped behind a chair that stood between him and Mason, curling his chubby fingers over the back rail. "I should have had it yesterday, but it seems you Indians are too lazy to tie up your loose ends around here."

Mason stared hard at the man, clenching his fists. *This son-of-a-bitch would like nothing more than for me to drive my fist into his ugly face so he can throw me in jail,* Mason thought. *Well, I won't give him the satisfaction!*

"I already told Ryan all you need to know." Mason retorted, kicking the chair hard enough so that the chubby fingers had to release it, "and if I that's not good enough, too bad!" He tilted his head to the side and deliberately looked at the man as if he were a sideshow oddity. Tarkington backed up a step and Mason breezed past him, eager to be out of the confines of the bar.

"Crow Walker, I need it on paper!" Tarkington yelled after him. "You might be a lawman, but I can still throw your ass in jail if you're deliberately withholding evidence!"

"Kiss my ass!" Mason yelled over his shoulder as he walked out the door, sprinting the rest of the way to the Roadkill. He knew Tarkington couldn't do anything to him regarding the report, but he could sure trump up a host of other charges if it suited him.

He hoped that Chase had had a chance to fill out some of the paperwork last night, saving him the task of trying to explain his theory of the killings to the FBI. He didn't intend to lie to them, after all. If he filled it out, he would write in the facts of the Ghostkiller legend and tell it like it is. *Yeah, the FBI would love that!* He thought.

The sharp scent of frying bacon reminded Mason he hadn't eaten since the fry bread Rosie had given him yesterday. The thought of Rosie's fry bread mixed with the smells of the restaurant made his stomach growl loudly. He scanned the room for Chase and saw him sitting alone at a table by a far window. He was surprised he had gotten there so fast.

It was quite crowded, mostly with local Indians, but to his relief, there were no FBI agents lurking around. He knew most of them were still at the police station and at least four were at Grady's bar. As he made his way to Chase's table, he heard a few hushed comments about Sam and hoped no one would stop to ask him about it. He got a few nods from some familiar faces, but that was about it.

Chase was smoking a cigarette and nursing a cup of coffee as Mason approached. He immediately noted the dark smudges under Chases' eyes, along with the ashtray that overflowed with his cigarette butts. Apparently he hadn't gotten much sleep the night before, either.

"Mornin'," Mason sat down, motioning for the waitress to bring some coffee. He waited for Chase to reply or to start hammering him with questions, but they didn't come.

"Rough night?" he asked after a few minutes passed.

"You could say that," Chase answered quietly, staring into his cup and not looking up at Mason.

He's probably still sore about yesterday, Mason thought.

"Listen, Chase. About yesterday…" Mason began, thinking about the argument they'd had the day before.

"Forget it, Mason," Chase interrupted. "We have more important things to worry about than a stupid disagreement."

Mason's brow furrowed. Chase was right, he had to admit. The events of the past two days were enough to strain even the strongest of friendships, and Chase was his friend, after all. Just because Mason was his superior didn't mean he thought himself better than Chase or above him in any way.

He studied Chase thoughtfully. The poor guy had no idea what was going on, and it really wasn't his fault that he didn't believe in the legend. Chase was from a different world and knew nothing of Dakota beliefs.

The waitress approached and sat a cup and saucer on the table along with silverware wrapped in a napkin.

"Anything else?" She asked, smiling down at Mason. She poured him a cup of steaming hot coffee and then sat the decanter down on the table. She was an older woman with dyed, bleach- blonde hair and red lipstick that feathered out around the lines of her mouth. A blue bandana tied in her hair matched her low-cut uniform that had obviously been altered. Mason recognized her as Mitzy Hollinger, who usually worked the drive-through window, and who always leaned out far more than necessary to hand him his coffee every morning. She was notorious for bedding Indian men, and just about everyone on the reservation had had her. All except the traditional Natives, that is.

"Yeah, I'll have two eggs over easy, bacon and wheat toast," Mason told her, amusement in his eyes.

"Terrible news about Sam, isn't it?" Mitzy said as she wrote down his order. "How many murders does that make this week?"

Chase looked up at Mason. They both knew what she

was doing. It was well known that Mitzy was not only the town slut but the town gossip, as well.

"Yes, it is terrible, but we can't discuss the details, Mitzy. You know that." Mason said crisply.

"Oh, I know." She mused. "You want anything else, sugar?" She asked, turning to Chase.

"No, thanks."

"Let me know if ya change your mind!" She winked at Mason before turning and walking away, sashaying her hips suggestively. He watched her, glad that he'd never been desperate enough to take her flirting seriously. That had never stopped her from trying to bed him, though, and she made no bones about the fact that she wanted him.

"You saw Sam, then?" Mason asked, turning his attention back to Chase.

"Yes," Chase answered, not looking up. Then clearing his throat he added, "Lee Tarkington hammered me all the way over here about it."

"Yeah, he cornered me in Grady's, too. It seems he wants to compare notes," Mason studied Chase's face. *What was wrong with the kid? He looks like he's seen a damn ghost!*

"Are you okay, Riley?"

"Mason, I had a dream last night that shook me up pretty bad."

"Yeah?" Mason refilled his cup.

"There's some weird stuff going on around here," Chase said, "and I need some answers."

Mason stopped stirring the sugar he had spooned into his cup and looked up at Chase.

"Answers about what exactly, Riley?"

Chase looked up at him and then diverted his eyes while he nervously lit another cigarette. How was he going to explain that he didn't feel the curse theory was ridiculous anymore? That after having a dream, his whole outlook on things had changed? Not to mention what he'd found in his room when he woke up. At that moment, he didn't know what was real or imagined. He was shocked to hear about Sam, but his death fit the pattern Chase had already suspected and it scared the hell out of him. He decided to tell Mason everything and hoped he would believe his change of heart once he heard all the details and saw the lance.

As Chase related the dream to him, Mason saw the warrior he described materialize right beside him, then vanish abruptly. He thought the warrior resembled Kyle, but couldn't be sure.

"Kit Fox Warrior," Mason said matter-of-factly, "you were visited by a Kit Fox Warrior. They paint themselves yellow and carry lances just like the one you described. They were the buffer zone for the tribe, facing attackers first so the women, children, and elders of the village could escape. What did he say to you again?"

Chase stumbled over the Indian words from his dream and Mason corrected him, translating what they meant.

"It roughly means, 'Get out.'"

"Yes!" Chase said slowly, "that's what I heard in my head, but he spoke it in Sioux. What do you make of it?"

Mason rubbed his jaw and looked at Chase for a long moment. The spirits were giving Chase a message — one that he may not want to hear.

"Well," Mason began, reaching for his coffee cup, "you may not want to hear this, but I think you were asked to leave, as in, 'butt out of the investigation.'"

He brought the cup to his lips, ready for the fallout, but Chase surprised Mason with his reply.

"Oh, yeah? Well, my white ass ain't goin' nowhere, Mason." He leaned forward, adding quietly, "We have a ghost to catch!"

"Whoa now," Mason sat his cup down and held up his hands. "What's this *we* shit? You don't believe in the legend, remember? What about the hokey-pokey shit I heard from you all day yesterday?"

"I know what I said yesterday," Chase admitted, "but something happened to me last night, Mason. I feel differently about things today." He looked at Mason through bloodshot eyes. It was obvious Chase hadn't gotten much sleep and he did seem to be thinking differently today, that was for sure. Maybe the dream really had changed his mind, but that still wasn't enough to convince Mason.

"Look," Mason began, "ya can't just have a dream about Indians and then all of the sudden —"

"I know that," Chase interrupted, "there's more."

Mason sat back and crossed his arms. "Go on."

"You all talk about having visions all the time. Don't they come in dreams, too?" Mason could already see where Chase was going with this and was surprised. "They can," he mused, "but I have to impress upon you that one dream does not a vision make!"

"Oh, okay," Chase said, seeing the look on Mason's face. "You're gonna tell me now that it's impossible for a white guy to have a vision?"

"No, not impossible."

Mitzy arrived with his order and Mason scooted back in his chair, studying Chase while she laid out the food in front of him. He couldn't believe this was the same guy who'd given him so much grief yesterday about the legend. Chase was actually arguing with him about a dream that he thought might be a vision. *Incredible.* He decided to hear him out.

"Thanks, Mitzy," Mason picked up his fork and dug in, sopping up yellow egg yolks with his toast. She stood there watching him eat, taking her time while filling his coffee cup again.

"I'll just refill this for ya'll, okay?" she said, holding the coffee pot.

"Okay," Chase nodded, and then stared hard at her until he made her so uncomfortable that she left. She took so long Mason almost had his plate cleaned before she finally walked away.

Sheesh, has she no shame? Chase thought.

"Still waiting..." Mason drawled in between chewing.

"Well," Chase began, "I wrote down the other words I heard him say, but I'm sure I didn't spell them right." He reached into his shirt pocket and unfolded a piece of paper, handing it to Mason. At first, he couldn't make out a single word, but as Mason looked at the scrawled letters and voiced it out loud, it wasn't too hard to figure out.

"Give this to my grandson."

It suddenly dawned on Mason, and he looked at Chase in astonishment.

"This can't be..." He stared at the paper in bewilderment. "Give what?"

Chase leaned forward and whispered. "I have something to show you. It's in my trunk."

Mason looked around and saw Mitzy watching them. "Let's not get up too fast. I don't wanna draw attention from Miss Peyton Place over there. Listen, I got a similar message last night, too," Mason told him. "I think the warrior you saw was Ghostkiller himself. Didn't you think he looked like Kyle?"

Chase remembered he did look familiar, but he hadn't been able to put his finger on why, or who the ghost warrior had resembled. Chase sat there wide-eyed and speechless; he knew then he had seen Ghostkiller too.

"I know just how you feel," Mason said when Chase didn't say anything. "Got any suggestions as to what our next move should be?"

"Well…" Chase thought for a moment. "Neither one of us are religious men, as far as the *wasichu* believe anyway, but I would really like to talk to Father O'Rourke about all of this – you know, get a religious stance on the whole thing," Mason smiled at Chase's use of the Dakota word.

Just then, Mitzy came by their table again to clear the dishes, overhearing what Chase had said.

"Father O'Rourke left town," she stated flatly, knowing that would get both men's attention.

"Sorry, I couldn't help but overhear."

"I'll bet," Chase muttered.

Mitzy ignored Chase. "The good father left this morning to go back to Montana."

"Montana?" both the men said in unison.

"Yeah, he stopped in here for coffee right before a cab showed up to take him to the train station." Leaning in, she winked and half whispered to Mason, "He asked if he could pray for me before he left, but I told him there was no saving my soul at this stage of the game."

She paused, looking from one man to the next, then stood upright and thrust out a basket with a red checkered towel draped over the sides. "Biscuit?" she offered. Chase took one, but Mason declined.

"Did he say anything else?" Chase asked.

"No, but I saw him talking to some of them agents before he got in the cab." She picked up the plates, and batting her eyelashes at Mason, asked, "Ya'll need anything else?"

"No, thanks," Mason answered, raising his eyebrows and turning back towards Chase, ignoring her.

"Nothing else for me, either." Chase dismissed her with

the wave of his hand.

"Well, kiss my ass," Mason said as Mitzy walked away. "The old padre done skipped town."

"So much for that," Chase threw down his napkin. "But what I'm wonderin' is, what did O'Rourke tell the FBI?"

"It goes without saying Kyle Ghostkiller's name came up," Mason said. "Everyone knows how close the padre was to that family."

Chase sighed, swallowing the last bite of his biscuit and slurping down his now-cold coffee. "Let's get out of here. You need to see what's in my trunk."

Mason threw a few dollars on the table and followed Chase to the front of the restaurant. Mitzy watched with a sneer on her face as the two men stood at the cashier counter.

"That half-breed must think he's too good for me," she spat out to a dark-haired girl filling water glasses.

"I'll bet he's gay," said the other girl, and they both giggled hysterically as the bell on the door jingled, signaling Chase and Mason's departure.

The streets were full of traffic. Horns blew and dust swirled as yet another unmarked car full of FBI agents pulled up in front of Grady's.

This had better be good, Mason thought as they approached the cruiser. He hoped whatever Chase had would exonerate Kyle. They needed something to take the heat off him because it sure wouldn't look good to have him get into town just as the killings began. In fact, as soon as the FBI was informed of that, they would head straight for him.

He watched as Chase slid the key into the trunk lock, wondering what in the world to do next. Chase lifted the lid, and what Mason saw inside almost physically knocked him off his feet. It was a bow lance in the shape of an S, about six feet long and wrapped in buffalo fur. It had an eagle feather tied on one end and another eagle feather tied just below the spear point. Three groupings of golden eagle feathers adorned the curves that formed the S shape, and it had numerous notches at one end, which Mason knew signified the number of coup that had been counted with it. This was no cheap reproduction from the *Wampums R Us* in China. This was the real thing. Mason recognized the lance immediately as being from the Kit Fox Society.

"I wanted you to see it before I turned it in," Chase leaned in to pick it up, but Mason grabbed his arm.

"Wait!" he snapped. "Where the hell did you get this?" He looked at Chase in astonishment.

"From the dream!" Chase said, jerking his arm out of Mason's grasp. "I told you when I reached for it in my dream the phone woke me up! After we hung up this morning, I saw it sitting in the corner of my bedroom by the door."

Mason was stunned. "How in the hell…" he began, and then the other words Chase spoke sunk in. "Turn it in? Are you nuts? Do you know what this means?"

"Look, I don't know if someone is just messin' with me or what," Chase said, "but I thought if I couldn't find someone who could explain it to me and give me a damn good reason not to, I'd have to hand it over to the feds."

"What?" Mason hissed. "I explained everything to you! Do you have any idea what this is?"

"That's why I showed you!" Chase exclaimed through gritted teeth. "Tell me!"

Mason looked around at the cars parked up and down the block, and at the FBI agents lingering around Grady's, and then turned back to Chase.

"No one's messin' with you," Mason hissed. "This is a lance used by the Kit Fox Society warriors – an old lance, an *original lance*," Mason insisted in a half whisper, "and to have had it materialize on this side of the veil is unheard of, especially being given to a white guy!"

"This side of the veil? What the hell are you talking about?" Chase demanded.

"Ghostkiller asked you to give this to Ghostkiller's grandson, right? It came from the other side!"

Chase balked, "The other side? You mean like the spirit world or something?"

Mason had a look of 'duh' on his face. He whispered, "You dreamt about it and then it showed up in your room. Where the hell else do you think it came from? Who could have possibly known your dream?"

"But how can this be?" Reality dawning at last for Chase.

Just then, Mason caught sight of Agent Tarkington lighting a cigarette and leaning lazily against his car, taking great pleasure in the scene unfolding in front of the Roadkill between Chase and Mason.

"Not here," Mason nodded his head slightly in the agent's direction. "Let's go somewhere else." Mason slammed the trunk closed. "You drive."

Chase slid a glance towards Grady's as he slipped behind the wheel of the cruiser. Mason climbed in on the passenger side and shut the door.

"Where to?" Chase asked, his heart racing.

"Remember how to get to Rosie's?"

"Ya damn skippy, I do," Chase answered.

23

Agent Tarkington watched as Chase and Mason drove away, noting they headed down Highway 13, which he knew led to the reservation. He wasn't stupid. Highway 13 was the only way out there, and they sure weren't headed to New Ulm unless that's where Ghostkiller was holed up. He chuckled. *Do they think they're being slick?*

Once they were out of sight, Tarkington found Agent Ryan.

"Follow them. I'll catch up."

He then made his way into the Roadkill, and after learning Mitzy had waited on Mason and Chase, he asked to speak to her. He came alone because he knew he couldn't trust the majority of the agents sent from Washington. Besides, he planned to bag both Crow Walker and Ghostkiller himself. He had an ax to grind with Mason anyway, and planned to enjoy every last second of the pursuit and arrest, and retain all the glory. He really hoped this waitress had dirt of some kind for him. Mason had been a boil on his ass for far too long, and if he could find something on him, he damn sure was going to do it.

Mitzy turned out to be the best stroke of luck he'd had in a while. She was an easy target for him – always the kind of witness he liked to talk to. As they sat down at one of the tables in a far corner of the restaurant, she told him what she'd overheard. When the name Kyle Ghostkiller came up, he really perked up his ears.

"When did you say he got back into town?" he asked.

"Just yesterday," Mitzy told him. "It was so funny to see him riding that old nag of his grandfather's. We all got a kick out of it," she laughed, "cuz that horse has gotta be two hundred years old!" Then she leaned over to him, purposefully exposing her ample bosom.

"Kyle is all Indian you know," she said in a hushed tone, reaching out to touch his knee. "He'd live like them savages used to if he thought he wouldn't get hassled for it." Tarkington raised his eyebrows. "Is that so?"

"Well, heck yeah," she exclaimed, "he's practically lived in a tee-pee his whole life! He carries those dead bird parts and feathers around, even wears them in his hair! It's so disgusting! And he always carries a knife, too. I heard it was one of them – whaddaya call it – Bowie knives," she fondled his knee. "And you did know that these murders are being blamed on the curse of the Ghostkiller family, didn't you?"

"Curse?" he asked, amused at her obvious attempt at flirting, but more interested in what she was saying. He thought he might take her up on her invitation to screw later, but right now he wanted to hear about this Ghostkiller curse.

"Why, yes!" she enthused, uncrossing her legs to give him a flash of chubby thigh as she scooted closer to the edge of her seat. She thought Tarkington was attractive enough and she took the opportunity to screw an agent every chance she got. It came in handy having friends in high places. Besides, her ego needed soothing after Mason Crow Walker had blown her off.

She looked around, making sure no one was listening before she continued. "That whole family is supposed to have some kind of special powers!" she exclaimed in a gritty whisper that came from smoking way too many cigarettes. "Even that horse is supposed to have some kind of magic!"

Agent Tarkington studied the waitress in amusement as she babbled on about Kyle's family and the curse of Ghostkiller, keeping one ear open to the important details while the rest of his mind calculated her words. Perhaps in some sick way Kyle Ghostkiller was killing people in an effort to keep the curse story alive. What better way to have control over the people on the reservation? Maybe he headed some sort of scam to steal money from the poor souls who believed him? He'd heard about those medicine men who charged for their services. *Kyle Ghostkiller is probably one of 'em*, he thought. *Those damned Indians with their mumbo jumbo bullshit, preying on whites for the last two hundred years!* He'd had all he could stomach of it, and it was time to avenge a few deaths of his own. Yes, he would make an example out of Kyle Ghostkiller all right, and take down Crow Walker at the same time. All he would have to do is bust Kyle for some Eagle feathers or other bird parts. He knew most Indians didn't bother with permits, thinking they were above the law for some reason. Once he arrested him for that, he could build his case for the murders – *maybe even get the death penalty for his prairie nigger ass,* he thought. He could possibly get that executive position he'd been passed over for last year in Rapid City.

"Imagine," Mitzy babbled on, "a spirit murderin' people! 'Course, none of us white folks believe in that kind of stuff." She smiled at him. Clutching at her neck, she suggestively ran her hand over her breast. "And we're sure glad we have you here to protect us!"

Agent Tarkington rose from his chair with a smile on his face. Despite his anger, her huge tits staring out at him still managed to turn him on. Hopefully, his clipboard was hiding the swell in his slacks. He certainly would take her up on what she was so eagerly offering later, but for the moment, it was time to make a trip out to the Stillwind camp. He reached into his shirt pocket and retrieved his hotel card, which he pressed into Mitzy's hand.

"Thank you, Mitzy," he smiled warmly. "I can't tell you how much you have helped. I'll be in touch." He winked at her as she took the card, looked at it, and then licked her lips suggestively. "I'm in room four," he whispered as he leaned in. Then he turned on his heel and walked away.

24

Rosie's was an hour away, and though the two men were careful as they left town, they were foolish to think they could stay very far ahead of Tarkington. They both knew he would follow them, and if Lee Tarkington followed them out to the reservation, Mason could imagine the firefight that would ensue. It could easily turn into another Waco or Ruby Ridge. It was one thing to arrest an Indian in the city, but to come onto the reservation in hot pursuit of one was just asking to get shot.

Mason kept those fears to himself as they drove down the deserted road. Chase had enough to digest without having to worry about something that might never happen anyway. He decided instead to talk about the significance of the showing up on this side of the veil. Chase, in turn, told Mason all about what he had found about the other killings on the Internet, as well as details of the hanging itself. However, the lance's significance was the highlight of the conversation.

At first, Chase had trouble swallowing the fact the lance came from the other side, but by this point he'd decided he wasn't going to question anything anymore. He had seen enough to convince him that any doubts he'd had about there being life after death, or the existence of a spirit, world were shattered when the lance had showed up out of nowhere in his room. As Mason said: no one knew what the dreamt, so how could it have been planted before he even woke up?

"I just can't get over the fact that it made its way to this dimension," Mason said again. It was such a high honor. Only Kit Fox Warriors carried that lance. "The Kit Fox are the first to go into battle, the buffer between the enemy and the rest of the tribe," Mason told him again.

"So what? Does this mean I've been made an honorary member or something?"

"No," Mason answered. "Ghostkiller asked you to deliver something, that's all. You certainly can't dispute the fact that the lance is here, but Kyle and Rosie will have to interpret that. They are Ghostkiller's direct descendants."

Soon the conversation turned to Sam's death, and the two men began to realize Chase's theory of there being thirty-eight murders to avenge the Indians' deaths might not just be a theory after all.

"So, if they're gonna kill every night now that Kyle has turned twenty-five, there are three more murders that are going to take place!" Chase exclaimed. "How do we stop it?"

"We go find Kyle Ghostkiller," Mason told him, "and we have to believe." The men exchanged glances. Mason waited for an acknowledgment and got it when Chase slammed the accelerator to the floor just as they passed a sign that read: Lower Sioux Indian Reservation 25 miles.

25

Kyle and Nina rode into Rosie's yard and Kyle dismounted, tying Macedone to the porch post. He reached for Nina, lifted her off the paint's back, and sat her feet gently on the ground. He leaned in to kiss Nina, but she balked when Rosie stepped out just in time to see it.

Rosie cleared her throat loudly. "A-hem. Don't mind me!" She smiled, happy to see Kyle and Nina were together.

"Sorry, Auntie," Kyle said sheepishly, as they both jerked back and then laughed liked giddy teenagers. He took Nina's hand, and they walked up the porch steps.

"Me too, Mama." Nina gave her a peck on the cheek.

Rosie smiled at them in turn. "It's about time you two made up." She squeezed their hands. "Come on in for some breakfast."

Kyle held the door open for the two women, and they chatted about Nina's adventure on Macedone.

"You are lucky Kyle found you," Rosie scolded, "or you might have been having breakfast somewhere far, far away." She winked at Kyle. Nina didn't respond, but excused herself instead to freshen up. She had stopped trying to figure out Aunt Rosie's riddles long ago. Kyle helped Rosie bring out the food, but they didn't talk about what had happened last night; there was no need. It was a longstanding rule that you talked if you felt the need to; otherwise, Rosie left you alone and didn't pry. She always knew what was going on anyway, whether you told her or not. The thought made Kyle grin.

The table was set for five, and Kyle didn't question Rosie about that, either. She always had a reason for everything she did, and he had learned a long time ago that she was always right.

"Your throne, my love," Kyle smiled as he pulled out a chair for Nina as she reentered the dining room. He took a seat opposite her, "so I can look at you," he whispered. Nina blushed hotly at his words.

The table was crowded with bowls of food, and Nina smiled as she heard Kyle's stomach growl loudly. There were scrambled eggs, fried potatoes, a huge platter of bacon and homemade biscuits – enough food to feed an army.

"Who else is coming?" Nina asked as Rosie sat a pitcher of freshly-squeezed orange juice on the table.

"Mason and that nice young man, Mr. Riley, will be along soon," she answered as she hummed her way back into the kitchen. Just then, they heard a car pull up outside, and a moment later Mason and Chase entered the house, calling out Rosie's name.

"How does she do that?" Nina asked, not really expecting an answer. She knew as well as anyone else that Rosie had a special way of knowing things.

"Kyle," Mason walked into the dining room, "thank God you're here. There's something…."

"Not before breakfast!" Rosie interrupted, standing in the doorway with one hand on her hip and the other holding a huge bowl of steaming milk gravy. "You boys sit down and eat!" she exclaimed.

"But Rosie," Mason began, "this is too important —"

"Not a word until you've eaten!" Rosie reiterated, giving him a scolding look he knew so well. There was no arguing with her and he knew that. Mason, defeated, sat down beside Nina, motioning Chase to sit opposite him.

"Now," Rosie said as she joined them, setting the bowl of gravy on the table and taking her seat, "who would like to say the prayer?" she asked, looking up at each of them.

"I will," Kyle offered. They all joined hands and bowed their heads.

"Tunkasina, we thank you for the food we're about to eat, we thank you Unci, and for the richness of her soil with which to grow it in, we thank the animal who gave its life for us today. Bless our children and our elders, and be with us today as we go about our tasks, however difficult. Mitakuye Oyasin."

"Aho," everyone said in unison, the events of the past twenty-four hours having had such an effect on Chase that even he said it.

Mason and Chase devoured their share, despite Mason having already eaten in town. It seemed he could always find room when it came to Rosie's cooking.

He broached the subject of the dream and then turned the floor over to Chase, who began relating the details to everyone as they filled their plates. Kyle was a bit skeptical about the dream of the lance at first, asking Chase questions again and again until he was satisfied with the answers. When Chase retrieved the lance from the trunk, however, Kyle knew at once the story was true. Ghostkiller had visited Chase.

"Understand that I would never question Ghostkiller," Kyle told him, "but you have to be careful; spirits have a way of toying with people, too. There also are people who would try to take medicine and abuse it. Even though it would be their mistake and they would suffer greatly for it, it is still up to me to know who is who. By keeping the medicine safe, I protect it and save them from themselves at the same time. It is my responsibility. I don't believe you would do that or even know how, but I'm just telling you. Just know it is nothing personal against you."

Chase nodded his head. He understood. There were many things that were making sense to him now, although he wasn't sure why, and he certainly couldn't have explained it to anybody. Mason breathed a sigh of relief as he watched the understanding wash over Chase. Maybe now they could really get down to business.

They brainstormed while they ate, planning their next move.

Mason's cell phone rang. He listened, then hung up quickly.

"We have to go. Now!"

It was decided Mason and Chase would follow Kyle and Macedone to Redwood Falls, making sure the feds didn't interfere. Rosie and Nina were to stay home and pretend they hadn't seen the other three, although Nina didn't like that idea much.

"I don't see why I can't ride along, too," she pouted.

"When the feds show up and you're not here, they may become even more suspicious," Mason told her.

"They don't know a thing about me!" Nina retorted.

"If they've done their homework, they do," Chase interjected, "and they've certainly done that by now, especially with five murders in two days."

She knew she shouldn't argue, but she couldn't help herself.

"But I don't —" Nina began.

"Look, cupcake, there's no sense in arguing," Mason said. "You don't understand how thorough the feds are. They already know everything about you, believe that, and they'll be out for blood to arrest someone, even if they have to trump up charges to do it. With news of the killings being blasted from here to Timbuktu, they're gonna have to arrest someone soon or face the government to answer why. We've got to get Kyle out of here now!"

Nina knew enough about criminal investigation to know Mason was right, but it still didn't make it any easier to have Kyle leave her again.

She looked at Kyle and he nodded, "He's right, honey. You stay here with Rosie and don't fret. Everything is going to work out, you'll see." He reached across the table and gave her hand a squeeze.

With that, the three men rose from the table. "You ready?" Mason asked Kyle.

"I was ready two days ago," Kyle answered. "Let's do this."

Kyle stood and rounded the table, pulling Nina to her feet. He held her in his arms for a long moment then gave her a lingering kiss. "This will all be over soon," he smiled down at her.

One last squeeze, and then he released her and turned to Rosie, whose short frame barely touched the bottom of his chin. He gave her a bear hug, whispering so only she could hear him, "Make sure she stays here." He leaned in and kissed her cheek. Rosie looked at him with a knowing gleam in her eye. Chase was already out the door revving up the cruiser's engine when Mason and Kyle emerged from the house. Macedone stamped restlessly as if he knew where they were going.

"Let's ride," Kyle untied Macedone from the porch post and swung effortlessly into the saddle.

Nina rushed to the front door with Rosie following closely behind.

Kyle mouthed to Nina, "I love you." Mason jumped

into the passenger seat of the cruiser and Chase began backing out of the dirt yard.

Rosie and Nina waved as Kyle turned the huge stallion in the direction of Redwood Falls and took off at a dead run.

"I love you, too!" Nina whispered. She didn't stop waving until they were out of sight.

26

Agent Lee Tarkington had made his way back to Grady's, thankful the swell in his pants had dissipated almost as soon as he'd left Mitzy and the Roadkill. He certainly didn't want to walk in there with a boner; he would save that for later. She wasn't the best-looking woman, but he hadn't been laid in a while and she beat a blank.

Agent Ryan radioed that Mason and the others were at the Stillwind camp.

"Damn injuns still causing trouble," one agent grumbled.

"We need to even the score for Custer!" another laughed.

Tarkington picked ten men to follow him to the Stillwind residence but warned them all to not to get trigger-happy. He himself had no problem shooting an Indian — he'd certainly shot a few in his day — but he didn't want a war on his hands either.

"That's all we need, another Wounded Knee. Now, let's mount up!" he said as he strode towards the door.

His mind was racing before he ever made it to his car. The drive to the reservation reminded him of when he'd first become an agent and had been assigned to Pine Ridge, South Dakota to keep order on the reservation there. He supposed it was being in this town and having to deal with that damnable

Mason Crow Walker that was the catalyst.

It had been a free-for-all on the reservation back in the seventies, and many agents had adopted the same mentality as their forefathers: "The only good Indian is a dead Indian." That was especially true when the Indians fought among themselves. It had been easy to let them kill each other back then. The traditionalists had wanted to go back to the old ways, and the American Indian Movement had been right there to back them up.

Their own tribal leader had been a corrupt sonofabitch who'd been taking kickbacks off land leases near and on Pine Ridge. All hell would have broken loose if that news had gotten out, and more than a few key government agents would have lost that extra blood money they loved so well. Discretion was a must.

He remembered Mason from those days. He had been right on the front line with the traditionalists, acting as spokesman, stirring up trouble and coming just a wee bit too close to what the agents were trying to hide. Tarkington had often wondered why the Indians couldn't just leave well enough alone and give up peacefully. They knew they would all be jailed or killed if they didn't, but Indians didn't care about going to jail. They lived better in jail than they did on the reservation, and many said they would rather *die like warriors* than to give up. A few of them did die, but so did two agents who were friends of his – family men who had their heads blown off in a field in '75. Arrests were made, and one conviction, but it wasn't enough to satisfy the agents who were left to go to the funerals, least of all Lee Tarkington. Mason Crow Walker had been one of the accused but was acquitted.

Tarkington laughed to himself as he thought of the old adage, 'what goes around comes around.'

"He won't get away this time," Tarkington snarled aloud. Mason, the damn militant half-breed. He always found a way to avoid a bullet and get out of trouble, more often than not making Tarkington look like a fool. He'd even somehow managed to get the charges dropped for illegal possession of eagle feathers that Tarkington had filed against him. *He's still trying to outwit the law!* Tarkington thought. Well, this time, he'd file charges that would stick. He'd get him on being an accomplice to murder as well as aiding and abetting. That'd keep him in jail for a good, long time. Tarkington smiled to himself as he slammed his foot on the accelerator. *Yes, Mason Crow Walker will pay dearly for his love of those damn redskins.*

27

The ride to Redwood Falls seemed to take longer than usual. They would have made much better time had they not had to stop for a flat, but Mason and Chase changed it in record time and caught up with Kyle in no time. Macedone was running right alongside the cruiser when Chase decided to clock him.

"Jesus! He's running sixty miles an hour!" he exclaimed. Mason just grinned.

"Yeah, and he can keep it up, too. This car would run out of gas before Macedone stopped!"

Chase didn't even bother to ask. He had already seen so much he didn't understand that asking about Macedone would only add to his already overloaded circuits.

Mason was gearing up to tell Chase about Macedone's special powers, but all thought ceased and a panicked gasp escaped his lips when he happened to look in the side mirror.

"Holy…" He cast a sideways glance at Chase. "Do you see that?"

"Hell, yes," Chase answered, slamming his foot down hard on the gas pedal, "but I've already got it to the floor now!"

Swirling in a cloud of dust, a wall of black cars filled with federal agents was less than half a mile behind them, closing in fast.

"Shit!" Mason hissed. "Looks like a swarm of locusts!" He glanced out the window at Kyle who was staring straight ahead, determined to reach the river. The speedometer read sixty-five, seventy-five, and then eighty-five miles an hour and Macedone still kept up.

"Redwood Falls is just over that knoll!" Mason yelled as they raced for a small grade before the water's edge. Mason kept an eye on the side mirror until he could see the figures in the cars. Peering closer he could make out the face of the one in the lead.

"Holy shit! It's Lee Tarkington!" Mason exclaimed. "Kyle's got to get away!"

"I know! I know!" Chase thought fast, and then without knowing what else to do, he yelled, "Hang on!" and slammed on the brakes, cutting the wheel and skidding a full donut, forcing the cars behind them to slam on their brakes, as well. The two men braced themselves for the impact, but it never came. The FBI vehicles skidded and swerved to avoid hitting them, kicking up a hailstorm of dust and rocks in the process. Mason and Chase both looked up in time to watch as Kyle and Macedone emerged from the dust cloud and approach the top of the hill.

What happened next seemed like a dream. The men could see what looked like a silvery mirror forming over the top of the hill, sinking downward toward the water on the other side. A misty blue light mingled with dirt and leaves swirled itself into a huge vortex, and the noise it made grew louder as it churned. It sounded like a freight train bearing down on them, but the men hardly noticed that; it was the blue mist that had their full attention. Kyle and Macedone raced up the hill towards the swirling colors and leaves, which shimmered like the aurora borealis.

Suddenly, yet as if in slow motion, Macedone jumped,

and to their astonishment, both horse and rider vanished through the mirrored blaze of color.

Abruptly all was quiet, and Chase sat with his mouth hanging open.

"What the..." he began softly, his mind not really registering what he had just seen, or what he was looking at now. "Mason?" He said the name intending to form a question but stopped.

Mason sat quietly beside him, his own mind scrambling. He let out the breath he'd been holding, relieved that Kyle and Macedone had finally made it through, but what next? If they stayed here, they'd go to jail and it really was that simple; but if he went through the veil with Chase, what would happen then? He knew despite all Chase had said with reference to changing his mind about the curse, this was something on a whole other scale. Chase might not survive the transition through time, and Mason would be left with a babbling idiot on his hands. Hell, his own mind would have trouble handling the aspects of traveling through time, not to mention the reality of finding himself a hundred and fifty years in the past. But if they stayed...

Before he could gather his thoughts, he realized their pursuers were now attempting to box them in. Chase looked in the rear-view mirror and saw the agents slowly beginning to circle their cars around them. The two men looked at each other, and no words were needed; Mason simply nodded his head and Chase slammed the accelerator once again and took off for the hill.

"You better brace yourself, Riley!" Mason yelled.

"Yeah?" Chase answered, "Well, you better explain all this to me if we make it through!"

Mason braced himself on the dashboard and Chase had a death grip on the steering wheel as the cruiser sped up and sailed over the hill. The mirrored veil was clearly visible from the top – a bluish glow with prisms of light dancing all around it, as leaves and dust swirled and mixed up the elements of earth and color. Both men yelled a collective "Oh Shit!" as the cruiser launched up and into the veil, passing through the beautiful portal. The veil was immediately sucked up into the heavens and the leaves scattered, floating gently to the ground, the only reminder of what had just happened.

Seconds later the agents reached the top of the hill, and a few sailed over too fast, their cars landing hood first into the shallow part of the river. Tarkington slammed his car into park and got out, pausing to run a hand through his hair. *Idiots!* As he pulled his gun from the holster tucked under his jacket, he could hear water splashing and noted the coughs and sputters as his men made their way out of the river.

"Morons," he muttered.

He was anxious to make his arrests and get the damned reports filed so he could get DC off his back. Then he could go to the hotel and finally relax and see if that waitress had called. Hell, at this point, he was so frustrated he was ready to shoot the three suspects where they stood. The bumbling fools in the water surely wouldn't question him about it. He started down the hill, fully expecting to see Chase, Mason and Kyle Ghostkiller; but as the dust settled around Agent Lee Tarkington, he realized the cruiser and the horse had vanished, along with the trio of men he so hotly pursued.

28

Macedone hit the ground running and Kyle never missed a beat with the rhythm of the horse.

As they raced through the field across from Redwood Falls, Kyle noticed the landscape hadn't changed much, but the Redwood Falls sign was gone, as was the mini-mart and the houses that lined the road. And there were no roads. He'd made it! He let out a whoop, shrill and high, so relieved to have finally made it this far.

"HIIIYAAAAA!"

He was anxious to see his great, great grandfather, anxious to do what he had prepared for his whole life. The chance to save his people had finally arrived. He openly wept with relief as he thought about all he had learned and was now going to put into practice, but he smiled through his tears as he rode on, never questioning Tunkasina would protect him and that Macedone knew exactly where they were going.

Chase seemed to be floating in a dream state, somewhere on the edge of reality. His mind felt a peace he never wanted to wake up from, but his body felt as if it were being torn into a million pieces. He could almost feel his blood cells racing to keep up. Somewhere, off in the distance, he heard what sounded like thunder, and he felt his body tremble from the sound. His eyelids felt like lead, and although he could hear what was going on around him, he felt he couldn't have opened them if his life depended on it. But that was okay because this was just a dream. The tranquility enveloped him like a comfortable old coat, and all he wanted to do was nestle into it; but the sounds grew louder, disturbing his comfortable slumber. Something in his mind told him the thundering sound was horses' hooves digging into the earth beneath him, but as hard as he tried to identify the other sounds, he could not. Firecrackers? Clanging metal? Loud knocks and pings that threatened to wake him at any moment continued as his body was tossed and jostled about, roughly shaking him out of his serenity. He thought he heard Mason's voice from somewhere above the din. Where was he? What the hell was going on?

"Go, go, go!" Mason yelled, and when Chase was finally able to open his eyes, he had four leather straps wrapped in his hands in place of the steering wheel. He jerked his head around to discover instead of the cruiser, they were sitting in a covered wagon. Suddenly wide awake, he looked ahead, and to his astonishment, he saw a team of six horses pulling the wagon, with Kyle and Macedone clearly visible about three hundred yards ahead.

"Holy shit!" Chase burst out, realizing this was no dream at all.

He almost lost his balance when the wagon hit a rut, but Mason steadied him while simultaneously jerking the reins out of his hands. *What are we running from?* Chase thought, but as his disorientation started to subside, the loud crack of gunfire was easy to distinguish. He swung around to look behind them and saw a wall of mounted Cavalry was gaining ground.

"Holy shit!" He cried out again. "What the hell is going on? Where are we?"

"No time!" Mason called out over the loud gunfire and

thundering horses' hooves. "Return fire!"

Chase raised his eyebrows and looked at Mason, the Cavalry, and back at Mason again. "I can't shoot at the Cavalry!"

"You either shoot and drive 'em back or we'll both be caught and hanged," Mason yelled.

This was too much. Chase couldn't even comprehend what had just happened, much less what was going on now. He wasn't sure what to do next, but a bullet whizzing past his ear didn't give him much time to think about it. He ducked and then quickly drew his gun and began returning fire.

"If we can make it to Yellow Medicine, they can't follow us in!" Mason yelled.

"What's Yellow Medicine?" Chase hollered.

"It's a river," Mason yelled back, "and it's our only hope!" He didn't bother trying to explain the magic of Yellow Medicine. He figured Chase had enough to deal with for now. He was just relieved to see how close they were to it and thankful they had both made it through the veil in one piece.

Up ahead, Kyle had heard the gunfire and was looking back to see what was happening. He slowed Macedone to a lope when he saw a covered wagon fast approaching. As the wagon drew nearer, he could see Mason and Chase inside. *They've come through the veil!* He wheeled Macedone around and backtracked towards the wagon at a dead run, catching them in a matter of seconds. He had to think fast. The Cavalry was still far enough away that they might have a chance if they cut the horses free. Turning Macedone in line with the wagon, he shouted the plan to Mason.

"I don't have a knife!" Mason yelled to him. Kyle untied the sheath hanging at his side that held his Bowie knife, tossing it to Mason.

"Cut the harnesses once you're aboard!" Kyle shouted.

Mason tied the horses' reins to the back of the seat, shouting at Chase to follow him. He carefully settled himself on the back of the big bay closest to the wagon. Chase watched in shock as the plan was being put into action; he had no doubt he could pull it off, but it had been years since he'd ridden, and bareback was a whole other story. He stood unsteadily in the bouncing wagon and started to climb aboard the closest horse. Suddenly, he remembered the lance that was in the cruiser's trunk

. A deeper panic began to rise anew; he had to have the lance. If he and Mason went through the veil and the cruiser became a wagon, did the lance make it through too? Hope struck Chase when he realized it might be in the back of the wagon.

"Mason!" he cried, "the lance!" But even before Mason could answer him, Chase hastily climbed over the wooden seat and into the back of the wagon.

"What's he doing?" Kyle yelled.

In his frustration, Mason could only shake his head. "I don't know!"

Kyle looked back and saw the Cavalry gaining ground fast. "Mason! Cut the horses loose!" Kyle cried.

"C'mon, Riley! There's no time!" Mason yelled, already cutting the leather straps connecting his own horse.

Chase's instincts had been right. He saw the lance lying between the spare tire and jack. He barely spared a sideways glance for the implements from the future, deciding he would try to figure it out later. Grabbing the lance, he climbed back over the seat, maneuvering himself onto the back of the horse beside Mason's. Now that he was holding the lance, holding the harness one-handed was no small feat. *How did the Indians do it?*

Mason and Kyle smiled to each other as they realized

what Chase had done. The fact that the lance had traveled with them was enormous. Mason slapped Chase on the back and handed him the knife.

"Cut your horse free!" he yelled to Chase, as he grabbed his own reins and pulled away to ride up alongside Kyle and Macedone. The Bowie knife sliced effortlessly through the harness, freeing Chase's horse just as the wagon hit a rut. The three men raced ahead, as the remaining horses scattered and the wagon tumbled down a ravine, the Cavalry was left in the dust.

29

From her hiding place in the closet, Nina could hear the continual drone of Agent Tarkington's voice. Poor Aunt Rosie! Tarkington had made her answer the same questions over and over, yet continued to persist as if her answers might change. Thank God they had no idea Nina was hiding upstairs.

The agents had searched the house but hadn't found the trapdoor in the floor of her closet. It had been built as an escape route for this very reason, and Nina was glad it had been. She had retreated to it at her aunt's insistence when they'd seen the house being surrounded by unmarked police cars. The opening was just big enough for her to fit through, with a small landing about four feet wide below and narrow steps that led down to the storm cellar. An escape door that led to the outside was hidden behind a star quilt on one wall, and unless they knew to look behind it, the FBI would never know it was there.

From what Nina could gather, they'd lost the trail of Kyle and the others and had come here to look for them, but she knew Kyle had more sense than to come back here. Rosie's voice remained calm as the questioning continued. Nina knew it was only for her benefit. Rosie was deliberately being evasive so the agent would continue to ask questions, giving Nina time to get away. She had to do something, and soon.

Her thoughts raced as she sat crouched in the hole. If

she could sneak out, she could make a beeline for the pasture they shared with the neighbor's horse farm. It's where her horse Dapple was grazing with about fifty other horses. But where would she go for help? How in the world could she find Kyle? If he had gone to the river, there were tons of hiding places down there and it wouldn't be hard to find him. They'd spent their childhood playing there together, after all. She knew every nook and cranny around those parts. That's where she intended to start, but first, she had to make it out of the house and to the river. Her legs and back ached from squatting on the landing for so long, and she knew she had better make her move while she could still feel her limbs.

She heard Agent Tarkington's voice boom once more and caught the tail end of what he was saying. "...I'm going back to town. If you see or hear anything, radio me immediately." She heard heavy footsteps cross the hardwood floor, and the front door slam behind them. Silence followed, but she knew there were agents still in the house.

She very quietly eased the trap door open, leaning it against the wall. Sweat popped out on her brow when the door squeaked slightly. She hardly dared breathe as she waited to hear something, anything. *Why isn't the radio on or something?* She screamed in her head. Just then, she heard Rosie's voice, and after a few minutes, the sound of country music wafted up through the rafters. *How did Rosie do that?*

She stood still for several seconds, willing herself to stay calm. She simply had to get out of here without panicking. *You can do this,* a little voice told her. *Just have faith, Nina!* Taking a deep breath, she reached up through the trap door opening and found her riding boots. Next, she carefully removed a pair of jeans and a sweatshirt off two hangers hanging overhead. Placing the articles at her feet, she slowly eased the trap door shut, praying the second squeak it made wouldn't alert the agents. Tiptoeing down the steps, she collapsed to her knees with relief when she made it to the bottom. Gathering her things, she tiptoed towards the star quilt and peeked behind it out the cellar door. There was no way of knowing how many agents were in the house, but she could see how many were out back through the cracks in the door. Three were out by the barn, and two were near the west corner of the house. As luck would have it, the pasture ran behind the barn and up along the east side of the house nearest to the storm cellar. It was near dusk and Nina decided to wait the remaining few minutes for nightfall before making her move.

    She inspected the room, looking for anything she could use for her trek. The last rays of sunshine streaming through the cracks offered her just enough light to scan the contents of an old rickety shelf lining one wall. There were labeled jams and jellies of all varieties in mason jars on the top shelf, along with beans, turnips and even a few jars of pigs' feet. Besides those, she saw cans of sliced fruit, a few pouches of buffalo jerky, an old-fashioned can opener and a case of bottled water. A flashlight and extra batteries were on the second shelf, along with a couple of stacks of dusty Life magazines, an old Army canteen and her backpack she had used in school. A dusty sleeping bag lay rolled up in the corner beside the shelf.

    Nina briefly thought how funny it was that everything she might need was right there in front of her as she scooped it all up and stuffed it in the sleeping bag: a few bottles of water, the flashlight, and batteries the buffalo jerky, and a few cans of fruit. She wriggled out of her clothes, pulled on her jeans, sweatshirt, and boots, and stuffed her discarded clothes behind an old dusty armchair in the corner. With that done, she crept back to the cellar door and waited for darkness to fall.

30

Thunderclouds gathered overhead and lightning danced across the sky as the trio approached a path that Kyle said led to the river. The wagon horses were tiring, but as they drew near the trail, they pranced as if they could sense they were a part of something very exciting.

Yellow Medicine River lay about a hundred yards ahead, and as they approached a clearing dotted with cottonwood trees, they decided to camp there so they could rest and water the horses. They had outrun the Cavalry, and because this was reservation land, Kyle said he didn't believe they would follow them here.

It was a gorgeous spot, flat and dry with small bunches of purple and yellow wildflowers scattered about, whose fragrance permeated the air. Sprigs of sagebrush grew on top of the giant boulders surrounding this bit of paradise. The men could not remember when they had ever seen such beauty, and it dawned on them they probably never had.

"This place was gorgeous when I was a kid, but I've never seen it like this," Kyle said.

"Yeah," Mason agreed. "It looks cleaner and brighter, almost as if the colors in the future have a cloudy film over 'em." They all agreed they probably did.

Kyle reached out and touched the bark of a cottonwood tree. The knots were shaped like human eyes, detailed right down to the pupils that seemed to watch them as they rode past. He marveled at the splendor he knew only God could have created. These same trees were long gone in their own time — this was a neighborhood now. It seemed everywhere he turned lately he was reading about or seeing a new subdivision going up, destroying the natural beauty of the landscape all across Minnesota.

"Wow," Chase said simply as they dismounted, breathing in the sweet scent of sage and flowers and river.

"Yeah," Mason agreed. "It sure is 'wow'."

They led the horses to the water, and Kyle walked a little way upstream to fill two canteens he had pulled from his saddlebags. *God love Rosie*, he thought.

Chase watched as Mason leaned down to get a drink for himself.

"Is it safe to drink?" he asked, remembering that he read somewhere that ninety-five percent of the earth's water was polluted.

"It is in this time," Mason smiled. Chase knelt down and hesitantly took a sip from his hand, marveling at how sweet the water tasted. He drank his fill, sighing deeply as he looked out over the water, finally allowing himself to relive the past couple of hours. The reality of the time warp and the Cavalry chasing them seemed no more than a dream now. Maybe it was the taste of the water and the beauty of this place that made him realize he really was in the past.

What a ride! He thought to himself. Strangely, he wasn't freaked out by any of it, although a part of him said he should be. In fact, at the moment, he felt absolutely at peace, which he hadn't for a long time, if ever. He knew he was supposed to be here. He took a deep breath and got another drink of water while Mason watched him. Kyle strolled up then, and he and Mason exchanged glances. The look on Chase's face was serene enough, but both of the men were thinking the same thing.

"Hey, Riley," Mason called as Chase stood back up, "you okay?"

"Sure," Chase answered, looking from one man to the other. "Why?"

"No reason. Don't be so paranoid, Riley!" Mason chuckled.

"Well, you did just come through a time warp, Chase," Kyle said. "Are you feeling okay?"

"Yes, I'm fine," Chase chuckled, rubbing his backside gingerly, "though I can't say if I'd ever ride in a wagon again." They all laughed at that.

"We'd better set up camp," Kyle said, noting the rumble of thunder in the distance. He pointed behind one of the boulders. "There's a cave right up there. That'll be the safest place in case of rain, and we can have a fire inside, too."

Chase took the horses up the small incline while Kyle and Mason gathered firewood.

"You really think he's all right?" Kyle asked Mason. "I mean, physically?"

"If he says he is, I guess he is."

Kyle grunted. He was sure things had worked out this way for a reason. Why else did they end up going back in time with him?

The cave opening was narrow, just wide enough for the men and the horses to fit through. It was pitch black inside, so Kyle went in first to get a fire going. After a few minutes, Mason followed him in while Chase tied the horses to a nearby tree.

The river appeared to be moving slowly in the distance, but even from this vantage point, Chase could hear the water rushing over the rocks and knew it ran much faster than it looked. *Creator's power.*

The red and golden leaves of the trees burst with color and fluttered down with every sigh of the breeze. The rays of the late afternoon sun weaved in and out of the limbs and made beautiful patterns of shadow and light on the ground. Chase took a deep breath and closed his eyes; he couldn't remember when he had ever smelled such clean, sweet air or seen leaves look so vibrant. Mason touched his arm. "C'mon in, Riley."

Chase ducked through the opening and was surprised to see it opened up into a huge cavern with a ceiling that easily reached fifteen feet or more. Stalactites and stalagmites strained towards each other in one corner like long, pointy daggers. A fire blazed in the center of a large clearing. The dirt floor had been tamped down many years ago, forming a floor as hard as concrete. It told Chase they were not the first inhabitants of this cave.

In the golden hue of the firelight, he noted a familiarity in the cave, and a sudden hot-cold flash of reality hit him hard: it was the same cave in his dream. He stood for several seconds taking it all in, and then hesitantly joined the other two men at the fire. His emotions threatened to overtake him. How could this be the same cave from his dream?

Sitting down cross-legged in front of the fire, he handed the lance to Kyle. The cave was quiet, save an occasional swish of a horse's tail that drifted in from outside. Chase almost jumped when Mason began speaking to Kyle. He spoke in Dakota, and Chase couldn't make out a single word.

"Okay, what's up?" Chase interrupted, nervously looking from one man to the other. "Or is this a private Indian party?"

"No," Kyle spoke first, "this is about you."

"Well, ya mind letting me in on it?"

"You know this place, don't you?" Mason asked him, although it was more a statement than a question.

"Yes," Chase answered slowly, "this is the same cave from the dream I had last night."

Kyle and Mason exchanged glances. "There are certain things you need to know, Chase, things that I normally wouldn't tell you. But since you had a dream that produced Ghostkiller's lance on the other side of the veil, you'll need to know them. Not only that, but you need to adhere closely to what I say."

Chase sat in humbled silence. He knew the reverence of what he was about to be told. He didn't know how or why, but he just knew.

Kyle took a deep breath. He had come this far, and evidently Ghostkiller had had enough faith in him to send the lance through the veil. He bowed his head and said silent prayers for what he was about to do. The lance on his lap began to feel warm.

He reached for the medicine bundle and opened it carefully. He withdrew an abalone shell and filled it with sage, and lit it with a long stick from the fire. Next, he unwrapped a red bundle that held a pipe. With each step he took, he smudged everything with the smoke from the burning sage. Every piece and movement had a purpose, Kyle told Chase. He prayed quietly as he filled the pipe with the contents of a small pouch, something he called *cansasa*.

"White people think we smoke dope in our pipes, our *canupas*," Kyle said. "That's Hollywood thinking. We use a special blend of sacred herbs, but not that kind. And those drumbeats you hear on TV are not the right way, either. The drum is the heartbeat of our people," he told Chase.

"If your heart ever beats like the ones on TV, go to the

emergency room," Mason said. They all chuckled at that.

"We say a prayer with everything we do," Kyle said, "it's all sacred." He started singing softly as he lifted the pipe and offered it to the four directions, then towards the heavens and then downward towards the earth. Chase had never heard a song like this, but as he listened to the Dakota words, he found he understood every one of them this time.

When Kyle was finished, he pulled the hot stick from the fire once again and lit the pipe. He pulled the smoke over his head, held up the pipe and said *Mitakuye Oyasin*, all my relations, before passing it to Mason.

As Mason smoked, he quietly explained to Chase that everything in the circle moves clockwise, and showed him how to hold the bowl in his left hand as he passed it to him. Chase did as Kyle and Mason had done, and then passed it back. Kyle nestled the pipe in the crook of his arm and held onto it gingerly, almost like holding a baby.

"You were given the task of delivering that lance by a very powerful *wicasa wakan*, a medicine man, who was my third great grandfather," Kyle said. "All of the research you did in relation to the legend revealed much, except for one important detail: Ghostkiller did not curse the town of Moccasin Flats, he simply stated an evil would be unleashed after the hangings. The curse itself was brought upon the citizens of that town from the evil deeds of the greedy traders and military. Innocent lives were lost on both sides because of the selfishness and greed of the *wasichu* in power. There were many whites who befriended my people, and vice-versa; many Indians tried to save their white brothers during the raids, yet it is many of those same names that make up the final list of those who were hanged."

Chase felt as if his eyes were suddenly opened, and for the first time since all this had started, everything fell into place.

It was time for healing, a time to save innocent lives from death in Moccasin Flats!

Kyle and Mason began to sing quietly, and as Chase listened to them, he found himself singing along, knowing it was a song of prayer.

The fire suddenly flared up, startling them, but they continued to sing. Kyle closed his eyes, his senses were heightened and he smelled wood smoke and sweet grass. He heard the wings of a giant bird flapping gently to his right; the breeze its wings generated fanned his face, ruffling his hair. He heard a rattling sound above his head, beating fast and then faster as it moved down in front of him. *Sacred*, a voice said. He knew it was right for all of them to be here.

Suddenly, he sensed the pain in the hearts of the slain Indians and white settlers, and tears began to sting his eyes. In the dark recesses of the cave, he heard the clacking sound of horses' hooves echoing against the wet cave walls, saw Chase running and slipping with the lance in his hand.

Kyle opened his eyes to see Ghostkiller standing at the cave entrance. He worried that Chase would panic when he saw him, and he stole a glance to see Chase with his eyes closed, too.

"Open your eyes." The voice did not belong to Mason or Kyle, yet it was a voice Chase recognized. The voice repeated the words, and when his eyes fluttered open, he found staring into the face of Ghostkiller. The resemblance between Ghostkiller and Kyle was striking, and Chase quickly averted his eyes. *This is a ghost! A sacred ghost!* Was he supposed to look at him? Was it disrespectful to just sit there, or should he stand up?

"Relax, Riley." Mason touched his shoulder and then offered a hand to Chase, who quickly took it and sprang to his feet. The two Ghostkillers had stood as well, and were talking quietly on the opposite side of the fire. *How could all this be real?* Would they change the course of history by being here? *Change the course of history! That's what Rosie said would happen!* But, how could both Ghostkillers be standing there? As the questions turned repeatedly in his mind, the elder Ghostkiller turned and spoke to him, as if reading Chase's thoughts.

"Many things are possible in the spirit world."

"But how?" Chase stumbled over the words, swallowing hard. "I mean, how is it possible?"

"Anything is possible as long as you have faith," Ghostkiller told him. "Come," he gestured towards the ground, "let's sit and talk a while."

31

Agent Tarkington hurried to his car, eager to get to his hotel room and away from the prying eyes and ears of the Indians who were still hanging around Grady's. It was next to impossible to find a quiet corner to tell his partner the details of what had happened out at Redwood Falls, but he had managed to say enough to satisfy the other agent. He had to lie, of course, saying they had all escaped to the woods; he knew he couldn't tell him what had really happened. How was he supposed to explain the suspects had simply vanished into thin air? And along with a police cruiser and horse, for that matter? He couldn't figure it out himself, much less explain it to someone else. His partner took him at his word, and Tarkington had exited Grady's without a backward glance.

He drove past the police station half expecting to see the cruiser parked outside but saw nothing. How had they escaped? It had to be some kind of trick of light or something, a smokescreen of some sort to help Ghostkiller get away. *They all work together,* Tarkington sneered to himself, *those filthy redskins. They had practically the whole town eavesdropping, too, trying to find out all they could so they could warn that murdering prairie nigger. Oh, Ghostkiller was guilty all right; why else would he run?* It irked Tarkington how the Indians all stuck together. "Like flies on shit," he muttered. To top it off, that damned

Mason Crow Walker and his partner were in on it somehow. He didn't know how they had all managed to vanish, but he refused to believe it had been anything other than smoke and mirrors. He'd figure it out soon enough, and then he could take his revenge how he saw fit.

He dreaded the call he was going to have to make to Washington. He had sent a fax that things were under control and he had a suspect under arrest. Now, he would have to explain that Ghostkiller was still on the loose and why. His office would send more agents, *and then the whole thing would turn into a freakin' circus*. He decided then to put off that phone call just a bit longer. *I can take care of this in short order,* he thought, touching a hand to his revolver that hung in the holster close to his chest. It would sure beat all the paperwork he would have to do. *A firefight is not an uncommon thing,* he reasoned, *and who the hell outside of the reservation would care if two Indians were found dead?* Yes, he would find them, and when he did, he would simply eliminate them himself. *That'll be two fewer redskins to deal with,* he thought, *and Chase Riley will be, unfortunately, caught in the crossfire.* He smiled to himself as he pulled into a parking spot at the local motel.

All thoughts of his ingenious plan left him immediately when he opened the door to his room and was greeted by the sight of Mitzy lounging in his bed, wearing little more than a smile.

"Hi, handsome," she purred as she sat upright, letting the covers slip down, exposing her huge breasts to him. Agent Tarkington got an instant hard-on.

"Well, well," he said as he closed and locked the door behind him. "What do we have here?" He smiled.

"As if you didn't know," she cooed. "C'mere," she crooked her index finger. "You look like you could use a diversion."

He approached the bed, shrugging out of his coat as he went, throwing it over a chair. Mitzy looked up at him, grabbing the belt buckle of his pants and tugging at it feverishly. Agent Tarkington paused for only a second or two as visions of his wife crossed his mind. *That fat bitch will never know*, he thought.

Slapping Mitzy's hands away, he undressed quickly and slid into bed beside her. He was smarter than his wife, smarter than the Indians, smarter than his bosses in Washington. He felt invincible, and at that moment, he didn't care about anything else.

Clasping his hands behind his head, he gave a deep satisfying sigh as Mitzy proceeded to give him the best blowjob he'd ever had.

32

Chase felt himself getting lost in the coal-black eyes of Ghostkiller as he spoke. He wasn't sure he should be looking him in the eye, but Chase couldn't help himself. The shock of Ghostkiller being there in the flesh was beginning to wear off, but now it was the things Ghostkiller said that had Chase mesmerized.

He switched between English and Dakota, and Chase found himself understanding both, although he didn't know how. And it really didn't matter. What mattered was the fact that Ghostkiller was speaking of the past, which was now the present, and Chase had to start thinking that way, as well.

Ghostkiller explained that he, along with the other chiefs of his region, knew all along the whites were coming to steal their land. The Dakota had found that out early on when the first treaties were not honored. This summer had been particularly hard on his people. Many were starving, and without means of hunting for food, they had no hope of getting anything to eat. This fact alone was plenty of fuel to fire the resentment that was already burning out of control for the Dakota. This catalyst had led to the uprising a few weeks ago. Ghostkiller had seen all of these things during visions he'd had in his youth, and he knew things had to change now before their land was lost to history forever. "But visions only tell one story," he said. "The outcome can change if we do things in another way."

Kyle felt his life come full circle as he listened. He realized at that moment everything that had brought him to this point in his life, and to this place in the past, had prepared him for right now. From the rigors of learning ceremonies, learning the songs, leaving Nina, all of it was instrumental.

As they sat talking with Ghostkiller about what their roles would be in the next few days, Mason admitted he wasn't sure what part he was to play.

"We all have a role," Ghostkiller turned to Mason, "and your role was told to you upon the scattered leaves. Did you not think you had an important job, as well?"

"I never knew I was supposed to come back, too," Mason answered, lowering his eyes.

"We all play a part in life. Every action we take has a consequence, which is why we all must tread softly. If you disrupt one aspect, it upsets all aspects of life. Does this make sense?"

Mason thought back to 1973 and what had happened out at Wounded Knee. His thoughts turned to Anna Mae and all the others who had died senselessly. Ghostkiller told him the past was the past, and he had to be stronger now than he had ever been. They all had to be. The future generations depended on them.

"Up until this moment the past could not be changed, but by adhering to the prophecy, Kyle has opened the door that was closed here when the hangings took place. To cross the veil as the three of you have done, and to bring that lance back across it, enables us to change things permanently. There are a few old Indians of your generation who knew about this. My great grandson James knew, as did Fools Crow, and although they did not live to see what was accomplished through your journey, they will see it from the spirit world.

They smile down on us because they know that their lives on earth will have been different because of changes you make now." Ghostkiller's smile faded slightly. "Now the veil is open, but it is only open for a short time. We must use this time wisely."

He explained prophecies foretold by other Nations, ones that included a time when all colors would share the pipe to spare the world of the evils committed against the earth.

"Our Mother is tired," he explained. "The sacred sites have been violated for far too long. Sitting Bull spoke of the colors coming together so all could understand how to understand Creator's plan. This will happen by remembering there are many religions all over the world, but they all point to one God. Even the Bible of the Christian faith speaks of things that happened long ago and prophecies that will come to pass unless things are changed. But now to the present: The army is ordering all of the Santee to report to a place called Camp Release to turn over our prisoners and then peace talks can begin. Little Crow has decided not to go. What do you know about all of this?" Ghostkiller asked the men.

"I know they can't do it!" Chase exclaimed.

"He's right. It's a trap!" Mason chimed in.

Their reaction startled Ghostkiller.

"Tokoja?" Ghostkiller turned to Kyle.

"Grandfather," Kyle answered, "the whites are only interested in rounding our people up to exterminate them. There will be no peace for the Santee if they go to Camp Release."

He explained the fate of those who stayed – they would be chained together and put into prisons where they would have little food and water, how there would be short trials and convictions of innocent men accused of the massacre.

"General Sibley's word is no good, he refers to the people as *devils in human shape*. The women, children, and elders will be beaten and pelted with stones as they walk down the streets, chained together. It won't matter that they are innocent, and it won't matter that the ones chosen to be hanged were among some of the ones who saved the *wasichu* from their own brothers' wrath."

Ghostkiller nodded. "Yes, I have seen this. No matter how many treaties we have signed with them, they starve us and steal our money, then hang us when we try to take back what is rightfully ours."

"That is the way of the *wasichu*," Kyle said bitterly. "Unless we change things, many will die. Our great chiefs, Sitting Bull, Red Cloud, Black Kettle, Crazy Horse, and many more will die in the near future, trying to save the land of our father's father. We must stop this! Thirty years from now, all our people will be crowded onto reservations and there will be very little land left for us."

Ghostkiller looked thoughtfully at Kyle and nodded. "You have taken a great risk coming here, *cinks*. This is the chance to set things right for the people. We will take this to Little Crow, and from there it will be up to you to undo what was done to the Dakota."

As the conversation continued, it became clear things were going to be much more difficult than Kyle had originally thought. But, as they listened to Ghostkiller in front of the crackling fire, he told them things that made it all at least seem possible.

33

Nina whistled softly and watched her little gray Arabian quietly make her way through the herd towards her. She slipped a hackamore from a gatepost around the mare's soft nose, thinking her years of riding bareback were going to come in handy now. She grabbed a handful of mane and swung herself onto Dapple's back, keeping low to the horse's withers as they made their way slowly towards the south side of the pasture. Once the house was out of sight, Nina dug her heels into the mare's flanks and headed for the back fence. Dapple cleared it easily, and the two raced off into the surrounding woods.

Nina wasn't sure where to look first but decided to go to Redwood Falls because that's where the men had been headed when they'd left Rosie's. From what she had overheard the agents saying at the house, Kyle, Mason, and Chase had escaped, so she doubted they would still be at the falls, but she figured it was a good starting point.

She turned Dapple in the direction of the falls, and as they loped their way quickly towards the north, she was thankful she had gotten away so easily. Kyle had taught her how to mingle quietly among the horses so as not to spook them.

It was full dark when she finally reached the falls, but this was her old stomping ground and a place she could have found blindfolded. She slipped off Dapple's back at an outcropping of familiar willow trees that sat near the water's edge. Peering into the moonlit night, she searched the horizon for any sign of movement, hoping against hope she would see Kyle or the cruiser. At this point, even the creepy blue mist would be a welcome sight. Scanning the landscape, however, she saw nothing and sighed deeply in frustration.

It was a beautiful night, chilly, but crisp and clear. She took a deep breath of the sage and wild autumn flowers that hung heavily in the air and allowed the sound of the rushing water to bathe over her. It reminded her of the many nights spent out here with Kyle. The thought was calming and offered her comfort.

She sank back remembering those times, all the nights she'd ran to the huge willow trees after the nightmare. Nina remembered thinking as a child that the trees' "long hair" would hide and protect her from her bad dreams. A sad smile tugged at the corners of her mouth as she remembered the look of concern on Kyle's young face when he had come upon her that first night so long ago.

"White Horse?" he had called softly. "Little White Horse?"

"I'm here," she sniffed.

He'd pushed the willow limbs aside, and without hesitation, gathered her into his arms and held her as she cried long into the night. She remembered waking in the morning, lying in his arms under the trees, and watching the warm sunshine cast haphazard shadows through the branches on his handsome face. Upon waking, Kyle caught a few fish, built a fire and cooked them. As they'd eaten, the sound of rushing water and bird calls orchestrated their plans for the day ahead. They never spoke about the nightmares.

She smiled as an owl hooted in the distance, and she

heard the lonesome cry of a wolf echoing her own feelings of loneliness. She closed her eyes and imagined Kyle's arms around her now. The hours they'd spent together the night before had been sweet, and she wished he was still with her now. Wherever he was, she knew he was all right and he could take care of himself. The numerous hideouts around the falls were spots known only to the locals, and she just knew Kyle and the others were hiding in one of them now.

She and Kyle had spent countless summer days exploring those hiding places together. One of her favorites was a cave near a bend in the Yellow Medicine River, which was only a few miles away. The cave had been a hideout for the Indians who'd escaped after the Great Sioux Uprising in 1862. She recalled Kyle telling her that before they had scattered about the plains and Canada, Chief Little Crow and some of his band of Santee had holed up in that cave to escape General Sibley and his murdering army. He told her his third great grandfather, Ghostkiller, had decided not to go with Little Crow and had subsequently been hanged in Moccasin Flats. She shuddered as she remembered what Kyle had told her were Grandfather Ghostkiller's last words from the gallows:

"You're building a Nation upon greed, and will reap what you've sown."

He'd told her his grandfather had visited him in a dream once telling him they would meet one day. Nina thought at the time the dream meant Kyle was going to die, but he assured her that was not what it had meant at all. She wished now she had paid more attention to those stories he told her during their outings in the cave; it might help now to come to terms with what was happening, as well as hold a clue as to where she could find him.

The cave! She thought suddenly. *Of course that's where*

Kyle would go, especially now that the time had come for him to dispel the curse!

She looked up at the sky and saw a million stars shining brightly overhead like glittering diamonds scattered across black velvet. She knew somewhere up there God was looking out for Kyle, and it gave her hope.

She turned Dapple and started for the Cave of the Old Ones.

34

The nude man was tied spread-eagled to the bed, his hands and feet bound to the bedposts with leather straps whose knots were nothing if not sheer genius. An FBI agent was taking pictures from every angle and the flash from his camera gave the scene an almost strobe light effect, making it all seem to move in slow motion. The man's throat had an ugly, jagged wound from ear to ear and his eyes held a look of absolute horror as they bugged out unnaturally from the sockets. As one agent took notes, he grimaced as he scribbled the words, "The corpse has a smile on its face."

The blonde-haired woman in the next bed was lying on her stomach with her face turned to one side. She wasn't tied up and appeared to be just sleeping soundly. As the coroner turned her over onto her back, the men gathered around the bed saw that she too, had the jagged gash in her throat. A few of the agents moved closer, noting the similarities between this and the most recent murder victims. Suddenly, a nerve twitched unexpectedly, vaulting the woman into a sitting position. The men gasped and jumped back, practically tripping over one another. In their haste to get away, coroner Whitey Smiley ended up on the floor. If it hadn't been such a serious moment, it would've looked like a stunt out of an *Abbott and Costello* movie.

A few shrieks rang out and one agent actually vomited

while stumbling out of the room. The hideous smile on the woman's face silently laughed at the FBI agents, who would swear later that her eyes had not been open when they'd first turned her over. Suddenly, the body fell backward onto the bed and lay perfectly still, the eyes staring unblinking at the ceiling, empty of life except for the look of sheer terror that was evident in their empty depths.

Whitey cautiously approached and felt for a pulse, immediately pronouncing her dead. He quickly placed one hand over her eyes, forever shutting out whatever they had seen.

Dan Tarkington was huddled in a far corner of the room. A small group of men crowded around him. He was oblivious to any other activity and completely inconsolable after seeing the dead man tied to the bed. It was his father, Special Agent Lee Tarkington.

35

The Upper Sioux Indian Reservation was abuzz with activity. Children played while dogs yapped noisily at their heels. Women were busy cooking over open fires while some sat in the shade sewing or nursing babies. Some men stood talking in small groups while others sat in front of their lodges, sharpening weapons or creating new ones. A larger group was riding horses in a nearby field, whooping and hollering in a game of what looked like tag, and as far as the eye could see, there were tipis set up everywhere.

A hush fell over the camp as the strangers on horseback rode in. Women cautiously called their children to them and took them inside the lodges. A few more stopped to stare curiously at men. A group of warriors began to assemble near a huge painted tipi. A handful of elders looked on from a distance, whispering quietly among themselves.

Several warriors on horseback approached the men. A few more came from behind, following them as they rode out of the woods, effectively boxing them in. The resemblance between Kyle and Ghostkiller caused a few gasps. One of the warriors on horseback approached and spoke to Ghostkiller, who was riding double with Kyle. It was easy to see Ghostkiller was highly respected, as his request to see Little Crow was honored immediately.

They rode slowly towards the center of the village, and along the way Mason told Chase a bit about Little Crow. He said his Dakota name was Ta-oya-te-duta, which meant "His Red Nation" in the Dakota language. He became known as Little Crow because of a mistranslation by the *wasichu* of his father's name, Cetanwakuwamani, which literally meant "Hawk that chases or hunts walking."

Little Crow was the chief of the Mdewkantons. He always wore long sleeves to cover up a disfigurement from badly healed wounds he had gotten in his younger years. It seems his half-brothers had tried to kill him when he had been first in line for the position of chief, but were found out and executed. He was about sixty years old in the year 1862 and had been chief for quite a few years already. He was the one who'd signed both of the treaties that had tricked his people out of their land. None of them were sure what to expect when meeting him but was sure Little Crow's disillusionment with the government probably had him upset at all whites.

"Here, take this." Mason offered Chase a blue pouch of Bulgur tobacco, explaining what it was for when he saw the look of bewilderment on his face.

"When you visit an elder, you always offer tobacco for their wisdom and knowledge that they will undoubtedly pass along to you. It's a sign of respect."

"What about these?" Chase asked, pulling his Marlboro reds out of his shirt pocket.

Mason rolled his eyes then dismissed the cigarettes with a wave of his hand. "Little Crow's not gonna know what to do with those, and besides, unless you wanna learn to roll your own, you better ration those out."

Chase nodded mutely and took the pouch.

When they approached the lodge, Ghostkiller told the rest of them to wait outside while he ducked in to speak to

Little Crow. Chase looked around, not really believing where he was. The events of the past twenty-four hours were hard enough to swallow, but to have actually traveled through time one hundred and fifty years to the past was almost too much to comprehend. How often did anyone get a chance like this? *Is this where all those people missing in the Bermuda Triangle disappear to?*

Mason looked around at the way the Indians were dressed. He thought about how some of these same elaborately fringed and beaded articles of clothing could even now be encased in glass at some roadside museum or airport that dotted countless western towns in the future. *What about the people who wore them?* It was all going to change now, however, and the future will know who they were.

Ghostkiller emerged and they were ushered into the tipi by two shirtless warriors. Little Crow was sitting towards the rear of the lodge, facing the door. The men filed in, forming a circle around the fire that burned in the center. Kyle and the others glanced around the lodge in awe, determined to remember every detail. There were containers that looked like huge, gray water balloons hanging by leather thongs near the door. Wooden bowls and plates were stacked neatly under those, along with furs of various sizes. Backrests fashioned from tree branches sat off to the side. Two stacks of neatly folded clothing were sitting in one corner. A huge crow perched over the doorway watched warily through its empty black eyes while various other birds hung from the lodge poles overhead. They appeared to be stuffed, and Kyle absent-mindedly wondered about taxidermy services in 1862.

Little Crow did not speak for a long time; he simply sat filling his pipe, murmuring quietly as he did so. When he Little Crow was finished, he cradled the pipe in the crook of his arm, just as Kyle had done in the cave, and began to speak in English.

"Hau, mitakuye oyasin. I am Ta-oya-te-duta. It's good to see you all here," he said. "I am anxious to hear what you have to tell me, but first, I'm going to explain some things to you about how I came to be here so that you can understand more fully what has happened and why." He paused as if collecting his thoughts.

"I once lived like a white man and even became a member of the Episcopal Church. I put away my traditional clothing and traded them for white man's clothes. I built a house and farmed the land as the whites did. I was told by the Great White Father in Washington this was what he wanted for the Santee; to live and work and farm, and if we did this, we would be allowed to live harmoniously with the whites. This is why I signed the treaty. I thought I was doing something good for my people. I made friends with many whites and lived a good life for a while, but the Great Father still wanted more land. He promised the Santee would be taken care of if I signed again, but shortly afterward I knew I had been betrayed; the father did not send the money or food that was promised to the Santee in the treaties, and when it did come, it was late or the food was rancid."

He said his people had lost respect for him when they'd found out he had signed away their land, so he thought if he could get food for them they would respect him again. He had failed. He was now a man who felt cheated and deceived and had finally called for war when the greed and deceit of the *wasichu* had forced his hand. He explained the events that had led up to that fateful day in August which started the uprising in the first place. It had been a month, he said, since they were to have received the annuity funds as payment in accordance with the provisions of the latest treaty. In late July, he and some of the other chiefs went to see their agent, Thomas

Galbraith, and asked why they could not have some of the food in their warehouse that was bulging with food and supplies. Galbraith told Little Crow he could not give them any because the annuity payment had not yet arrived, the same thing Little Crow had heard a countless number of times in the past. Galbraith then ordered one hundred soldiers to guard the food stores. The next day, five hundred Santee surrounded the soldiers and broke in the warehouse taking sacks of flour to feed their families. Instead of firing upon the Santee, another white soldier chief named Timothy Sheehan talked Galbraith into giving them pork and flour and taking it out of the payment when it arrived. The rest of the party left peacefully, but Little Crow stayed until he got Galbraith's word that the same food would be given to the Santee at the Lower Agency, as well.

Little Crow's village was near the Lower Agency, but Galbraith took his sweet time in arranging a council. Finally, on August 4th a meeting was set up at Redwood where Little Crow again asked for food to feed his people. Galbraith told him he did not intend to give them any and then turned to ask the traders in attendance what they would do if they had to make the decision. Andrew Myrick, one of the lead traders, had said that as far as he was concerned if they were hungry they could "eat grass or their own dung." He made this statement right in front of the chiefs at the meeting.

"When Myrick was found dead a few weeks ago, he had handfuls of grass stuffed in his mouth," Little Crow told them.

Another man named Long Trader Sibley was a soldier chief that the Santee knew well. He had stolen $145,000 of the $475,000 they were to receive in their first treaty, saying they owed his company, American Fur, money for overpayments for furs he had bought from the Indians. Little Crow said he underpaid them, but their agent at that time, Alexander Ramsey, accepted Sibley's claim, along with claims from other traders. In the end, the Santee received almost nothing for their land.

Chase remembered reading about some of this on the Internet. Colonel Henry S. Sibley was appointed by General Ramsey to be the Eagle Chief of the Minnesota regiment after Ramsey became governor.

"Now Sibley is calling for all the Santee to report to a place he calls Camp Release to bring in our captives," Little Crow said. "I have decided not to go to the camp, but to leave and go west instead."

"You mustn't let your people go to Camp Release, either," Kyle warned. "They must go with you, or they will all suffer greatly."

"The people have lost faith in me," Little Crow spoke sadly. "How can I convince them to leave with me now?"

"That is why we are here," Kyle told the Chief. "I was given the lance of Ghostkiller by my brother who received it in a dream. When the people hear of how it came to me, they will follow us."

Little Crow turned Ghostkiller, "Did you give it to him?"

Ghostkiller shook his head. "*Hau*," he answered. "It left my tipi with me when I dream walked."

Little Crow turned to Chase with raised eyebrows, the enormity of what Ghostkiller told him showing on his face. "Is this so?" he demanded.

Chase cleared his throat, "Y-Yes, Ghostkiller gave it to me in a dream two nights ago," he answered, suddenly feeling like he did something wrong by taking it.

Little Crow sighed deeply, nodding his head as if he finally understood a secret he had been trying to decipher.

"You have done nothing wrong," Little Crow told him, reading his thoughts. "Tunkasina is at work here."

The Chief turned to Mason. "You are here to help the half-bloods," he looked directly into Mason's eyes. "Though your heart is bad because of the FBI, it is still so. You have fought your own battles with the *wasichu*," Little Crow smiled knowingly, "and that part of your past will disappear from history."

Mason was shocked. Little Crow knew about the FBI? Except for the few things he had told Chase, no one knew how he really felt about them, and couldn't know unless they had been at Wounded Knee, or in his head. He had been afraid that those feelings of hatred would interfere with his walk in the past, but apparently, they did not.

"We must hold a council," Little Crow announced. "The other chiefs must be prepared so they can inform their people."

With that, he lit the pipe and the men smoked it in the same manner as they had done in the cave. With the pipe smoked out, Little Crow tapped the ashes into his hand and then dug a small hole and buried them. Mason leaned over and quietly explained to Chase that by doing so the prayers in the pipe were given to Mother Earth. "Just like we did as children, going to our Mother to help solve our problems." As he told him this, the men realized their own fears had drifted away on the rising smoke.

36

The list of chiefs who assembled at Little Crow's tipi that night was an impressive one: Shakopee, Mankato, Wacouta, Medicine Bottle, Big Eagle, Lightning Blanket, and Wabasha among others. They were from four of the Santee divisions: the Mdewkanton, Wahpeton, Wahpekute, and Sisseton. These chiefs and their people had been forced onto a tiny stretch of reservation land that ran along the Minnesota River. They were woodland Sioux, known as the frontier guardians of the Sioux domain, and shared strong ties and tribal bonds with their blood brothers of the prairies, the Yankton, and Teton. Chase, Mason, and Kyle knew what would become of all of them unless the chiefs listened to what they had to say and acted upon that information. They also knew it was not going to be an easy task.

 The trio gazed in amazement at the powerful leaders as they filed into the lodge. Kyle guessed their ages ranged from around thirty and older. One by one they entered and Little Crow said their names as they took their seats around the fire pit. Most of them wore bonnets, the kind you saw on old westerns, but these were far more elaborate – exquisite headpieces adorned with eagle feathers and long strands of horsehair that cropped out on top. They all wore leggings and moccasins, some wore shirts with bright ribbons sewn on the front and back, others were bare-chested. One wore a long, blue officer's coat over his breechclout and had his face painted half white and the other half black; two white strips were drawn from his hairline over one eye, and down to his jaw line. He looked very intimidating. Kyle told Mason and Chase that the Indian was heyoka, a contrary, and had very powerful medicine. "His name is *Wakinyan Sapa*, Black Thunder."

"How do you know him?" Chase asked.

Kyle smiled. "There are things that go on in our ceremonies that cannot be explained, but let's just say I've met him before."

Chase shrugged. Nothing would surprise him after the events of the past twenty-four hours.

Ghostkiller directed Kyle to sit facing the door. Mason explained to Chase what the honor seat represented. "It's for the person who is being honored or prayed for, a person who deserves honor."

Kyle felt a wave of emotion as he sat down. He had worked his whole life to save his people from certain banishment to reservation life and even death. He grasped the lance tighter in his hand and could feel the power within it.

Chase stole a nervous glance at Kyle and Mason, who thankfully were seated beside him. He noticed that Kyle seemed relaxed as he chatted with Mankato as if it was something he did every day.

Mason had confided to Chase earlier that although he knew time travel was possible, it was another thing actually being here, and as Chase looked at him now, Mason seemed a bit tense. He was seated next to Lightning Blanket and sat fiddling with a lace on his moccasin as the chief watched intently.

"Moccasin Palace," Mason smiled stiffly, referring to the company logo. The chief grunted and shrugged, but smiled back.

Mason noticed Chase scanning the lodge and looked around himself at the chiefs assembled. He thought Chase was doing a great job at keeping it together and was proud of the fact that his respect for the ways had grown so quickly. He thought about what Little Crow had said to him earlier about the scattered leaves giving him messages. He told him the Creator had given him that medicine and it was His will that the spirits came through that way. He said Mason would learn more about his medicine as he grew in the ways of his people and that the Creator would let him know when the time was right. He hoped that his alcohol consumption had not deterred the spirits from showing him what he needed to know now.

The general mood inside the lodge was a bit distrustful at first. Chase was grateful that when Little Crow addressed everyone, he spoke in English so Chase could understand. But as Little Crow spoke about calling a council of the four divisions to talk about moving the camps to the flat water, which was Nebraska, shouts rose up from Medicine Bottle and Shakopee.

"Why should we listen to Taoyateduta when it is your fault our lands are gone?" Shakopee shouted angrily.

"Yes! Why should we follow you anywhere?" This from Medicine Bottle.

"Our relatives are here from the future and they have told me the fate of our people if we stay," Little Crow said evenly.

"Bah," Shakopee spat, "there is no proof that what they say is true! And you have a stranger in the honor seat! What great medicine does he have?" He stood then, looking ominous and lethal, directing his gaze towards Kyle. Kyle stared back, looking up at the Indian. Shakopee was tall with a rutted complexion and intense black eyes that clearly showed the hatred he felt for all whites.

"I hold the lance of my grandfather, Ghostkiller," Kyle spoke up.

"Still, there is no proof of where or how you got it," Medicine Bottle jeered, standing up to join Shakopee. "He probably stole it or bought it from a white trader!"

"You go against my word of honor?" Ghostkiller stood then and faced Medicine Bottle, a dangerous look in his piercing, black eyes.

Tension mounted as the two men stood glaring at one another and more shouts rose up as other chiefs stood and tempers began to flare.

"Don't listen to what the *wasichu* has to say!" said one.

"Give Taoyateduta a chance to speak!" said another.

Chase looked at Mason and Kyle, but they sat still. One looked to the other, but neither spoke. *Why don't they do something?* Chase screamed to himself.

It was clear that a dividing line was forming between Little Crow and Ghostkiller supporters and those who agreed with Shakopee and Medicine Bottle. Kyle knew of Shakopee's treachery. The stories had been handed down to him over the years. During the Great Sioux Uprising, Shakopee and his warriors were ruthless in battle. Near the end of the war, it was reported that he was on the verge of hating Little Crow, but it was apparent that he already did. Shakopee, Chase read, had been a traitor and had gone behind Little Crow's back to General Sibley. He'd lied and told the General that he wanted protection from Little Crow and that he had not taken part in the killing of the whites, but wanted to be friends with them.

Kyle knew that was far from the truth just by looking at Shakopee in real life. He seemed ruthless enough to kill any one of the men in the lodge and not lose any sleep over it. Still, something had to be done before it escalated to that. With a deep breath, Kyle stood up.

Kyle fiddled in his shirt pocket, finding the lighter Chase had loaned him earlier.

"Quick, give me a cigarette!" He whispered to Chase. Chase slipped him a Marlboro from his pack. He kept it hidden in the palm of his hand.

"Show me how you make fire!" Kyle shouted to Shakopee. The group fell silent. Shakopee glared at him but did not answer. Kyle rose and walked to Shakopee, handing him the cigarette.

"Where I come from, this is a tobacco offering," Kyle said quietly. "Show me how you make fire."

The conflict was now between Shakopee and Kyle. Realizing this, Ghostkiller and Medicine Bottle nodded to one another and sat down. Mason stayed Chase when he started to get up. "*Hiya*," he whispered, "wait and see what he's up to first."

Shakopee looked around the circle and saw all eyes were on him. The future man was coming to him in a respectful way; to refuse the white stick he called tobacco would certainly cause him to lose face with the other chiefs.

He snatched the cigarette away, smelled it and then ripped the paper open. He examined it for a long moment; it was indeed tobacco. Without speaking, he shoved the cigarette into a pouch tied around his waist and then looked around, spotting a small pile of kindling near the flap of the lodge. He stalked over and, grabbing a handful, knelt down and placed it on the ground. He produced a flint and a rock from another pouch, and after a few minutes of striking them together managed to ignite the kindling. He blew it lightly, coaxing a flame to spring to life after several more minutes.

He raised his head and stood, and with that same,

detestable look in his black eyes he hissed, "Now, what is the point of this?" He then took one moccasined foot and viciously ground out the flame.

Without speaking, Kyle walked over and picked up a handful of the dried kindling. He knelt down and sat it next to the blackened earth where Shakopee's fire had been. Next, he placed both hands over the kindling and with his right hand still holding the lighter, he struck it. The kindling caught instantly and the flame rose and danced in a matter of seconds. Mason nudged Chase, and the two men looked on, amusement dancing in their eyes. They heard the collective gasp from the men in the lodge and watched Shakopee stumble back in fear.

"What is this medicine you have?" Shakopee demanded, panic in his voice. Kyle approached him and struck the lighter again, close to the Indian's face. "It's fire medicine," Kyle announced, holding the lighter high above their heads. He walked around the lodge showing it to the men. The chiefs in assembly grunted and nodded their approval, all talking at once about the future man's medicine.

Once Kyle was satisfied he had won them all over, he returned the lighter to his pocket. Leaning close so only Shakopee could hear, he said, "I know about your message to Long Knife Sibley, but he will not save you and you will die later, three summers from now. You will run to Canada and they will hunt you down like a dog and haul your ass back to a place called Fort Snelling. There, you will hang with your friend Medicine Bottle." Kyle drew back from Shakopee's ear until his face was scant inches from the Indian's. "Be careful of what you say next."

Shakopee stood stock-still. There was no way this man who claimed to be from the future could know about the message he'd sent to Long Knife Sibley. He had sent it via a runner two weeks earlier, at the same time, Little Crow sent his asking for peace. This man had to be telling the truth. His eyes grew wide as he glared at Kyle and saw the spirits that were working with him. The orbs dancing around his face and head were unmistakable. Shakopee looked hard at Kyle, and then with a jerk he nodded his head, took his place in the circle and sat back down, ready to hear what the future man and his friends had to say.

37

Nina followed the Minnesota River for several miles until it forked and veered left, joining the Yellow Medicine. The sun was just beginning to rise and although she hadn't been here for a long time, the scenery looked very familiar; huge oak and maple trees towered above the riverbank, cottonwoods swayed in the breeze as their brilliant, yellow leaves fluttered and swirled down to the ground. The river looked narrower to her, but she figured that was because she now saw it through grown-up eyes.

It was a beautiful day and she breathed deeply of the sweet scent of dampened earth and leaves, laughed when a spray of cool water sprayed up near the water's edge. She was surprised they had not passed any hikers or campers along the way, but figured it was so late in the season, all but the die-hards had probably cleared out.

After a while, they approached a bend in the river and Nina turned Dapple to the right and up an embankment. There it was; the familiar grove of cottonwoods whose bark always reminded her of human eyes that watched her every move. The Indians used female cottonwood trees for their Sundance ceremony. The females had a fork in the center, and she always thought they had the most 'eyes,' as well. She remembered Kyle's scars on his chest from sun dancing. He was an eagle dancer and had also danced the spider dance his first year, so he had scars on his back, as well. The Sundance was done for prayers and each sun dancer's reason for dancing was different. It was the most sacred ceremony of the Sioux and not one to be entered into lightly. A person would sometimes have visions for years before ever committing to dance, and even then, they might wait for several more before taking it on. She knew that Kyle's vision to eagle dance had been with him his whole life. He'd talked about it since they'd first met as small children. He had shared most of his visions with her.

Nina had gone to the Sundance every year since she moved to the reservation. She never danced, but had learned the songs and sang with the women on the drum. It was just another way she and Kyle were connected. He told her hearing her sing the songs gave him the strength to endure the piercing and suffering he went through for those four days he danced. She was glad she had been there for him during those times, and it made her even more grateful now. No other woman shared that bond with him.

She could see the cave in the distance, and noticed little had changed there. The huge boulders that surrounded the grove of trees looked the same. She noted more sage growing and lots of Indian paintbrush. She had read the faces on Mount Rushmore had to constantly be repaired because the rocks they were carved into seemed to breathe – cracking as they expanded and retracted like lungs. The same principle held true with these boulders apparently, because they were huge and had cracks in them, as well. It dawned on her if more people saw the earth as a living, breathing entity like the Indians did, she was sure there would be a lot less damage done to it. The breeze picked up and the trees began to sway and sing their leafy songs. She almost felt like they were welcoming her home.

She stopped at the cave entrance, dismounted, and tied Dapple to the nearest tree. Retrieving the flashlight from her backpack, she walked inside. She flicked on the light, and the interior of the cave lit up immediately. The scent of smoke and ash assailed her nostrils, and as she showed the light on the ground near the center of the cavern, she saw blackened wood and ash where a fire had been. Placing her hand low over the black coals, she found they were still warm. Shining the light on the ground, she could just make out the imprints of human bodies scattered in the dirt that lay beside the small fire pit.

"Yep, they were here," she whispered aloud, imagining the three of them sleeping beside the fire last night. As she examined the marks further, however, she saw four body imprints and wondered who else could have been there with them. Her first thought was Thorn Rivers. If anyone would help the three men escape and hide out, she knew it would be him.

She hadn't seen him around the reservation recently, but Rosie had mentioned he'd gone to Rapid City for a relative's funeral a few days ago. She decided he must have gotten back and ran into the three fugitives on their trek last night. *Fugitives?* How could she think such a thing! *Kyle is innocent and so is Uncle Mason and his friend Chase!* She thought.

Still chiding herself for her bad thoughts, she went back outside and searched for tracks in the immediate vicinity. She saw a few, but the pattern was haphazard and didn't really follow a path of any kind. A whinny from Dapple interrupted her and she chuckled at the horse.

"You're probably getting hungry, huh, girl?" Dapple nodded her head as if she understood.

"All right," Nina sighed, "c'mon."

She stuck the flashlight back inside her backpack and led the horse to a patch of sunlit grass near the water.

Suddenly feeling ravenous herself, she sat under a nearby cottonwood tree and dug through the backpack to find something to eat. The footprints weren't going to go anywhere, she reasoned.

She settled on a jar of pears and the buffalo jerky. She sat back enjoying the woodland sounds as she ate. Birds chirped, two squirrels chattered and then gave chase to one another, leaping from tree to tree in a figure eight. She smiled as she watched them, permitting herself to relax a little. The long hours spent on Dapple had been hard on her, and she was still sore from her ride on Macedone. It made her wish she had taken more time to ride in the past few years, but between school and studying there just wasn't enough time. She vowed to get in better shape, which she'd always swore she'd do before she had any kids. She thought of Kyle and pictured what their children would look like – dark-haired, blue-eyed babies that would be the most beautiful kids on the planet, no doubt — and she smiled.

After she finished eating, she settled back against the tree, allowing the river sounds to sooth her. She closed her eyes and imagined her body floating on the passing water, and before she knew it, she was fast asleep.

She saw herself flying over the treetops, looking down at the earth and watching it glide quickly past. It seemed she was going somewhere important and, with a determination she knew all too well, was heading there in a hurry. She landed at a spot beside the river and stood for several minutes, feeling the warmth of the sunshine on her naked body. She hadn't realized she was naked until now, but it didn't seem to matter. She felt free and alive and closed her eyes as she stood there listening to the water rush past. Suddenly, she heard voices and thought to cover herself, but instead found herself staring in shock as she realized she was hearing voices from the past – her past. She watched as an imprint from her own memory replayed itself right before her eyes. She and Kyle were arguing the day he left for Pine Ridge all those years ago:

"Nina, you must understand why I have to do this!" Kyle pleaded with her. "I have to prevent any further deaths, and try to preserve our spirituality! It's been taken from us. That's why the curse has fallen on this town! I must make things right!"

"How? How are you going to make things right? By leaving me and running off on some wild goose chase? Chasing ghosts? What do you hope to prove? That those Indians were innocent? You can't change the past!"

"The past is not an illusion! It really happened! It's how we came to be where and who we are! You included! If I have been given the gift to change it, I have to take it! Why can't you see what is at stake here?"

"Because I see *us* at stake here!" Nina said hotly. "I see us ending right here, right now!"

The sun was low in the sky when Nina awoke. Startled and sweating, she momentarily forgot where she was. She sat up and saw Dapple still grazing where she had left her, and with a shake of her head, she rose and walked to the water's edge, dipping her hands in the cool water to splash some of it on her face. It felt good and refreshing and helped to bring her out of the fog of sleep. Once the disorientation fully subsided, her determination to find Kyle renewed with a vengeance. It dawned on her then that she had to remember the past in order to realize what was at stake. She chided herself for the selfishness she had shown in her arguments with Kyle. She realized that all the preparations he'd had gone through and everything he was doing now, was for the people, and not to stroke his own ego. Her eyes filled with tears, and when they fell from her eyes, she watched as her reflection in the water shattered on the ripples they created. She had to find Kyle! She simply had to, and the sooner the better.

She sprang to her feet and dashed back to the cave entrance. Scouring the ground, she noticed that the hoof prints did indeed follow a path and she set about following them. Upon closer inspection, she saw that there were prints from at least three horses, along with a couple of sets of boot prints, and the unmistakable print of moccasins, but they were two different sizes.

"Two people wearing moccasins?" she said aloud.

Of course! She thought, *I was right about Thorn being here!* He probably brought the horses from his ranch, too.

She wasn't sure what her next move was going to be, but she followed the tracks to get a general direction of where the men had been headed. The funny thing was the tracks disappeared just beyond the cottonwood grove. She circled back, and then circled again, and still she could not pick the tracks back up. She walked the perimeter five more times but continued to come up empty. How could the tracks simply disappear?

Where the hell did they go? She thought.

Blowing out a sigh, she came to rest beside the tree where Dapple stood grazing. She was confused, tired, and at a total loss as to what to do next. Should she go home? No, home was out of the question. The FBI would be waiting for her, ready to interrogate her, just like they did poor Aunt Rosie. Stroking the mare's neck, she looked around. The sun was setting; she would never make it back home before darkness set in anyway. If Kyle were in her shoes he would keep searching for her and that's exactly what she would do, too.

She decided to spend the night in the cave. It offered

better cover than being out in the open, and what's more, it would help her feel closer to Kyle since he had been there so recently. It might be a little creepy at first, but it wasn't like she'd never slept in it before. Of course, it had always been with Kyle, but she was a big girl now and had Dapple with her, too.

A short time later, she was making her way back into the cave, dumping armloads of twigs and sticks near the entrance. It took several trips, but she managed to collect enough wood to last her throughout the night. Taking it all inside, she went back out to get Dapple. The horse shied away from the entrance at first, but once inside seemed to relax, and dozed lazily once Nina got the fire started.

She opened a jar of Rosie's and set them near the coals to heat, then spread out the sleeping bag and settled down in front of the fire. As she watched the flames lap at the wood, she allowed her mind to relive the days spent here with Kyle.

She had been about eleven when he'd first brought her here. Rosie had thrown a fit when he'd asked if he could take her so far away from the reservation. Uncle Mason had intervened and assured Rosie that the children would be fine.

"That cave's as safe as a mother's arms," Uncle Mason had said, "but if it'll make you feel better, I'll take them myself." And so, with Rosie's blessing, Nina and Kyle had packed all their gear and had gotten an early start the next morning with their uncle. Once Mason had their assurances that they would follow all the rules he'd laid out for them, he left them at the cave and said he would be back for them in the morning. As soon as he'd left, they'd set to work laying out their sleeping bags, flashlights and gathering wood, all per Uncle Mason's instructions. When that was done, they'd grabbed their fishing poles and headed for the river. They cooked and ate the fish they'd caught and then swam in the river later when the temperature climbed into what they called 'swimming range.'

The cave became a favorite place for the two of them, and as they got older, it became a weekend ritual. Often they came with friends, but it was during a time when they had come alone that Kyle had first declared his love for her. That was one day Nina would never forget. Innocent kisses followed his announcement and they'd both gotten nervous, caught up in feelings they didn't quite understand. Kyle had broken the tension by telling her one of the famous stories about the cave. Nina had heard it before, but it was one she never tired of. "This is about our people," he announced. Kyle always said "our" people when telling Nina the stories, making her feel even more like a member of the family.

It was about an Indian named His Red Nation, or Taoyateduta, in the Dakota language. "The whites called him Little Crow, but whatever he was called, he was a great chief among our people. His Red Nation had tried to get along with the whites, and even lived among them for a while in the *wasichu* way, but months of watching our people starve to death had caused him to turn away. Some warriors from his band had called him a coward because he argued with them at first about calling for war, but in the end, he told them, 'I will die with you.'

"After the war, he and his people hid in this cave for a few days before going north and finding safe refuge at Devil's Lake. He returned to this area later to steal horses for his family. One morning while he and his son picked berries near here, a rancher named Nathan Lamson shot and killed Little Crow. His son Wawinape was injured but got away.

"Later, his son was captured and sent to Iowa, and Wawinape's children had to fight to get their grandfather's bones back from a museum. They say that Little Crow haunted this very cave for years, looking for his bones."

Of course, the ghost story didn't scare her anymore, but Nina never forgot how horrible she'd felt to learn that Little Crow's family had to fight a museum for his bones. *And the whites called the Indians barbaric!* She certainly couldn't remember ever hearing about white people's graves being dug up and desecrated, their bones kept and sold or put in a museum. It reminded her of the rumor regarding Geronimo's grave that was supposed to have been dug up and his skull taken to some secret society at Yale University by prominent, rich white guys in the 1930s. It was just another example of why Kyle fought so hard, and how much he loved his people and why he wanted to make things right for them. It was one of the many reasons she loved Kyle so much.

Nina stirred the warmed beans and ate them straight from the jar, allowing her mind to wander back to the other nights they'd spent here— nights when they were a bit older.

It was an innocent time, a time when they longed for each other, their young and desperate teenage hunger threatening to consume them. The passion that had smoldered between them had been all-encompassing, and she smiled to herself because it was still as alive today as it had been all those years ago. Even now, nothing had changed between them, despite the circumstances of their separation. The years spent apart had melted away last night, and she knew he still loved her.

She snuggled inside her sleeping bag while those thoughts danced in her head, and soon she was fast asleep with a smile on her face.

38

Kyle and Mason both agreed that they had never seen such a huge gathering of Indians, not even at the Gathering of Nations in Albuquerque, the biggest powwow in the world.

They had all congregated at the Lower Sioux agency to hear what the men from the future had to say. The chiefs in attendance sat on fallen logs, blankets, or stumps situated around a huge central fire, while hundreds of other Indians gathered around behind them, crowding around in the hopes of hearing what was said.

Kyle and Mason explained to Chase what was going on, as most of what was said was spoken in Dakota.

"I've gotta keep that fire trick in mind." Chase chuckled as he tapped his breast pocket that held his cigarettes.

"Yea, good thing I forgot to give your lighter back." They all chuckled at that.

All three men agreed that the hour was upon them and they had to use any means necessary to convince the Indians to leave here before it was too late. The men now stood beside Ghostkiller, and a hush fell over the crowd as he began to speak. His voice was powerful, yet he spoke kindly as he told the story of a vision he'd had in the cave at Yellow Medicine several months earlier.

An eagle had come down and told Ghostkiller he was going to show him a place where a great council meeting was to be held. Eagle said the Indians of the Sioux Nation must meet there in the Moon-of-the-Changing-Season. This gathering must happen before they could make demands on the Great White Father in Washington.

"I climbed upon his back and Eagle took me far up into the sky," Ghostkiller explained. "I flew away from the Sundance and saw thousands upon thousands of lodges camped where the rivers meet in the land of the flat water. Eagle then took me even higher up into the heavens and when I looked down at the grass and the water and the dirt, I saw that the place we were to meet was in the shape of an eagle's head and its beak where two rivers joined. He said I could name it and I chose to name it Eagle's Beak, in honor of the Eagle. He flew with me up and down the big river, and I saw many more lodges all along its banks – too many to count.

"Eagle told me that the lodges were guarding the gates to the west and no white man was to be allowed to cross. He said if all tribes joined as one, the Great White Father in Washington would have no choice but to meet the demands for a meeting with us, and he would sign a new treaty that would protect us forever."

Kyle knew the rest. The first treaty stated, "No white person or persons shall be permitted to settle upon or occupy any portion of the territory or without the consent of the Indians to pass through the same," which was bogus. However, with the new treaty all other treaties would become invalid, including *The Treaty of Long Meadows* — also known as the Fort Laramie treaty of 1851 — and the Horse Creek treaty of 1868. Ghostkiller admitted he did not know what the Horse Creek treaty was until the three men from the future had told him.

"I did not fully understand the vision when I had it, but I do now. My grandson and nephews have traveled a great distance to help us. They are going to tell you what our future holds unless we do something to change it. It is up to us to listen to what they have to say." Kyle then stood and addressed the group.

"The Horse Creek Treaty goes by another name; it is also called the Fort Laramie Treaty of the white man's year of 1868. It was supposed to have been signed by many of our brothers of the plains – the Cheyenne, Arapaho, and Lakota, among others – but some of the men whose signatures are on the paper were not even at the meeting. They supposedly had representatives there, but their names were written falsely. The white man just wanted it signed and did not much care who wrote the names down. No matter who signed it, it was not going to stop the *wasichu* from taking the land because they came despite the treaty. They came because they learned there was gold in the Paha Sapa; therefore, the army did not even try to keep the whites out. The Fort Laramie Treaty was full of lies. Red Cloud and Sitting Bull found that out. And any part of it that was to benefit the people was never honored at all," Kyle told them. "When the whites came flooding into our country, we complained to the agents, the army, but it did no good. The long traders then began killing all our buffalo so we could not eat or have warm robes for the winter, and by the white man's calendar year of 1880, almost all the buffalo were gone. Can you imagine that? Millions of buffalo slaughtered so Indians would starve!"

A collective gasp shuddered through the crowd followed by shouts of anger from several in the group. The crowd was asked to quiet down and then Mason took his turn.

"When our people had enough, that's when wars broke out against us and genocide was spread far and wide, not just here in Minnesota Territory. The Great Father in Washington wanted all Indians to be crowded onto reservations and would do *anything* to get the land. Once they did, they starved us and gave us blankets with diseases hidden inside to kill us. According to the treaty, they were supposed to give us food, but handed out rotten meat instead! Thousands of our people everywhere starved or were slaughtered; Black Kettle's band of Cheyenne will be slaughtered at Sand Creek in two winters, and that's just the beginning. There's a slaughter at the Washita too, and the final fight comes in the white man's year of 1890 at a place called Wounded Knee, where Big Foot and his band are gunned down in the snow while waving a white flag. Just like at Sand Creek, those who were killed at Wounded Knee were mostly women, children, and elders!"

More shouts and wails rose up. The people gathered could not believe their ears!

"These things will happen. We must move now, go to the meeting place in my grandfather's vision, and fight for our land!" Kyle exclaimed.

The crowd roared. Cries and whoops rose up from the young warriors, and old men sitting side-by-side nodded and whispered among themselves. Little Crow stood then, holding up his hand to quiet the crowd. "If these things are to come to pass, is it possible to stop it...and if so, is it wise to change the facts of history?"

"Little Crow is a coward!" Shakopee spat from his seat. "He did not want to go to war against Galbraith, even though he did bad things to the Santee!" Some of the other chiefs nodded and grunted in agreement.

"Little Crow is not a coward!" the chief thundered back, "but just as I said before this war if you kill one *wasichu*, more will come! They will come like locusts that cover the prairie! What if we change the course of our future and anger the Creator by doing so? These things must be thought out carefully!"

"I have seen the future!" Chase stood, and then gesturing toward Mason and Kyle, he continued, "My brothers have seen it, too! We live in it!" The crowd quieted down.

"We were never meant to live the way we do in the future. Even in your own time, some of the nations to the east have been driven to extinction, and for others, they have been forced to go to a land unknown to them in the west, a place where they believe spirits go when their time here is up."

Mason and Kyle nodded as they looked out at the anxious faces in the crowd. All was quiet as Chase continued.

"We were sent here to stop the killings that are taking place in our own time by bad spirits. An evil spirit is killing people because it has been given power by the way you were all treated by the whites. It does not discriminate between women and children. It kills to make a point. We know that many of you sitting right here will be hung in Moccasin Flats if you stay."

Kyle shot a look at Shakopee, "How do we know that *Wakan Tanka* did not send this spirit when you all died? How do we know that He is not already angered, not by what we decide to do now, but by what the *wasichu* have done in the past and will do in the present and future? In our time, the white man has been here over two hundred years already. It is not a nice world to live in. The water is sick and you cannot drink it, the air is dirty and thick with black smoke that makes us cough. Unci Maka is dying a slow and painful death. If we were sent here to change things, what good will it do if we don't change it all?" He paused then and looked at Ghostkiller, who gave him a nod of approval. "The answer is that it will be worse for all people if we don't."

Faint murmurs and whispers fluttered up from the chiefs. The huge crowd that huddled around was silent as they waited for Little Crow to respond. Mason, Chase, and Kyle stood beside Ghostkiller, holding a collective breath.

Little Crow looked thoughtfully around the circle. What was he to do? He had already lost so much. The next decision he made would not only affect his own people but all of the plains people. The chiefs looked anxiously at him, and Little Crow could see in their eyes the answer they wanted him to give. He looked beyond them and out to the people gathered. A baby cried. He saw the women, children and elders and their expressions of fear and uncertainty, the pain of starvation and abuse evident on their faces. Those looks were the deciding factor.

"If it is at all possible to change these things," he spoke at last, "we must do it for our future generations."

The crowd cheered then as each chief stood, one by one, clapping Little Crow on the back. Even Shakopee gave Little Crow a stone-faced nod of agreement.

The decision was made to move the camp immediately. Runners were sent out ahead to the camps on the plains – Sitting Bull of the Hunkpapas, Red Cloud of the Oglalas, Standing Elk of the Brule, and many others – to meet at the place where the Platte and Loop Rivers joined in Nebraska on a modern map. The next step was to break camp before Long Knife Sibley had a chance to catch them, and within the hour, two thousand Santee Sioux were on their way to Eagle's Beak.

39

  The sun was setting fast, and Little Crow watched from the back of his pony as streaks of red and gold stretched against an endless vault of light blue sky. The trees along the Missouri riverbank were alive with color as brilliant crimson and orange leaves danced and fluttered in the light breeze. In one of his visions, he had heard a voice telling him that time would speed up when the men from the future arrived, and as he watched the sunset move quickly from light to dark, it was easy to see that it was coming true.

  It was the Moon of Falling Leaves, the time when they should be moving to their winter camps. He knew they had to hurry to the meeting place, but the trek to Eagle's Beak was not going to be an easy one. Nebraska territory was Crow country. Several bands of Crow had already signed over their lands to the government, and a great many of their warriors had taken jobs as scouts for the army. Even worse, the Crow were a bitter enemy of the Sioux, and if the Santee were spotted, their scouts would report them to the nearest fort. Even though the white man's Civil War was raging in the south and it would be easy to think that the army would be short on manpower, Little Crow knew that the Crow would gladly kill as many Sioux as they could, if for nothing else but the sheer pleasure in doing it. However, there were other Indians in that area with whom the Sioux had good relations.

The Omaha and Winnebago were brothers to the Santee, and he was sure that they would all join up together soon. That would reinforce their battlefront quite a bit. There was still the issue of food, however, and although the *wasichu* food stores near the reservations had been taken by the Santee, it wasn't going to be enough to feed all of the people for very long.

I must not lose faith, Little Crow thought, and decided instead to call a council meeting with the men from the future. He knew one of them would have an answer. He turned his red pony toward Ghostkiller's lodge, where he and the men from the future were setting up their camp.

Chase and Mason were struggling with tipi poles while Kyle hollered instructions. Ghostkiller had a smile on his face as he watched the trio. Macedone was oblivious to the goings on as he dozed lazily under a cottonwood tree.

"I thought this was woman's work," Chase grumbled.

"Well, you see any women around here willing to do it?" Mason growled back.

"Hau," Little Crow approached, and the men stopped what they were doing.

"Come to my lodge. We will have a meeting now." He didn't wait for a reply, and as he rode slowly away, the four men stood and watched after him.

"His heart is bad," Ghostkiller said.

"He's got a lot of responsibility on his shoulders," offered Chase.

Kyle grunted his agreement. "Yes."

"Well, let's go see what's up," Mason replied, dropping the end of the lodge pole he'd been holding onto Chase's toe.

"Ow!" Chase yelled. "Dang it, Mason!" He dropped his end as well and grabbed his injured foot, hopping around while grunting and groaning exaggeratedly.

"I thought there weren't any women around here."

Kyle laughed and Mason and Ghostkiller joined in.

"Yea, yea, laugh it up," Chase grimaced. The others walked towards Little Crow's camp while Chase hobbled along to catch up.

A handful of chiefs sat in a semicircle in front of Little Crow's lodge; others clustered a short distance away, but still well within earshot. Chase, Mason, Kyle, and Ghostkiller sat on one side of Little Crow near the lodge entrance. Two of his wives busily stacked firewood while a third sliced vegetables over a pot hanging above the fire. Little Crow waited until the women were finished before he started speaking.

First, he thanked the women for their hard work and then invited them to take a seat near him. He spoke of his concerns in a quiet voice, about the food shortages and the inevitability that the food they had would soon run out.

"We are concerned also," Big Eagle agreed. "There is very little game to be found here. Our hunters were gone for two suns but came back with only a few rabbits."

"The food my camp has left will run out in one day's time," Wabasha added.

"This was not such a good idea, maybe?" Shakopee sneered as he sat cross-legged in the grass nearby.

"He still has that damned negative attitude," Chase hissed to Kyle under his breath. "How much food do you have for your people?" Chase challenged him.

Shakopee glared at Chase with a hatred Chase had seen only once before. It had been on the face of a serial killer he had arrested back in 1999. The man had no conscience, and the psychiatrist who had evaluated him had declared him a sociopath. Kyle touched Chase's arm in a warning gesture for him to back down.

"It seems we are all losing heart," Ghostkiller said, "but we cannot forget that our Creator is taking care of us and will provide. We cannot lose faith." He looked at Little Crow, who nodded towards Mason, and the two men exchanged knowing glances.

"Crow Walker, can you help us?" Little Crow turned to Mason. Mason looked at the men and women seated but wasn't sure what was being asked of him. *Remember Taoyateduta's words*, a little voice said. Mason remembered what Little Crow had told him regarding the scattered leaves, but had no idea how that had anything to do with finding game for the people.

"I...uh," Mason began, and then stopped as Ghostkiller's words echoed in his head – *we cannot lose faith* – and he knew he couldn't lose faith either, not in the Creator. Mason stood and began to speak, hoping the right words would come to him.

"Ghostkiller's right. We can't lose faith. If the Creator sent us back in time to do this, then He must have a plan for us, and along with that plan is a way to take care of us. We cannot lose sight of what we came here to do. The Creator is far greater than we, and it is through His power that we will have the strength to make a difference."

As Mason spoke those last few words, a gentle breeze grew into a gust of wind that sent the mighty cottonwood and maple trees groaning and swaying all around them. Leaves swirled and fluttered creating a beautiful kaleidoscope of colors, and when Mason saw them, he acknowledged in a prayer that their beauty was something only God could have created. *We cannot lose faith.*

Kyle leaned over to Chase with a smile. "He's dialing up the leaves," he whispered. Chase grinned back, more with appreciation and wonder that his friend had such a gift. He had learned over the course of the past few days that the Creator indeed had all the power and man was helpless to try to defy it.

All the people gathered around and watched curiously as Mason walked to a clearing a few feet away. He stood with his arms outstretched toward the heavens, letting his spirit direct him. The people watched in awe as the leaves danced their graceful colors down towards him from all directions, surrounding the man from the future. Mason repeated Ghostkiller's words aloud like a mantra:

"We cannot lose faith! We cannot lose faith!"

The leaves helped me before, he thought. *They gave me messages.* "Creator, please help me now!" he prayed.

The wind began to howl, intermittently cool then hot, encircling the people seated in camp. Baffled, they all looked towards the sky to see if a storm was building, but the sky was clear and the sun was on its way towards a brilliant sunset.

"We cannot lose faith! We cannot lose faith!" Mason yelled above the howling wind, as the men and women gathered gazed in astonishment at what was happening. "Tunkasina! Omakiiyo!" Grandfather, help me!

The colorful leaves began to swirl around Mason, kicking up dust and dirt that made him cough, but he stood strong. Faster and faster they spun, and within the twisting mass of leaves, the soft whispers began to speak to him.

"Go to the west, Crow Walker. Go to the buffalo. They are waiting on the other side of the river."

As quickly as it had spun up, the cyclone was gone, leaving Mason gasping on the ground in a heap of leaves and dirt. Each man in camp simultaneously jumped up and ran to Mason, crowding around him.

"Give 'em room!" Kyle bellowed as he and Chase ushered Ghostkiller and Little Crow in to kneel beside Mason. The chiefs began a quiet prayer of thanks as Kyle and Chase helped Mason to sit up. He coughed and gasped until finally someone passed a water skin to Kyle, who gave Mason a drink.

"Drink it slowly, nephew," Little Crow soothed as Mason sipped the cool water, smiling weakly up at the old man.

A crowd gathered as everyone from the village came out to see what had happened. As word spread, whispers and murmurs drifted through the crowd about the powerful medicine of the men who had come from the future.

"Tantanka," Mason breathed heavily. "They're waiting for us on the other side of the river." Immediately each chief sent word to their hunters to cross the river and search for the buffalo. Little Crow smiled at Ghostkiller. Crow Walker's medicine was true, and he was happy he had made the decision to take his concerns to the men from the future.

Once he'd regained his breath, Kyle and Chase helped Mason to his feet and took him into Little Crow's lodge at the chief's instruction. "He will stay here and rest," Little Crow announced to the crowd, and then he and Ghostkiller ducked inside the tipi. Shakopee and Big Eagle asked the women to send word to their lodges as soon as the hunters returned, and then they turned and left, dispersing the crowd as they went.

Later, as Mason slept in the back of the lodge, Little Crow's wives served up a vegetable stew to the men, and as they ate, they discussed the events of the day concerning Mason and the leaves. Unbeknownst to him, the people had given him a new name: Rattling Leaf.

40

The long line of men and horses stretched for miles, and for every mile they traveled, more Indians joined the line. By the time they reached the outskirts of Nebraska, several more bands, including the Brule and Cheyenne, had joined the Santee. In modern history books, it would be known as the largest concentration of Indians ever to congregate on the plains in one place.

The runners reported to Little Crow that what should have taken days had only taken them a few hours, and the message to Lincoln was delivered in record time. They were told that Lincoln would arrive at Eagle's Beak in three days. Little Crow nodded. Time was speeding up, something he had suspected anyway.

Five thousand Indians now gathered at the western fork of the Little Sioux River, with more on the way, all heading directly to the land of the flat water, Eagle's Beak. The afternoon sun was high in the sky, its golden rays stretching like graceful fingers through puffy cumulus clouds.

Mason seemed to have recovered from what had happened earlier, and Little Crow watched as he and Chase sat together on a fallen log. He was proud of Mason's abilities with the leaves and was glad the white man was here, as well. Kyle's medicine had given Shakopee a different perspective on things, which was important too, as some of the people were still unsure as to whether or not he could be trusted. Little Crow smiled. He was happy his people were looking to him for guidance once again.

The women began the task of packing up the massive amount of buffalo meat they now had, thanks to Mason. The hunters had not only found the buffalo, but had reported that while they were hunting, a great thunderstorm that had loomed on the horizon had split, and they were able to hunt unseen within the storm's protection.

They were on the outskirts of Crow country and had to be wary of the Crow scouts that may have already seen them. With the large group that had joined them this afternoon, the risk was becoming greater that they would be reported to neighboring agencies and military posts. Little Crow called a council to discuss the trek to Eagle's Beak. The lodge was crowded with the newly arriving chiefs, and after they were told about the men from the future, the chiefs confronted them with their concerns.

"If even one Crow should see us, they will tell the white soldiers," said one chief.

"They probably already have!" said another.

"Then we will fight them!" shouted Shakopee. "There are many more Santee than there are scrawny Crow!"

"All you ever want to do is fight," Lightning Blanket said. "There can be peaceful resolutions, too."

Ghostkiller stood and held up his hand. "There is no need to shout!"

He looked at Shakopee. "To fight the Crow will surely bring the *wasichu* from their war parties in the east. It is too risky."

Kyle, Mason, and Chase sat in silence alongside Little Crow, listening to the exchange. They each knew that the fears of the Indians were well founded. If they were caught up in a fight with the army, it would end their hopes of saving the people from prosecution and then the subsequent genocide that followed. Their plan was to change history, and that is what they were going to do, one way or another. Kyle rose and stood beside his grandfather.

"I wish to speak with my brothers privately," he said. Little Crow stood up to leave, but Kyle asked him to stay, as well.

"Wonder what he has in mind?" Chase whispered to Mason as the tipi emptied out.

Mason grimaced, "That's what I'm afraid of."

After the three men sat back down, Kyle cleared his throat and spoke softly. "There is a way to get past the Crow and anyone else that might cause trouble for the Sioux," he said, "and it won't matter if we travel by day or by night."

Before he could speak any further, there was a rap at the door. Little Crow said something in Dakota to the person on the other side of the flap. In the split second that it took Kyle and Mason to realize why Little Crow had spoken in Lakota, the man who'd rapped on the flap had entered the lodge and was shaking hands with the two older chiefs. He then took a seat across from Kyle.

The words Kyle had been about to speak stuck in his throat as he gazed at the man seated across from him. Chase and Mason could only stare in shocked silence, not realizing both of their mouths gaped open. Recognition dawned on the three of them simultaneously, and Kyle immediately reached for his tobacco pouch while Chase fumbled with his cigarette pack in his shirt pocket. Mason patted himself down, and then realizing he didn't have any tobacco on him, nudged Chase to pass him a cigarette as well.

"*Hiya*," the man said. "We do not have time for formalities." He smiled, then he spoke to Kyle. "You were about to tell them your plan to use the veil's passageway as a better way to protect the people on their trek to Eagle's Beak."

"Yes," Kyle spoke slowly, "I was."

"But how did you…" Chase began.

"It doesn't matter," the man smiled at Chase, and then looking at Kyle he said, "But as you know, it does need to happen like that."

"Yes," Kyle repeated, a slow smile crossing his face.

"Now," the man said, "introduce me to your friends."

Gesturing towards Mason and Chase, Kyle said, "Mason, Chase, I'd like you to meet Chief Sitting Bull of the Hunkpapas."

Once the shock of the introduction had worn off, the men decided on how they would organize the massive amount of people. Chase, of course, had a slew of questions, and Kyle, along with the other men in the lodge, answered them as patiently as they could.

"Can you just conjure that gate up anywhere?" Chase asked.

"Yes," Kyle smiled. "If we travel to Eagle's Beak through the veil, we will be there in an instant. No one will see us at all."

"But what about the people?" Chase asked. "There's more to going through the veil then just taking a stroll through it, Kyle."

"The people will be safe," Sitting Bull said. "The visions have been too strong for the outcome to be any different. Creator gave young Ghostkiller the medicine."

"Yes, let me worry about the people this time," Kyle smiled. "Grandfather?" Kyle looked at Ghostkiller in question, for traditionally he had to have the go ahead before he would be allowed to take on such a task. After all, it was Ghostkiller's vision they were following.

With a nod, Ghostkiller agreed and along with Sitting Bull and Little Crow, they called the remaining chiefs back into the lodge and told them of the plan. They would leave at dusk, forming a line behind the men from the future. Each chief was instructed to explain to his people that they were to go through the veil, single file, no matter what. It might be frightening to them, but the veil was offering safe passage to the meeting place, and no matter what happened, the people were to go through it, running if they had to. Shortly afterward, they all filed out, moving to their respective camps to pack up.

Mason and Kyle took the next hour practicing their horseback riding skills. Chase tried to keep up, but he was no match for the two Indians who'd obviously been riding all their lives. They jumped the horses over fallen logs, galloped around large boulders, and raced the horses at break-neck speeds. Macedone was always declared the winner. Ghostkiller observed the three young men from under the shade of a cottonwood tree and chuckled to himself. It was good to see the future through his great, great grandson's eyes.

After an afternoon filled with feasting, games, and plenty of celebration, it was time for the people to prepare for the journey through the veil. The sun was a deep red and sat low in the western sky when Kyle, seated on Macedone, took his place on a hill overlooking the river. Chase and Mason stood behind him, each seated on the wagon horses they had ridden in on.

The line was long, but formed in record time. Ghostkiller, Little Crow, and Sitting Bull sat on their horses behind Chase and Mason, and each camp lined up behind them in a double line. Most were on foot, but they placed the warriors on horseback behind the women and children for protection. All was quiet as they watched and waited in anticipation.

Kyle raised his arms high above his head and began singing a song that was familiar to all: a thank you song that he sang in Dakota. As he sang, other voices joined in until the whole mile long group was singing together. It reminded Chase of *Horton Hears a Who*, the Dr. Seuss book he remembered reading as a child. *'We are here, we are here, we are here!'* the song seemed to be saying.

Kyle reached into the medicine pouch that hung around his neck and withdrew something that he put into his mouth. After a few moments, he blew into his hands, creating a blue orb that he threw up and into the air. A collective gasp rippled through the crowd as a loud roaring sound began to surround them, but the people continued to sing.

All at once the portal opened, no bigger than a dot at first. The wind gusted and lightning crackled inside the hole as it grew larger. Suddenly, the swirling vortex became a bright, rectangular doorway, large enough for man and horse ten deep to fit through. With a cry coming from deep within him, Kyle drove his heels into Macedone's flanks and ran towards it, leaping through and disappearing instantly. Chase and Mason then whooped and rode their own horses through, followed by Ghostkiller, Sitting Bull, and Little Crow, and then a sentry of warriors on horseback. The people followed and began to run towards the light, still keeping in single file as they had been told to do. It seemed everything was going as planned.

Kyle, Chase, and Mason hit the ground on the other side, and they quickly discovered themselves in the middle of an all-out battle. In the flurry of excitement, Kyle and Mason quickly assessed that it was Lakota fighting Crow, but they hardly had time to think as shots rang out from every direction. Mason drew his 9mm and began returning fire and Kyle drew his knife and let it fly, quickly finding its mark through the heart of a Crow who stood holding a raised club over an injured Lakota child.

Chase felt a bit disoriented from the trip through the veil. *Just when I thought I was getting good at this!* He shook his head slightly and then pulled his gun, but was unsure at first about who to shoot. *They all look alike!* Some faces were painted, some were not; some wore feathers, war shirts, others were shirtless; he saw long hair, short hair, but they were all Indians. It was too much! Before he could even decide, he was knocked from his horse. Fire shot through his thigh as he was hit by an arrow on the way down. He lay dazed on the ground, but saw an Indian with a Mohawk sighting down the shaft of an arrow pointed straight at Mason's back.

Chase hissed through the burning pain in his leg. "If I'm going to die here in the past, your ass is coming with me, you sonofabitch!" He took aim and fired repeatedly, emptying his gun into the Indian while crying out every curse word he could think of.

Mason turned and rode to Chase's side, quickly dismounting. He stood over him, firing as fast as he could, trying to protect him and the women and children as they came rushing through the veil. The Crow in the immediate area began to panic and turned to run as they saw the Sioux emerging from out of a seemingly empty blue hole in mid-air. The battle was over almost as soon as it had begun. The air was thick with the pungent odor of gunpowder and the metallic scent of blood.

Little Crow and Sitting Bull sent a hundred of their warriors after the terrified Crow, ordering them not to come back until they had found and killed them all and then stood with Ghostkiller as they waited for the remaining women and children to come through the veil. Kyle vaulted onto Macedone's back, rode back to the hole, and continued to sing until everyone was safely on the other side. As soon as the last moccasin-ed foot stepped through the vortex, the veil was quickly sucked back up into the heavens, leaving a few colorful leaves to flutter down to the ground. The clouds above seemed to heave a great sigh of relief as a giant wind *whooshed* and echoed, and then all fell silent. The wounded were taken away, along with those who had been killed, although the number was quite low.

The Lakota involved in the battle were a part of the group that had already gathered at Eagle's Beak, and once the battle was over, they began to surround the Dakotas who had emerged from the blue hole. Their initial shock at the vortex was quickly replaced by questions directed at Kyle and Mason. They had all heard rumors about the men from the future and were eager to hear what they had to say.

Macedone tossed his head restlessly as people began to encircle them. Kyle dismissed inquiries and ordered a travois for the injured Chase, who was swiftly loaded onto it, bound for the nearest camp. Curious eyes stared at the oddly dressed men, but as they made their way through the crowd, information rapidly spread that they were the futuristic trio, and they were all ushered forward with great speed and reverence. Little Crow, Sitting Bull, and Ghostkiller followed closely behind, answering questions as best they could along the way.

The men were shown into a tipi painted with various symbols – Indians on horseback, dead soldiers, arrows flying, the sun and the stars – all obviously depicting battles fought in the past. A fire burned in the center of the lodge, and the smell of burning sweet grass filled the circular structure. Chase was in a great deal of pain and Mason practically slapped his hands away when he attempted to pull the arrow out of his thigh.

"Let the medicine man do it!" he snapped, as he helped maneuver Chase onto buffalo robes which acted as a bed. Looking at the ugly gash and the massive amount of blood Chase was losing, Mason silently prayed the arrow hadn't pierced an artery.

The tipi door burst open and a young woman entered followed by an old man with two long gray braids. He was dressed in leggings, moccasins, and a wolf skin clout, his face painted half red and half black. He motioned for the others to step out, and Chase gave Mason a worried look. Mason assured him everything would be all right before following the others out of the tipi. Chase studied the pair apprehensively as they unloaded their wares; the woman appeared to be in her mid-twenties and was beautiful, with dusky skin, large brown eyes, a small nose, and full pink lips. The firelight cast blue highlights in her long black hair that was parted in the middle. She wore a buckskin dress adorned with small white shells that tinkled with every movement. Chase managed a weak smile as she moved to sit beside him.

She held what Chase now recognized as a smudge bowl in her hands, a large shell that Mason had told him was called abalone. The medicine man pulled a hot stick from the fire, lighting the contents of the shell and the sharp scent of sage filled the tipi. He fanned the smoke over Chase from head to toe, singing in a low tone. He worked quickly and in a motion that left Chase little time to react, he sat the shell down and grasped the arrow, snapping it quickly in half. Chase jumped, and then groaned as fresh blood pumped from the wound. The medicine man then pulled a knife from a leather sheath strapped to his side and held it in the open flame. The woman bathed Chase's perspiring brow with a cool cloth dipped in a wooden bowl of water. Clenching his teeth, Chase waited for the hot blade of the knife to pierce his throbbing flesh. The woman began singing softly and Chase stared at her, mesmerized by the sound of her voice.

The medicine man began to pry the arrowhead from the wound, but before Chase could react to the pain, he slipped into a deep sleep, mindless of what was happening. Floating to another place, it reminded him of the peaceful confines of darkness he'd felt when he'd passed through the veil the first time. A warm light began to gather around him and he could see figures of people, but no details of what they looked like. A calm, easy sigh escaped his lips, and all went black.

When he awoke, the medicine man was gone and he could see a star-filled sky through the smoke hole of the lodge. He turned and saw his friends talking quietly among themselves. He saw Kyle lying on his back with one arm thrown over his eyes. Mason, Ghostkiller, and Little Crow sat on the far side of the lodge, speaking softly. The woman sat to his right, watching him. She smiled and lifted a bowl of warm broth to his lips, and he drank it hungrily.

"Easy," she said, smiling as she set the bowl aside. He rose up when she handed him a second bowl. He was surprised she spoke English, but her next words were in Dakota and he realized that he'd probably heard the extent of her English vocabulary.

After drinking some of the water she offered, he felt a bit better, but trying to converse with her further seemed too daunting a task. Chase nodded his thanks and sank back down onto the buffalo robes, falling into a deep sleep, riddled with disturbing dreams of a beautiful woman with long black hair murmuring words to him he didn't understand.

41

Nina tossed and turned in the darkened cave. She thought she was dreaming, but couldn't be sure because the fire had gone out and the cave was black as pitch. She felt sure her eyes were open and even tried to open them wider, but it didn't do any good. *Surely, my mind knows whether I'm awake or not!*

She felt like she'd been in there for days. There was no light and no warmth as she struggled inside her sleeping bag, feeling as if she were tied down. She thought she had built a fire big enough to last most of the night, but the fire was out and she didn't even see a glowing coal.

She searched for the sliver of light that would come through the cave entrance if it were morning, but it had to be the middle of the night still, as she saw nothing there. Panic started to take over and the feeling of being suffocated was almost overwhelming. It was as if she was suspended in time, and she thought about the dream walkers she had heard about while growing up. *Could I be trapped in the dream world?* She called out to Dapple but got no response. Just then, a twinkle appeared some distance away. It was the same eerie blue color that had surrounded her and Kyle. Her eyes followed the blue light as it traveled upward, suddenly shooting sideways and then falling from ceiling height, settling on the ground beside her sleeping bag. The light grew, and then became more brilliant and she gasped as a beautiful woman began to materialize in front of her. Nina froze as she watched the woman hover in the air. She thought the woman looked familiar, but couldn't remember where she had seen her before.

The woman said her name. "Nina."

Who is that? Nina peered at her. *What is happening?*

"Who are you?" Nina asked, still trying to decide whether she was dreaming or not.

"Elisi," the woman replied.

All at once, Nina felt like the air was being sucked out from around her, depleting and swallowing her along with everything else, even the cave itself.

"Elisi?" Nina heard herself choke.

"Don't worry, he's coming for you."

Before she could think any further, everything faded to black.

42

Kyle dozed in Little Crow's tipi as low voices engaged in conversation drifted in and out of his consciousness. Ghostkiller, Mason and Little Crow were talking about the runner who had been sent to Washington to summon President Lincoln.

"Sitting Bull was really anxious to get that runner on the trail," Kyle heard Mason say. "All we can do now is wait," and from somewhere in the back of Kyle's mind he heard the words 'for a sign.'

"I don't think there were any survivors, so I doubt we will have any more trouble from the Crow after today," said Ghostkiller.

Little Crow grunted his agreement and they began discussing the Crow and the Pawnee, also bitter enemies of the Sioux.

Mason told Little Crow and Ghostkiller what the history books in the future said about the Crow and how they factored into the future of the Sioux. "They originally lived along the Missouri river and called themselves Absaroke, or bird people. Once they moved closer to the Rocky Mountains and became buffalo hunters, the trouble with other tribes started."

He told them that in 1873 the Crow would form an allegiance with the United States and send their scouts along with a man they would call "Yellow Hair," known in the white world as George Armstrong Custer. He and the Crow would hunt down the Sioux and engage them in battle in the white man's year of 1876, in what they would later call the state of Montana near a place called the Greasy Grass. "This was called the battle of the Little Big Horn," Mason said. "And Custer and his entire regiment was killed that day by us," he added.

Half awake and half asleep, Kyle allowed the words to drift through his mind. It had been a long day and his body was screaming for much-needed rest. He had plenty of time to contemplate what lay ahead of them with this meeting with Lincoln and his cabinet, but for now, he was going to sleep while he had the chance.

Kyle was glad he was used to the physical demands of riding after all that had happened. Mason didn't complain, but Kyle had seen him wince when he'd sat down in the lodge earlier and knew the older man was having a tough time with all the riding. Kyle smiled beneath closed eyes when he remembered racing each other earlier in the day. It was like old times, but the fun sure hadn't lasted long. He allowed himself to relive the battle that had taken place when they came through the veil. Had all of the Crow been found and killed? If not, they would have the army to deal with by this time tomorrow. Kyle would have to remember to ask Little Crow if he'd gotten word about that or not.

Kyle thought about Chase and about how bravely he had fought, the way he had saved Mason's life. He was glad Chase was going to be okay. *Chase turned out to be a pretty good friend for a white guy*, Kyle smiled to himself.

He breathed in deeply and let out a satisfying sigh, allowing his thoughts to turn to Nina. She was never far from this thoughts despite everything else that was going on. He wanted nothing more than for all of this to be over so he could get back to the future where he knew she awaited him. She was his love, his life and he had so much to tell her. When all this was over, maybe she would finally understand why he had left and had sought out his destiny with such conviction all those years ago. He allowed himself to relax and let sleep claim him, welcoming the darkness that swallowed him up. He lay in the comfort of its arms, content to just be lost within its warmth. He knew he had done all he could for today, as far as the legend was concerned.

    Kyle's dreams began as soon as he drifted off to sleep. He saw Nina's face clearly, and he allowed himself to absorb her essence. He felt himself floating while intertwined with her body. He could smell and taste her womanness, feel his body within hers, and then felt them drifting down onto soft furs that lay in front of a blazing fire. He had this dream of making love to her often, and it felt the same every time – a bit of resistance, and then he was deep inside of her, their bodies writhing together inside the warmth of buffalo robes. They belonged together, and he couldn't wait to marry her. A sigh escaped his lips as he lay in contentment with Nina in his arms. He saw her face in the firelight, felt the warmth of her body close to his, heard her whisper his name.

    Suddenly the images faded and he was taken to another familiar place. Although it was dark, he recognized the Cave of The Old Ones immediately and saw Nina lying in a sleeping bag. An inky black entity hovered above her with a hangman's noose dangling from its long, skeletal fingers. The figure was barely three feet tall, and he could not see its face or legs, just its boney hands. He watched, horrified as the gruesome figure slipped the rope over Nina's head and around her neck. Nina screamed a long, blood-curdling scream.

Kyle woke with a start and sat up. His heart was racing wildly, his breathing labored. He looked around the lodge – Chase asleep near the rear of the lodge, Little Crow's niece sitting beside him, the young woman tending to Chase. The other men, who were talking quietly, now turned their attention towards Kyle.

"Takoja?" he heard Ghostkiller softly call out the term for grandson.

Suddenly the images from Kyle's dream materialized in front of him. The lodge itself seemed to shudder as if being shook out like a dirty blanket, and Kyle blinked several times trying to make sense of what he saw on the tipi wall. He gasped aloud as he watched the image of the black entity pull the rope taut around Nina's neck. She screamed but the sound was cut off, which caused the entity to laugh a horrific, maniacal sound that sent a coldness rippling through the lodge unlike any wind chill he had ever felt before. Chase sat up, and along with the other men, turned towards the commotion. The realization was almost too much for them to comprehend at first, and then with shocked anguish, they watched as Kyle's vision played out before them, as well. Nina choked out Kyle's name and Kyle lunged forward grasping for her and fell face first into the dirt as the images vanished.

"Holy!" Mason exclaimed.

"Takoja!" Ghostkiller repeated, rising to his feet and calling out to Kyle, who was already pulling on his moccasins.

Kyle stood and turned to the older man, the look on his face grim.

"Go to her, *cinks*, take Macedone and bring her here quickly!" Ghostkiller urged.

"Kyle!" Chase grabbed the lance and tossed it to him when he turned in his direction.

Kyle caught it midair, nodding his thanks. Mason bolted to the flap and pulled it to the side. "Hurry!"

Kyle was out the door and on Macedone's back in an instant, heading for the woods at breakneck speed.

Hurry! Hurry! A little voice pleaded. There were certain times in Kyle's life when that inner voice spoke to him with an urgency that was hard to deny. More intense than that nagging little thought in the back of his mind spoken by his voice, this was the sacred voice that let him know something was amiss. Kyle knew that voice well. It belonged to the spirits who worked with him and had saved him on countless occasions, always put him in the right place at just the right time. He knew that particular voice he had heard all these years and he'd learned to trust it, and as he raced through the woods towards Nina, he awaited his instructions.

When he reached an outcropping of cottonwood trees, Kyle was told that this was the right place, and to his relief, it was not too late. With only a thought, the blue mist spun down and the veil opened for him immediately. Sensing the urgency of the situation, Macedone charged headlong into it, sailing through to present day.

In what had become the norm, the horse hit the ground running, but this time, he didn't have to run very far. That same outcropping of cottonwood trees surrounding the Cave of the Old Ones stood before them. The trees were bigger, but Kyle recognized them immediately and knew that the cave was less than two hundred yards away. He slammed his heels into the horse's flanks, urging him on. Kyle could hear Nina's screams and the desperate whinny of her horse echoing through the cave's opening as they drew near. Macedone barely had time to stop before Kyle dropped to the ground and ran inside, clutching the lance in his hand. What he found inside stopped him in his tracks, and he stood frozen as his vision in the tipi unfolded in front of him.

The hangman's noose tightening around Nina's neck did so of its own volition. Her eyes bulged in terror and her breath came in great gasps as the rope cut off her airflow. He watched her struggle inside the sleeping bag, and could see a thin stream of blood beginning to run down from under the rope as it tore into her flesh. He couldn't move, couldn't save her. A fire blazed in the center of the cavern, and Kyle saw dark shadows dancing in the flames, their movements joyous, as they celebrated what looked to be some sort of sick sacrifice.

The inky, black entity was laughing, and Kyle saw the glowing eyes and razor sharp teeth that dripped the blood of every man, woman, and child it had killed. As it hovered above Nina, it looked at Kyle and let out another hideous barrage of laughter that sent his blood running cold. The hairs on the back of his neck stood at full attention. *This is what you are fighting! This killing machine will murder everyone in Moccasin Flats!* He was face to face with what his Grandfather James and all his relatives in Pine Ridge and Moccasin Flats had told him about all of his life, and in that moment, he was frozen. The thing had complete control over him and he couldn't move.

They stared each other down, Kyle fighting with every ounce of willpower he could muster while the entity's hatred permeated him. Suddenly he could feel the pain and terror of every victim it had killed, along with the greed and loathing that had caused the Great Sioux Uprising. Kyle staggered and fell to the ground, crying out as the excruciating pain of what the people had felt gripped him, the horror of how it had killed them, the anguish and reasons behind it. He knew deep down inside that just as with any sort of evil, if he fed it, it would win. Just then, the little voice in the back of his mind cried out, *we cannot lose faith!* From deep within his soul, a war cry as old as the cave itself tore from his throat and Kyle was suddenly free. Lunging forward, he quickly drove the lance into the black entity, sending it screaming into the dark recesses of the cave with the dancing shadows following close behind. Its macabre shrieks mixed with the screams of the dead filled the cave with a deafening roar and then faded down one of the corridors.

Kyle rushed to Nina and knelt beside her, cradling her limp body in his arms. The horror of seeing the noose bound so tightly around her neck made him worry that it might be the only thing keeping the flesh of her throat together, but he had to get it off. Gingerly, he loosened it, relieved that blood didn't come gushing out as he feared it might. He was suddenly made aware of what had caused the ugly jack-o-lantern wounds on all those murdered victims.

Cautiously lifting the noose over Nina's head, he flung it aside and then ripped a sleeve from his t-shirt, carefully wrapping it around the rope burns. Tears streamed down his face as he looked in anguish upon her beautiful, pale face.

"Don't you leave me," he whispered to her, brushing back a lock of blonde hair from her forehead. Moving quickly, he unzipped the sleeping bag and pulled her out of it, gathered her into his arms and rocked her back and forth. He sang a prayer song as he held her, murmured her name, and told her how much he loved her, how he would never leave her or let anything happen to her ever again.

A tiny, blue light came flying out of nowhere and settled in front of Kyle. It startled him as he watched it form into the figure of a woman. She was dressed in a calico print dress and had long, black hair parted in the middle.

"Protect my granddaughter," The woman said. "She was given to your family for safe keeping."

Suddenly, he heard a chorus of voices mixed with the demonic laughter from far off in the distance. The woman looked in the direction of the voices and then vanished. The scrambled voices grew louder as they echoed from the corridor where the shadow people had vanished. Kyle didn't have time to digest what he had just seen. The little voice warned that the shadows were coming for them. He groped around for the lance, but it was gone. *Hurry! Hurry!* The little voice called desperately.

"Tunkasina!" Kyle cried out as he hauled himself to his feet with Nina in his arms. "Dapple, follow!" he ordered and the frightened mare trotted out behind him. He vaulted onto Macedone's back with Nina in his arms, a leap he couldn't have explained if he'd tried. It was as if something lifted them both onto the horse with as much effort as it took for the wind to blow. With no time to contemplate that, the lance materialized in front of him. He snatched it out of the air, gathered the reins and took off. The sounds from within the cave echoed loudly near the entrance and were suddenly right behind them.

No! No! His mind screamed! He couldn't have come this far only to be caught by these entities and have Nina die! This wasn't part of his vision! *We cannot lose faith!* He drove his heels into Macedone's flanks and they raced back towards the veil. Kyle could see the light growing dim, but the little voice told him there was still time. He glanced over his shoulder and saw a dark cloud of small black figures gliding along the ground at an impossible clip, their chilling screams of laughter growing louder.

Hurry! Hurry! The little voice urged. Kyle looked ahead and watched as the veil seemed to be racing towards them. He closed his eyes just as it swallowed them up, safely carrying them back through time.

As the shadow people poised themselves to hurl through the veil, it was quickly sucked back into the heavens, leaving them to wail in mourning for their victim who had just escaped her fate.

43

A crowd began to gather behind Ghostkiller as he and the rest of the men stood waiting at the cottonwood trees where they had seen the light of the veil flash. It had been no easy task for Chase to follow, but he was determined to see what was happening, and with the help of Tory, managed to limp along with the others. His leg was very tender, but the medicine man had done a good job. Chase didn't have a fever, which meant there was no infection setting in, and aside from a slight headache, felt as if he was going to be okay.

Although Kyle had only been gone a few minutes, it seemed like an eternity to the ones who waited on the other side. Suddenly, there was a flash and Macedone came bounding through the portal with the mare on his heels.

"They're running like the devil himself is after 'em!" Chase exclaimed.

"That may very well be," Mason answered as he moved into the path of the horses.

Questions formed on Chase's lips, but he chose not to ask them right then.

"Whoa!" Mason steadied the horses, soothing the frightened beasts in a low tone. Although he sensed Macedone's relief, the big stallion continued to prance and snort uneasily.

"How is she, *cinks*?" Ghostkiller asked as he and Little

Crow approached, casting a concerned look at the woman lying in Kyle's arms.

"She needs help, grandfather!" Kyle managed to choke out.

"Come," said Little Crow, "we must hurry!"

Little Crow noted Nina's long, blonde hair that cascaded to the ground, reminding him of the waterfalls he used to play in as a child. A distant vision from his childhood suddenly rushed into his mind of a woman with flaxen hair who was to be a factor in the lives of the people.

The group rushed back to camp with a large crowd following behind them. Hushed whispers and faint murmurs of the 'future people' carried through the masses.

Chase and Tory helped Mason tether the horses near the tipi and then ducked in after the others. Kyle carried Nina to the back of the lodge and laid her gently down on the buffalo robes. He sat beside her, cradling her head in his arms, praying harder than he ever had before. The medicine man seemed to appear instantly and ordered everyone out except for Kyle. Although the wound seemed to be healing as quickly as the minutes ticked by, the medicine man packed a sage poultice around it and tied it with a clean cloth. He smudged them both with sage smoke and then tucked Nina in amongst the robes, instructing Kyle not to let her out of his sight.

Once he received word that the woman was going to live, Little Crow sent several runners to the other camps, ordering an estimate of the number of people gathered in each. If everyone was in place, it would be time to take action. He'd known that the vision from his childhood would be a factor with the future people at some point, but now the woman with the white hair had arrived, the time had come.

When the runners returned, Little Crow consulted with Ghostkiller and Sitting Bull along with the other chiefs, and the decision was made to set things in motion for the arrival of Lincoln's party from Washington. The massive gathering of Indians was too numerous to count, much less fight. Even if Lincoln stopped the war and sent his whole army to Nebraska Territory, they would be no match for the Indians now gathered at Eagle's Beak.

A command for the various warrior societies came down, and all were given instructions to form a line along the Missouri River as per Ghostkiller's vision. The Kit Fox, the Braveheart's and the White Horse Societies were included, along with the Cheyenne Dog Soldiers and a host of other societies from additional tribes. These elite forces would have no problem following the order that was made crystal clear to them: No white men are allowed to cross the river. If any white man attempts to cross, kill them on sight. Whites who were already there were to be herded out, with no exceptions, but there was to be no killing unless fired upon first, and under no circumstances were women and children to be harmed in any way. The warriors quickly dispersed and began to gather their forces. Within a matter of a few hours, thousands of warriors whose only mission was to protect the people and all lands west of the river were guarding the entire length of the Missouri River from Oklahoma to the Canadian border.

Little Crow shared his vision of the white woman in Sitting Bull's lodge, and he agreed that her role was an important one. "It will take the effort of each of the future people to change what I have seen in my own visions. If they are successful, our people will live in peace forever."

The men talked far into the night finalizing the plans for the meeting with Lincoln, and once they were satisfied that everything was in order, Little Crow and Ghostkiller left Sitting Bull's camp and returned to check on Nina.

She was asleep on the robes, and Kyle sat beside her, stroking her head and singing softly. Mason bathes her head with a cool cloth. She never moved when they came in and seemed oblivious to what was happening around her. The two men knew she had no idea what her role in the past was going to be, or what her final destiny held afterward. They signaled to Kyle and Mason that they needed to speak to them. Chase was fast asleep, and Mason saw no reason to wake him.

"He needs that leg to heal or he'll be no good to us," Mason said. Kyle nodded. Mason joined the men at the fire.

As they waited for Kyle to get Nina settled, Ghostkiller and Little Crow considered the day's events and the future people's involvement in changing the future.

"It is good that she is here," Little Crow said.

"Hau," grunted Ghostkiller in agreement. "My nephews need to be told what is happening. As Tatanka Yotanka said, they are all a part of what is to be, as well." Little Crow nodded as he and Ghostkiller took a seat around the fire with Mason. Mason was curious as to what the men had to tell them. Once Kyle made sure Nina was asleep, he joined them.

After explaining to the group what had been set into motion with the warrior societies, Ghostkiller told them that when the President arrived there would not be much time for them to talk privately. "It is important that you understand the events that must take place now."

Chase awoke then and crawled over to the fire to sit beside Mason.

"You need rest," Mason told him

"I'm not missing out on any of this, "Chase whispered.

"You're nothin' if not resilient," Mason drawled.

Ghostkiller said that a new treaty had to be ready for the President to sign as soon as he arrived. "This will take the place of all of the future treaties you told us about, and it will be written in a way that all of our lands will be protected forever. The white woman will help with this."

Chase furrowed his eyebrows as he looked from Mason to Ghostkiller. "But what does Nina have to do with anything? I thought —"

Ghostkiller raised his hand, "The white woman's presence here is part of the prophecy," he interrupted, "and she will have a hand in drawing up the new treaty."

"What is the new treaty?" Chase asked.

"The All Nations Treaty of 1862," Ghostkiller and Little Crow answered in unison.

"But how did you know she would come?" Chase asked. Mason and Kyle looked at each other. They knew Chase had to have answers.

Ghostkiller looked at Kyle then. "Because of the love she has for my grandson. It is the love that only comes once and spans all generations," he smiled at Kyle, "and you two have that."

Kyle knew how he felt about Nina, how he had always felt about her. He had to admit he had been a bit surprised to learn that Nina was to be a part of the treaty-making, but guessed that it made sense since she had been to law school. She said she had specialized in Indian law. He realized then why things between them had happened the way it did. If they had gotten married, she probably would never have attended school, would never have earned her law degree. As hard as it was to leave her, it was necessary.

The hurdle of her past was another subject altogether, however. The message the woman in the cave gave him was pretty clear. Rosie had told him how Nina came to live with the Bolton's but were not her real parents. Who she was before she came to Rosie's was something he was not prepared to deal with yet. Nina would have enough to contend with once she woke up. They would just have to deal with the rest later.

He studied his great grandfather's profile in the firelight. It made his heart glad to know that even though more than a century separated them, he could still be a part of this with him. The spirits indeed worked in mysterious ways.

He smiled and formed a question on his lips, but Ghostkiller raised his hand again. "Now it is time for rest. Tomorrow will be a big day for all of us." Kyle decided to save his question for later — the next morning was going to come early.

Those lodged in Little Crow's tipi had no trouble falling asleep after the long day they'd had, all with the exception of Nina. As the night wore on, she came fully awake and as she lay there in the dim firelight, she retraced the events of the day. She reached up and touched the wound that curved around her throat, shuddering at the thought of the horrible shadowed creature that had come after her. She recalled the maniacal laughter of the black, inky *thing* as it had hovered above her, and of the noose as it tightened around her neck.

What in God's name was that thing? She thought, then it occurred to her that it couldn't be anything of God at all, and it would have certainly killed her if Kyle had not shown up when he did.

She looked over at him sleeping beside her, remembering what he had told her in her semi-conscious state. They had traveled back in time, he'd said, gone through a veil, the same doorway to the past he had tried to explain to her before, at Redwood Falls. *Back in time? How can that be?* Time travel was something she had always been fascinated with, but had never dreamed could be possible, even after hearing Kyle and Rosie talk about it for most of her life. She halfway thought it was just a metaphor. But it would sure explain a lot of things, like how the horse tracks had disappeared without a trace back at the cave, not to mention how she and Kyle had ended up here. It did feel different here, but being back in time? It couldn't be true, and her mind refused to accept it. She vowed then to look for telephone poles or other signs of civilization once it became light outside.

She suddenly felt the overwhelming urge to run. The thoughts she'd been having seemed almost mechanical, but as the realization of it dawned on her, anxiety began to wash over her. She had to get out of there, needed to get some fresh air and try to clear her mind. Near panic-stricken, she tried to sit up, but only made it to her elbows. Her head swam and her body ached too much to go any further. Kyle was instantly awake.

"Hey, hey," he said quietly, "where are you going?"

"I need..." she began, but he pulled her into his arms. Where was she going to go? There was no way she was going to try to take Macedone again, and she didn't even recognize where she was in the first place. Tears of frustration trickled down her cheeks. Even if she did just need some air, she couldn't even get up under her own power.

"Rest," Kyle pulled her close. "Things'll look better in the morning, I promise." His calming words did help her nerves some, and she snuggled closer to him and tried to close her eyes again. Within minutes she heard Kyle's steady breathing, telling her he was fast asleep once more.

Back in time? Her mind screamed it again, and she glanced around the tipi trying to find evidence to the contrary. She could see the lodge wasn't made of canvas, but animal hide – something that was almost unheard of unless you paid major bucks for it. It was very expensive to buy that much hide and was mostly seen in the movies or at rendezvous, rather than on reservations.

Back in time.

Gingerly poking her head above Kyle's shoulder, she waited for the dizziness to pass, and then realized she and Kyle were laying on buffalo robes. But that wasn't unusual. A lot of people on the reservation had buffalo robes.

Peering through the dim firelight, she spotted the shadows of containers hanging by the lodge flap and recognized them as water skins. *Buffalo bladders,* she thought. There were various lances, bows, arrows, and wooden dishes in one corner; backrests weaved from willow branches in another and sleeping bodies. *Sleeping bodies!* Nina looked anxiously around the lodge, relieved when she recognized Mason and Chase, and then her eyes settled on a man who looked like a slightly older version of Kyle lying not three feet from them. The resemblance was astonishing. She recognized him from an old Matthew Brady photo that Aunt Rosie had in the family album, and a small gasp escaped her lips. It was Ghostkiller himself, the ancestor who had spawned the whole legend or prophecy, however you wanted to look at it, seven generations ago. Her eyes lingered for a moment on his face.

He had the same strong jaw line, full lips, high cheekbones and, she guessed, the same black eyes his third great grandson possessed. She studied them both, looking from one man to the other, and she couldn't get over the resemblance between the two men.

If this is the year 1862, Ghostkiller is about 40, she thought and noted a bit of graying at his temples in the firelight. Her mind reeling, she allowed her eyes to travel across the fire pit and gasped when she recognized the man who lay on the other side. It was Little Crow. He had been a cousin to Ghostkiller and Crow Walker, Mason's ancestor, and the three of them were all in the same photograph Aunt Rosie had. She lay back down quickly, willing herself to remain calm. Taking a few deep breaths, her mind scrambled to retrieve what information she knew about Little Crow. He had been Chief of the Santee Sioux at the time of the Great Sioux uprising, had decided to join in with the fighting because of the treacherous dealings on the part of the government. He had headed Northwest after the conflict and was not involved in the army's round up of Indians, but had been killed a few years later by a farmer who'd said that Little Crow and his son had been trying to steal his horses. Kyle had told her the story a million times. It was Little Crow's descendants who'd had to fight to get his bones back for a proper burial.

Well, she'd always believed Little Crow had been on his way back to the reservation when he was killed, but she couldn't very well ask that since it had not happened yet!

Back in time!

Nina recalled her time in the cave. She had been thinking of that story about Little Crow. *Was that just last night?* She had been in the cave a lot longer than just one night, but it seemed like a lifetime ago now. She couldn't remember everything that had happened, but that misty, blue figure of that woman was still fresh in her mind. She said her name was Elisi, she at least remembered that much. Maybe Kyle would know more, maybe he saw something? She didn't want to even think about that now, forcing herself to accept it as just a dream.

She sighed heavily. Even if she did manage to come to terms with being one hundred and fifty years in the past, how could she possibly absorb everything else that had happened? She struggled to remember things she heard the men talking about, not knowing if what she did recall was real or things she'd dreamt. Someone mentioned something about a new treaty. *Was that Uncle Mason?*

She thought she'd heard that it was going to be up to her to write it. Is that what they wanted her to do? She had heard things as she'd drifted in and out of sleep – Kyle talking to her about it, her agreeing to it – but now that she was wide awake, she knew it was impossible for her to undertake such a thing. Yes, she knew a lot about Indian law, but she was no practicing attorney by any far stretch of the imagination. What if she made a mistake and had the great chiefs sign something that would end up with the Indians' fate sealed forever in some horrible way? *It couldn't be much worse than the way it turned out*, she thought. But this would put her smack dab in the middle of this whole prophecy business, and not in her wildest dreams could she ever imagine being a part of that, much less in this capacity. It was Kyle, not her, who had gone through the preparations and who had left her all those years ago because of it. He was the one sent to Pine Ridge to learn about the ways, because in Minnesota, hardly anyone on the reservation participated in ceremony anymore. There were no medicine men around, as far as she knew, aside from James. It seemed everyone had just let the traditional ways die off and she knew very little about them herself except for what Aunt Rosie and Uncle Joe had taught her. She knew how to smudge, how to make prayer ties and flags, knew not to splash water onto the ground during Sundance unless you wanted it to rain, and knew how to put out a spirit plate. Of course, Kyle had shared some things with her, as well. She'd been in *lawampi* and *inipi* ceremonies, but she'd always felt that those ceremonies were only intended for full bloods to run. So how could she be a participant in what was going on now? How could she possibly be the one to write a new treaty?

She closed her eyes and willed herself to calm down.

There was no way she could write up a treaty. She would just have to tell them that they had made a mistake. It would be far easier for them to accept it now and get someone else than to wait for her to change her mind because she wouldn't. She only hoped Kyle would understand. She turned to look at him, was a hair's breadth from waking him, but couldn't bring herself to do it. She'd talk to him in the morning and make him understand. Snuggling close to him, she tried to turn off her thoughts, but her mind was still reeling when the sun began to peek its head over the horizon.

44

The scent of roasting meat roused Nina from a fitful dream. *I guess I did sleep after all,* she thought. She had been having a nightmare but refused now to let it resurface. Her stomach growled loudly and she turned over, letting her arm fall across Kyle's empty spot beside her. Frowning, she forced her eyes open, and then remembering where she was, came fully awake. She looked around and saw she was alone.

She started to get up but was still a bit swimmy headed.

"Morning sunshine," Kyle's voice was liquid soft in her ear as he moved from the fire pit to sit beside her. "I've been watching you sleep since early this morning," he whispered, although watching her toss and turn was more like it. He took her into his arms and held her close. He had been gauging the severity of her nightmares by the faces she'd made, the tormented whimpers and moans, and was about to wake her himself when she had opened her eyes on her own.

"Kyle…I," Nina began, but she was so relieved to see him that she buried her face in his shoulder and didn't even finish what she was about to say. She kneaded her fingers into his back, feeling him as if she was afraid he wasn't real.

"I can't tell you how happy I am to see you awake," he breathed into her hair. Her stomach growled again and he set her back from him. "C'mon, let's get you fed."

"Wait, Kyle," Nina kept her hands on his shoulders. Leaning in, she kissed him hard on the mouth.

"My, my, are you feeling up to this?" he chuckled and pulled her to him, hugging her close.

"I'm just so glad to see you," she smiled up at him, "but I also want to talk to you about all this."

"We will, love," he told her, "but let's eat first, and there are some people you need to meet."

"That's what I want to talk to you about."

"I know what you're going to say, Nina, but your fears are unfounded. These things were set into motion a long time ago and by a power far greater than anything you are aware of. If you weren't meant to be here, you wouldn't be here." He tilted her chin up, "You, Little White Horse, are just as important as I am in being here. There's a lot I have to tell you, but first, I'm gonna feed you, okay? Can you just agree to that and trust me on the rest?"

Nina had to admit that he had pretty much answered her immediate questions and concerns, and her stomach was feeling like it was digesting itself. Perhaps if she ate, it would clear the rest of the cobwebs and help her think straight for what was ahead.

"Okay," she smiled weakly at him, "but you promise once we sit down and talk, you'll tell me everything?"

"Everything," he nodded.

"Okay, now one more thing," Nina asked. "Where are my boots?"

With Kyle's help, she sat up, groaning as her muscles screamed in protest, but managed to wiggle her boots on. Kyle helped her to her feet and she steadied herself against him, grateful for his support, but even more grateful that he was here with her. She knew he probably needed to be off somewhere doing something about the prophecy, but was here with her instead.

She didn't feel too awfully bad — her head didn't feel like it had traded punches with a hammer anymore. One thing she did notice was that the sores on her hands were completely healed. When she opened her mouth to ask about it, Kyle placed a finger over her lips.

"Later. I'll explain everything to you later." He held the lodge flap open for her and she flinched at the bright sunlight.

A young Indian woman cooking over an open fire smiled at Nina as she and Kyle emerged from the tipi.

"This is my cousin, Tory," Kyle said, introducing the two women in Dakota.

"Hello," Nina was disappointed that the woman didn't answer and obviously didn't speak English. Tory smiled and nodded to her, "Han," she said, and then turned to Kyle telling him something in Dakota.

"She said you are beautiful."

Nina blushed. "Pidamaye," she said, thanking Tory.

Nina looked around the camp. There were hundreds of people as far as the eye could see, tipis set up all over; kids played, dogs barked, and she felt like she had just landed on a movie set, half expecting to see Kevin Costner come around a bush any minute.

"Everyone is heading to a council meeting soon," Kyle translated. "We'll go over after we've eaten and bathed." Suddenly feeling too weak to argue with him, she simply nodded, telling herself that she would get a chance to tell him she was backing out of the treaty soon enough.

Kyle settled her down on a buffalo robe and handed her a wooden bowl piled high with meat and vegetables. Nina could smell the wild onions and turnips, and it was all she could do not to eat it with her fingers. Kyle joined her with his own bowl, passing her a spoon made out of a deer horn. She asked for seconds and ate every bite of that, as well. She was surprised to see a blue speckled coffee pot sitting in the coals, but figured it must have come from the supplies taken in Minnesota. She knew her history well enough to know that the Indians had to raid food stores in order to eat that summer and fall.

Kyle passed her a tin cup of coffee strong enough to float a bullet, but it was hot, and once she dropped in a few sugar cubes, it was drinkable and reminded her of really strong espresso.

After they ate, they walked hand in hand to the river that was just a few hundred yards behind the tipi. Kyle carried a roll of toweling and a yellow clump of what he said was soap, given to them by Tory. He told her that Chase and Mason were at the council meeting and had asked about her that morning before they'd left. Nina joked that Chase was probably freaking out about being here, but Kyle told her that he was taking it all really well. They sat on a log beside the water. Nina removed her boots and socks and dangled her feet in the clear water for few minutes, laughing at the story Kyle was telling her about the tipi poles and Chase's toe. The water was pretty cold; winter wasn't too far off in this part of Nebraska. Kyle explained where they were geographically in the United States they had come from and Nina remembered where the Platte and Missouri rivers met on a map indeed looked like an eagle's beak. She'd seen it in a book report for school. It seemed funny that that had caught her eye all those years ago.

She glanced around for telephone wires or any other signs of civilization but saw none. With a head full of questions, she decided not to ask them right now. Maybe she really was one hundred and fifty years in the past? Allowing herself to relax a little, she marveled at the vast cottonwood trees and at how clean and clear the water was. The sun was bright, a slight breeze rustled through the trees, and she breathed in deeply of the fresh air. Being in nature always brought her back to her senses, but being in the past with Kyle was a double bonus. Everything was fresher, cleaner. She stole a glance at him, studying his profile.

"We're too far back in time for anyone to have polluted it yet," Kyle told her, referring to the water as if reading her thoughts. "With the resources around here, the settlers and the government will get to it eventually." He paused briefly, and then added, "Unless we stop them." His gaze looked away from her. "The water is so pure and clean, it's hard to believe that in a hundred years it will be unfit to drink or even swim in. Hard to believe…"

Kyle's voice trailed off and Nina wasn't sure what to say in answer to it. She knew that west of the Missouri river settlers had gotten the best of the land, leaving the Sioux with the rest. In the treaties that were signed, they were stuck with the uninhabitable land, where nothing would grow on it, often located in parts of the country that had the harshest weather. They often had no water source fit to use. In the end, it hadn't mattered what the treaties said. She remembered one that stated the Indians could reside on the land 'as long as the grass grows,' but because no treaty had ever been honored, they may as well have all been written in Sanskrit. She tried to remember the total number of treaties there had been, but couldn't off hand, and it didn't matter. Only a handful of them were ever honored, and even at that, at the discretion of the government.

"It's okay," Kyle said, reading her thoughts. "Things will be different when we get back."

"Kyle, I really have to talk to you about all of that."

"In a while," he said, and then took off his boots and

socks, "Ready?" He stood and began to undress.

"Ready?" Nina repeated.

"Yeah," he pulled his shirt over his head then stopped to look at her, "to bathe?"

She looked around anxiously. "Kyle! Someone might come by!" she whispered loudly, and then cast her eyes to the ground as he shrugged out of his pants.

"No one is going to bother us out here. Tory knows where we are and won't let anyone come close." He walked into the water until it was waist high and began to lather himself up. It was so cold Nina needn't worry about him attacking her, he laughed to himself.

"You coming?" he called, knowing how terribly shy she was in the light of day. "Nina?" She didn't look up. "You can't see anything now. Look at me!" Nina slowly lifted her gaze to his. "You wanna take a bath don't you?"

"Yes." She looked at his soapy chest and imagined the way it would feel to slide her hands over it, remembered the feel of his warm skin against hers the night they'd spent together at Redwood Falls.

"Then come on," He coaxed. "Well, unless you're scared, that is."

"Scared?" She raised her eyebrows.

"Yea, scared," He teased. "I bet you won't even get in."

"You don't think so?"

"I know not," he answered. "Chicken!"

That was the magic word, and he knew it. From the time they were children, all he'd ever had to say was *chicken* and she'd cast all fears aside and join in whatever he'd challenged her to. In a move that both shocked and delighted him, she did something that was totally out of character, even for her; she stripped down butt naked and dove into the water without a backward glance. She came up for air a few seconds later, stifling the shriek that threatened to escape her lips from the cold water. She'd rather die than let him know she couldn't take it.

She faced Kyle, who was still standing waist deep in water with his mouth hanging open. "What?" she asked innocently, squeezing water from her eyes.

Kyle shook his head as if to clear it. "You just stripped naked in front of me and dove into a river."

"Yeah, so?"

"Yeah so? What do you mean, 'yeah so'?"

"Guess there's some things you don't know about me, huh, Ghostkiller?"

"And some I'd like to find out!" Kyle said, quickly diving under the water and coming up behind her, grabbing her around the waist and pressing his body intimately against her. He had no problem with the cold water now.

"Kyle." She leaned back against him, feeling the evidence of his arousal snake between her legs. She gasped as his hands cupped her breasts, sliding the soap over them as he kissed the back of her neck.

"Nina." He turned her around to face him and crushed her body to his, the bar of soap forgotten.

"I've wanted you all of my life," he breathed harshly against her lips, "and I mean to have you." Nina wrapped her arms tightly around his neck.

"Not until you make an honest woman of me," she smiled up at him.

"Yes," he drew back to look at her, searching her face, "and I intend to do just that. Will you marry me?"

Nina wasn't as surprised at the question as she was at how he asked it so quickly. She laughed softly up into his face. "Yes," she whispered, "yes!"

Kyle smiled down at her. "I'll ask my grandfather to

marry us tonight."

"Tonight?!"

"Yes. I don't want to wait another second for you to be my wife, Nina." Kyle's eyes burned into hers and she drank in the love as he slowly lowered his head.

Her eyes fluttered down as their mouths pressed together in a kiss that seared from her head right down to her toes. Kyle deepened the kiss, and as he did, they fell back into the water, coming up sputtering and laughing. They found the soap and Nina finished washing herself, all the while aware of Kyle's eyes on her.

"We'd better get going," he laughed after watching her rinse for the third time.

He took the soap from her and guided her out of the water, hardly able to take his eyes off her. She was all woman, with long legs, flawless skin, and the most gorgeous smile he'd ever seen. Beautiful. But more so than her physical attributes, he adored her loving and giving nature. Nina. Just her name, but it escaped with a sigh every time from his lips. He couldn't wait to marry her and was anxious to talk to his grandfather about it. He sat the soap on a rock and then handed her the roll of toweling, watching her dry herself through hooded eyes, imagining what it would be like to finally make love to her.

When she was finished, he used the damp towel to dry himself, then spread it out on a bush leaving it, along with the soap, to use later. They dressed quickly and headed for the council meeting.

45

President Abraham Lincoln answered his wife's questions, only half listening while she packed his bags. He was glad that she had something else to think about other than the loss of their son, Willie. He had died last winter and it had been a blow for them both, sending her into a deep depression. He couldn't help but smile a bittersweet smile as Mary Lincoln clucked around him like a mother hen. Yes, he wanted to take his best cravat; no, he didn't think he would need his pipe. *The Indians have plenty of pipes*, he thought. His brow furrowed then. *The Indians.*

They wanted to meet with him, wanted to hold a council about a new treaty, and wanted him to come to Indian Territory. The conflict in Minnesota had started this latest ball rolling, and he felt almost powerless to fight it. He had given approval to General Henry Sibley to round up the Indians after their rampage, only to learn in the latest telegraph that all but a few had escaped. It had been Sibley's wish to execute all of them, he knew, but it seemed the Indians had outsmarted him and his army.

Lincoln sighed heavily as he pulled his nightshirt over his head and tossed it on the bed. With the Civil War raging, there weren't any more men to send out west. If the Indians had found a way around the army already out there, what else could he do but give in to their demands? Perhaps he could convince them to sign another treaty, something written to their own specifications, but which would still confine them to a reservation. He sat on the edge of the bed and pulled on a pair of woolen socks as he vaguely heard Mary exit the room saying something about him needing long underwear.

He stared out the bedroom window, remembering the details of the Indians' demands. The runner who had brought the news last night, a half-breed named Henry Milord, had said that until Lincoln arrived for the council meeting, any white man trying to cross west of the Missouri river would be killed. He didn't understand why they had picked Nebraska for the meeting place, but it was the worst possible timing for a rebellion for three major reasons: The Confederacy had attacked and he had few troops to send out west for backup. He had just sent out a detachment from General George B. McClellan to oversee a wagon of supplies to Omaha, but they could hardly be considered backup by any far stretch of the imagination. Most of them were fresh out of West Point and barely teenagers. Then there was the Homestead Act and the Pacific Railway Act that had both been signed this past July. The Homestead Act actually encouraged pioneers and immigrants to settle in Nebraska! Thank the good Lord it wouldn't go into effect until January, so that was not of immediate concern, he could always rescind it.

He sighed heavily. That left the Railway Act, which opened up the plains west of the Missouri to the Pacific Ocean. Even now, he had railroad people heading out there to make maps of the route the train would take. His first order of business this morning was to send a telegraph telling the Pacific Railway people to hold off until they received further word from him, and another one to hold that wagon train heading west of the Missouri. He didn't want to think of what might happen to those men if he didn't intervene and stop that wagon train.

The tribes that encompassed the territory west of the Missouri River were numerous. He mentally clicked them off in his head as he tried to recall all the names. Besides the Sioux, there were the Cheyenne, Omaha, Arapaho, Kiowa, Blackfoot, Assiniboine, Shoshoni, and Gros Ventre, to name a few. If all of those tribes had congregated for this rebellion, there was no telling how many warriors were out there. His own men had telegraphed that the number of Indians camped along the river, at least from what they had seen, were too numerous to count. He positively could *not* put off this meeting. He had to go, and he had to go now. He stood and dressed quickly in his traveling clothes that Mary had laid out on the bed, not even waiting for the long underwear.

Ward Hill Lamon paced the floor of the entry hall, impatiently awaiting the arrival of the carriage that would take him and the President into town to catch the stage. A burly and good-humored man with a strong appreciation for liquor, he acted as a self-appointed bodyguard to President Lincoln. Lamon's love of liquor, arguments, and fist-fights made him a curious companion of the President, who was different in almost every way. Nevertheless, Lamon was staunchly loyal to him, and vice versa, and as Lincoln was his oldest and dearest friend, he was not above the good scolding, he was about to get. He was talking crazy and actually packing up to go meet with the Indians at this very moment. What was worse, he intended to travel without the protection of a cover, knowing how dangerous that would be. Fresh off the heels of the Emancipation Proclamation, where he stated that all slaves would be forever free as of January 1st. Many death threats were rumored. How foolish it was of him to think he was immune to a bullet. The words they'd exchanged the night before had been but a scrap, but Lamon couldn't stop them from echoing in his head.

"Abe, don't you remember the reason we had to disguise you on that train last year? Clearly, it is warranted again!"

"I am not going to hide myself away from my constituents, Hill," the President said, using the nickname he had given his friend long ago.

"Constituents?" Ward balked sarcastically. "Constituents? You mean the Indians? They're nothing but a bunch of savages!"

"They are citizens of this land," the President had reasoned, "and like all citizens, they deserve to be heard. Apprehension clearly exists with the Indians because of those treaties that were not honored with the Santee; otherwise, that war would not have broken out in Minnesota."

"That was no war!" Ward spat out. "That was a massacre!"

"Nonetheless, I shall get to the bottom of the whole sordid mess and with due recourse." Seeing his friend's anguished look, the President had continued, "You and I both know that the Indians have not been treated fairly, Hill."

"Who cares about their treatment? They signed treaties that were supposed to keep them confined and silent! That's what the Indian agents up there were hired to do, and now they're all dead, so clearly treaties don't work!"

"Perhaps it was the agents themselves who did not work. I should have had the foresight to send more reinforcements up there. It takes more than one honest man to watch one Indian agent," Lincoln replied. "I'll see you in the morning," the President said, signaling the end of their conversation.

Lamon had watched as Lincoln retreated from the oval office, quietly closing the door behind him. He admired his friend's ability to remain calm and focused, keeping things in perspective despite offending odds, but it was fleeting. He couldn't help his frustration with Lincoln's soft-hearted attitude towards the Indians. He was glad he had the power he did as United States Marshal of Washington DC because it afforded him inside knowledge that he would not be privy to otherwise. That, and despite the fact that he had to deal with Allan Pinkerton, whom he detested, he felt he had more of an influence with the President in the position he was in. He might even be able to stop this whole mess in spite of Pinkerton, especially since Pinkerton employed some not-so-honest officers.

If he were in charge, he would pull troops from the south and send them to Nebraska. No one was too worried about the Indian problem in this war, but they should be. Lincoln should spare no expense killing off these treacherous savages. He pictured enough gun powder to blow up a village or two. He smiled.

In the midst of his fantasy, he considered putting Lincoln on the wrong train, but the President wouldn't be stupid enough not to notice something so obvious. Short of kidnapping him, there was just no way to stop him from going to the meeting. However, he knew his Pinkerton contact would love to get his hands on a few Indians; in fact, around a few Indian necks was more like it. Yes, he was just the person to get involved and put a stop to this ridiculous farce once and for all. He was glad he'd sent had the foresight to send the telegraph to that particular agent last night. *With Herbert Tarkington on the case, things would be settled the old-fashioned way and without all the bullshit of trials and treaty talks.*

Satisfied with that thought, Ward sighed happily. There was no way he would miss this meeting. No way in hell.

46

At the council meeting, it was decided not to send any more warriors to maintain the perimeter of Indian country; the warriors who were already out there were plentiful and there was more than enough game to sustain them. They would have no problem fending for themselves, no matter how long it took the President to get to Eagle's Beak.

Runners were reporting that Nebraska's 2nd Regiment Cavalry was planning to set up at Fort Kearny, but that would be of little consequence to the thousands guarding the Missouri River. There was no way they could match the size of the army the Indians were gathering. That's exactly what it was, and it was the biggest Indian army the country had ever seen.

The warriors from the various tribes each had organized a sentry to take their women, children, and elders to settle in at Eagle's Beak before joining their comrades along the river. The vast amount of Indians now gathered at the main camp was not known, but Mason and Chase had discussed that it was at least in the tens of thousands, with more arriving every few hours. To try to estimate the number covering the perimeter was not possible, but judging by what Ghostkiller had seen in his vision, they figured the number astronomical. It seemed hard to believe that just a few days ago they had been living a quiet and relatively normal life in

Moccasin Flats, but Chase and Mason agreed that they wouldn't be anywhere else right now.

To her surprise, Little Crow acknowledged Nina's apprehension and assured her that she would not be making a mistake by helping to write a new treaty. Despite her misgivings, or because of them, she spoke about the new treaty with him for hours, telling him about the things it must include. The wording was crucial, she said, because in the future there were attorneys who had the ability to twist words, find loopholes and make the law fit their own agenda. If it were worded just right, they wouldn't be able to do that. He told her that he would ask one of the *iniska*, mixed bloods, who was fluent in the English language to write it out, and then asked if she would revise it in the right legal language. Nina agreed. She found Little Crow to be a charming and cheerful man with a quick smile and even temperament. According to history, Little Crow was killed while picking berries at a farmer's house with his son, and she was tempted to warn him about it. Of course, since that wouldn't happen now, she realized there was no need. It was sure hard to get used to being in the past.

Once the council meeting ended, Kyle asked Ghostkiller to marry him and Nina. With the anticipated arrival of the President, they had to move forward right away. They planned a traditional Dakota ceremony in honor of Kyle's father, Leonard. During a conversation regarding this, they figured out how the sixth generation of grandsons was calculated; counting backwards the family tree lined up like this: Kyle, Leonard, James, He Runs with Thunder, Black Ghost and finally Ghostkiller. Kyle was excited to meet Black Ghost and his son, He Runs with Thunder. Ghostkiller said they would be arriving soon.

Since Nina had no family here, the women in camp

immediately began gathering necessities for her. Before long, there were piles of buffalo robes, dishes, water skins, a sewing kit and enough skins to build another lodge, all sitting outside Little Crow's tipi. They gave her everything that a new wife would need, and with an unselfishness that was not familiar to Nina. She couldn't believe how eager they were to accept her, despite the fact she that was as white as the driven snow. She thought of how different it was in her own time, where prejudice ran rampant on the reservation and whole families would disown a son or daughter for marrying outside of their culture, much less a white person. She supposed it was to preserve what some thought of as a dying breed, but people were people, after all, and the Creator knew nothing of skin color, at least, that's what Aunt Rosie had always told her. But once she had gotten into college and learned what lies the history books told about the Sioux, along with other tribes, she understood why they felt the way they did about whites. Most of the books were far removed from the stories Aunt Rosie and the other elders had passed on to her. To have their way of life taken away, their ceremonies outlawed, it was no wonder the reservation Indians wanted little to do with the white world. It made her blood boil.

    She couldn't understand all of what they said, but as the women fussed over her, she knew that they were measuring her for a dress. The language wasn't so different, yet at the same time, and although she spoke quite a bit of Dakota, it was a bit confusing.

    She noticed that there were a lot of people in camp who were not full bloods, but no one treated them any differently than the next. It had been a lot different growing up on the reservation. She was often teased because of her skin color and it seemed someone was always picking a fight with her, either because she was white or because she lived with an

Indian family. Here it was so different, and as she looked around at the smiling faces that were becoming familiar to her, she couldn't imagine going back to the world as she knew it. She was with Kyle and he loved her, wanted to marry her, and all these wonderful people that surrounded her were helping her get ready. And just outside was a camp full of thousands of people working towards the same goal – a freedom not afforded them in the future. She vowed then to do what she could to help them. As she stood there being gently poked and prodded, she heard the word for 'sister' being spoken, and tears stung her eyes when she realized they were talking about her.

47

The train carrying President Lincoln and his entourage chugged down the track at a good forty-mile-per-hour clip. It was a warm day for late September, but the windows were only down a crack in the first class car because of the soot that sputtered out of the smoke stack. It generally wasn't of consequence for the first class passengers, but the rough winds were whipping some of the soot inside the car through the windows. The conductor had commented that it was an unusual time of year for thunderstorms, but it looked as though there was a whopper brewing.

The President sat forward with an elbow resting on the back of an empty seat and his chin in his hand as he watched the landscape rush past. The train would take them to East St. Louis, where they would have to ride a ferry on into the city, and then take a stage into Nebraska Territory. It would look more like a wagon train, what with all of the people going with him. Lincoln despised this kind of attention, but his aides assured him it was necessary and he had to agree. The Indians were in a frantic state if they were going to such extremes to have a meeting with him, and he couldn't blame them, really. He often thought of what it must feel like to have foreigners come into your country, be forced to do their bidding, and then be starved or killed for cooperating. This was partially why they were in the midst of a Civil War right now, for the freedom of human beings. He vowed that if he survived this trip and this war, the Indian system would be totally reformed.

The common dining car was just starting to empty of the dinner crowd when Ward Lamon entered and took a seat. He was thrilled that the President agreed to eat his meal in the first class car instead of eating with the regular diners. Lamon had his reasons for wanting to be alone, and wasn't in much of a mood for fighting about the President eating with his "constituents." He loved Lincoln like a brother, but the man could really be stubborn at times.

As the last diners left the car, Ward saw the man he was waiting for tip his hat to the young woman who was last in line, and then make his way down the aisle to where Ward sat. He was a short man with a plump belly and jet-black hair that was graying at the temples. He wore a tailored black, pinstriped suit, and it was obvious that the man had expensive tastes and the money to satisfy them. Ward watched him pull out his pocket watch and check the time just before sitting down across from him.

"Make it quick, Lamon. I don't want us to be seen together."

"Would it be so odd? You and I do work for Pinkerton, you know."

"Yes, but I have my reasons," the man said. "Now, get on with it."

Ward raised his eyebrows. "Certainly." He drawled. "You obviously got my telegraph?"

"Indeed, I did. Do you have the money?"

"I do," Ward answered, "but first you must tell me how you intend to get this done."

"How do one hundred kegs of gunpowder and sound

to you?"

"A hundred kegs —"

"Yes," the man interrupted. "And enough firepower to take down all those savages. Having stock in the railroad does have its benefits, you know." He smiled a smug smile.

Ward couldn't help but notice how much the man reminded him of Allan Pinkerton, and it irritated him immensely. He knew the man would get the job done, however, and with little or no backlash for it — no one cared if you killed Indians.

Fighting the urge to slap the smile off his face, Ward reached under the dining table instead, producing a red carpet bag and slid it across the table to the man.

"It's all there," he told him, "but wait 'til you get to your compartment before counting it, eh?"

"Of course," the man rose to his feet. "But if it's not all there—"

"It's all there," Lamon interrupted irritably. "I want this done right."

The man smiled, revealing perfectly white teeth, another sign of a man with a lot of money. "Oh, it'll be done right, don't you worry about that. Nice doing business with you, Lamon."

Ward tipped his hat. "And with you, Agent Tarkington."

48

The past two days had passed quickly with everyone getting ready for the impending visit from Lincoln, not to mention scurrying around in preparation for a wedding. It gave the people something else to concentrate on in the midst of such a formidable occasion as the visit with Lincoln promised to be.

A crier called everyone to the center of the village, and as early evening approached, a silence fell over the camp in anticipation. Even the babies did not utter a sound. It was as if even they knew the reverence of what was about to happen.

As the people gathered, a drum began to beat softly and they all formed a wide circle in the center of the village. Anyone who had seen the two young people together could see how in love they were.

As the drumming continued, a soft voice began to sing a song that sounded as old as the river and rocks that surrounded Eagle's Beak. As he took his place in the circle, Kyle recognized it as one his mother used to sing. The crowd parted and an old Indian woman, escorted by Ghostkiller, sang as she walked into the center of the circle. A pair of young boys walked behind them, loaded down with blankets and various other items intended for the ceremony. When they reached the middle ground, Ghostkiller stepped aside and the old woman had one of the boys lay out a buffalo robe, followed by bundles of sweetgrass, sage, cedar, and tobacco. She arranged the articles in traditional fashion on the robe, continuing to sing her song as she worked, her small, gnarly hands not at all hindered by the task.

When the old woman was finished, she handed Ghostkiller a medicine bag and then allowed the boys to escort her back towards the crowd. Kyle, Chase, and Mason stood opposite the place where Ghostkiller and the old woman had emerged. Kyle smiled at her as she walked away, noting her dusky skin and crystal blue eyes that were permanently crinkled at the corners. Deep lines from years of living out of doors etched her face, but it was a kind face, the eyes soft and clear. He knew her to be *Wanagi Duta*, Ghostkiller's grandmother, and a powerful force within the Dakota tribe. She was a warrior in her own right, and Kyle remembered his Grandfather James talking about her when Kyle was little. James spoke of her with reverence and a longing in his voice that was apparent even to Kyle at a young age.

Wanagi Duta was named for what James called her *red spirit*. Born of a Dakota mother and a fur trapper father, the name was an honor, for although she may have been a mixed blood, her heart was pure, her spirit red like her full-blooded relatives. She'd fought alongside the men in many battles, never showing fear or trepidation. In the old days, it was rare to be condemned by full bloods if you were a half or mixed blood.

"Indians in this timeline see you for who you are and determine that by how you act, not by the color of your skin," Kyle told Mason and Chase.

Mason leaned over to Chase and whispered that he'd

heard the old woman was a very powerful medicine woman who could turn leather hair ties into lizards that could suck cancerous tumors out of a person's body. Then Mason winked at Kyle as he walked past them to take his place beside Ghostkiller in the center of the circle, leaving Chase's mouth hanging open.

Kyle hadn't expected to be so nervous. He remembered an old saying of Aunt Rosie's about being as nervous as a long-tailed cat in a room full of rocking chairs, and now he knew just how nervous that cat felt.

The men at the drum were singing another song, and as they continued, Kyle watched as the opposite end of the circle opened once more. There, a handful of women stood with Nina, and after a moment, Wanagi Duta escorted her to the center of the circle. The whole crowd sang a wedding song as the two women walked towards Kyle and Ghostkiller. Kyle's gaze locked onto Nina. She was breathtakingly beautiful in an ankle length, bleached doeskin dress decorated with blue stones and small silver cones that jingled when she walked. Blue stones were attached to the fringe on the sleeves and bodice as well, and her feet were snuggled into matching moccasins. As she approached him, Kyle noted the stones braided into her hair that matched the color of her eyes. She smiled at him, but her lips trembled a little and he could see her eyes were moist. He knew she was as nervous as he was, but the shiver of anticipation he felt at that moment had nothing to do with nerves. The look of love in her eyes and the promise of forever held him there for a long moment. Wanagi Duta placed Nina's hands in his before kissing them both on the cheek.

"Wowastelaka ohinniyan." She murmured to them, which meant 'love forever.'

Kyle squeezed Nina's hands lightly, and as Ghostkiller

began to speak, he found himself swimming in the depths of two indigo pools, drowning out everything else going on around them. The love he felt for this woman was all-encompassing; no one would ever tear them apart. He knew this as he stood there holding her hands, drinking in the beauty of what made her Nina, inside and out.

Nina was shaking from head to toe as she searched Kyle's face. He looked so handsome, with his hair pulled back and two eagle feathers fastened on one side. He wore a wedding shirt made of bleached elk hide, beautifully decorated with red-tailed hawk feathers that hung from each shoulder. Tufts of horsehair were attached to the front and back of the shirt and it was painted with various red and blue symbols. A breechclout, leggings, and moccasins made up the rest of his wedding outfit. Around his neck hung a white bone choker adorned with an eagle plume dangling from the center. She gazed at him and felt faint with excitement. The fact that she was standing here ready to marry the man she had grown to love so much over the years was almost too much.

Kyle felt it too. He was looking at her intently, his black eyes holding her captive, drawing her into a world where they were the only two people in it. The years of longing and wanting were about to come to an end, and it was all they could do to contain themselves.

Ghostkiller had to nudge his grandson when it came time for him to light the pipe, signaling the end of the ceremony. Once it was smoked out, Ghostkiller smiled and encircled them with the buffalo robe, announcing they were now married. The crowd cheered as they walked briskly around the circle, accepting well wishes and thanking everyone for coming. The circle opened at one end and they rushed out, Kyle guiding Nina towards the wedding lodge that the women had erected down by the river. As they ran together with the blanket pulled around their heads, the gunshots at the other end of camp were drowned out by their laughter.

49

The horseman fired the army-issued rifle repeatedly, emphasizing to the crowd the power behind it while the rider next to him spoke in rapid Lakota. They were from Red Cloud's sentry that had set up just east of Eagle's Beak and were asking for Little Crow. Upon hearing the sound of gunshots, Little Crow, and Ghostkiller had each mounted the nearest horse tearing towards the direction of gunfire with Mason and Chase in hot pursuit. Little Crow and Ghostkiller hit the ground at the same time and quickly approached the two young men on horseback.

"Hau Hau! What is this?" Little Crow demanded.

"We intercepted a wagon!" the first rider explained excitedly. "It was full of guns and ammunition, enough for five hundred warriors! There were many white soldiers!"

Little Crow looked past the runner's head and saw the wagon. Sitting on the ground were six large wooden boxes, all marked with the white man's letters: "U. S." One young man held the reins of several horses with the same letters branded on their hindquarters. Little Crow turned to Ghostkiller and gave him a worried look. "Did you kill the men in the wagon?" Ghostkiller asked the young men.

Out of respect for the two elders, the young men dismounted before answering. The second Indian answered in English. He looked Ghostkiller square in the eye and seemed to be speaking only to him.

"Yes. One had yellow hair like him," he jutted his chin toward Chase, "and we killed the ones on horseback, too. They crossed over the river and our orders were that no one was to cross. We took the wagon and the horses and brought them to you." He gestured behind him, then turned back to Ghostkiller. "The yellow hair is dead." Ghostkiller raised his eyebrows and took a step back, almost a falter, but recovered before anyone noticed.

Mason and Chase observed the two young men, who appeared to be in their late teens or early twenties. The one who spoke English wore his long, reddish-brown hair loose, with an eagle feather tied at the nape. Two streaks of yellow lightning bolts bisected each of his cheeks. His skin was lighter than that of his companion, who had copper-colored skin, jet-black hair he wore in two braids behind his ears.

"Where is Red Cloud camped?" Little Crow asked.

"He is camped near the mouth of Horse Creek," the red- haired one answered.

"Go back to your camp," Ghostkiller ordered, "and tell no one what you have done."

The runners paused, and then scurried back onto their horses. "You will need these for the fight ahead," the red-headed one said as he moved his horse forward, handing the reins of the Cavalry horses to Ghostkiller.

"*Wakan Tanka nici un*," he nodded, and then with a shout, they turned their horses and were gone.

"Tasunke Witko is very brave among his people. I hope he has done the right thing," Little Crow said.

"He has," Ghostkiller replied, as he looked towards the path that the two young Indians took.

"Tasunke Witko?" Mason whispered, almost too low for Chase to hear.

Leaning towards him, Chase whispered, "What? Who was that? What did he say?"

Furrowing his brow, Mason turned to Chase. "That was Crazy Horse," he whispered hoarsely.

"Crazy Horse!" Chase blurted out.

"Indeed," Ghostkiller approached the two men. "Crow Walker remembers the language well."

"Grandpa, is everything okay?" Mason asked.

Ghostkiller nodded to him and said, "Yes, it is so," and then turning on his heel, he walked away. Little Crow fell in step beside him and the crowd began to disperse, leaving Chase and Mason sitting atop their horses.

"What did the other thing he said mean?" Chase asked Mason.

"You sure are full of questions all the time," Mason said irritably. He was still thinking about what Ghostkiller had said and the fact that that was all he'd said. He felt something ominous suddenly take hold of him.

"Mason?" When he didn't answer, Chase finally said, "If I knew the language, I'd stop asking."

With a sigh, Mason told him what the words meant. "*Wakan Tanka nici un*, means 'May the Great Spirit go with you.'"

"All that crammed in those four little words?"

"Uh!" Mason groaned and then turned his horse towards Little Crow's lodge.

"We must not lose sight of what we are here to do!" Ghostkiller told Little Crow once they arrived at his lodge. A few other chiefs followed them in, and the two men sat down with them to discuss what Crazy Horse had told them. Sitting Bull, Shakopee, Medicine Bottle and Iron Horse were among those in attendance.

Ghostkiller had no doubt that many council meetings

were held this night, what with the killing of the white soldiers and the taking of guns earlier. Of course, no one but Ghostkiller could possibly know the significance of Yellow Hair being killed. He reached for his pipe just as Mason and Chase quietly rapped on the lodge.

"Hau!" Little Crow called. Mason opened the flap and Ghostkiller waved them inside, motioning for them to take a seat. He thought briefly of sending them to get Kyle, but he would not disturb his grandson on his wedding night. Tomorrow morning, he would go to him himself and tell him about the yellow hair. He hated to interrupt them, but it was too important and Kyle and Little White Horse needed to be aware of what had happened, and most importantly, what it meant.

Ghostkiller thought of his grandson's wife. He had sensed her apprehension about the new treaty. Furthermore, he knew what she had overcome to get to this point, and knew that her struggles had been for the people, as well. She came from a place far from here, even further than she knew. Wanagi Duta spoke about people who traveled the *time road*, and that they could come from anywhere. Ghostkiller had seen Kyle in many ceremonies, which was common. One didn't have to be there to be seen. The ceremonies were so powerful, the spirits would show you many things, some would seem impossible to the average person, especially future people where the only thing they believed in was what they could see in front of them. Nina was from a different place. He knew she was unaware of where she came from, but that was something she would have to figure out on her own.

She had given Little Crow enough information about the new treaty for it to be effective in the future at any time. His future at this point, however, was not certain. He had seen what would come to pass if history replayed itself. It was not to be that way now, yet he did not know the details anymore. His visions changed slightly every night, and he was given clues, but no more. He did not question the visions because he had faith that the Creator would let him see what he needed to see when the time was right, and Creator had shown him a lot. He knew the entity responsible for the deaths since the hanging had not been obliterated, but White Horse surviving her fate had changed that part of the future to some degree. It was possible to keep their lands with a new treaty, he had seen this also, but with Yellow Hair dead, he wondered just how much of the future was changed. One thing was certain: Lincoln needed to sign that treaty. Without it, the future his grandson had told to him regarding the Sioux would not change very much.

Ghostkiller reached for his pouch of *cansasa* then, and Medicine Bottle began to sing a pipe filling song.

"*Tunkasila*, I pray for Lin-con," Ghostkiller whispered as he filled his pipe, using the name he heard Mason and Chase call the President. He took his time with his prayers, specifically praying for the outcome of the talks with Lincoln, praying that things would go as planned.

When he finished, he placed the *canupa* in the crook of his arm, and then looked at the men gathered together, gauging their faces one by one.

"There are many meetings being held this night about what happened today," he began. "Tasunke Witko shared my visions about that *wasichu* soldier with the yellow hair, and he did not hesitate when the chance came to strike him down. Killing the yellow hair was a good thing, but the Great White Father will be here soon, and when word gets out about what happened, more white soldiers will come. They will want to take the killers to the fort with the iron bars for trial." The men murmured their disapproval.

"No!" Shakopee spat out. "We made our terms clear. If those white men had taken us seriously, no one would have tried to cross that river. They did not take us seriously and now they are dead. They deserved to die!"

There were murmurs and grunts of agreement from the other men. This time, it seemed they all agreed with Shakopee. Ghostkiller thought he should be used to Shakopee's knee-jerk responses by now. It was true, however; the Great White Father obviously did not take them seriously. They didn't honor their own treaties, much less believe that Indian Nations were capable of defending their homelands. When their soldiers died they just sent more, but the Sioux had many warriors who were willing and able to die, as well – many more than the men in Washington were willing to believe.

Kyle had told Ghostkiller that their land, along with their way of life, would be stolen from them in the future, confirming his visions. The land would be raped and barren on the reservations and their ceremonies would be outlawed at one point. He knew that killing the Yellow Hair was a good thing because the yellow metal that makes them crazy could not be found in the Paha Sapa if he was not alive to tell it. However, was that enough to change things in the future? They needed to stand their ground and not let the killing of these men change their plans. Ghostkiller turned to Little Crow, who nodded his agreement.

"What Shakopee says is true, and we will not back down from the *wasichu*, but we need to be prepared for what will happen next – more white soldiers and Lin-con's arrival."

"Then we must call for everyone to prepare for war!" Shakopee said. "That is how the white man deals with Indians. He kills them! So we will strike before they can."

Little Crow looked at Ghostkiller who nodded his

agreement. As much as he despised Shakopee, Little Crow didn't question Ghostkiller's decision. He was a man who had cheated death at the hanging in Moccasin Flats, whose grandson was here from the future and a prophet in his own right. They were sent to them by the Creator and they were here to save the Indian race. He would not interfere with Creator's plan.

"Yes," Little Crow said, "send the runners as quickly as possible."

Later that night they sent twenty runners to spread the news of a chiefs' gathering.

50

    Someone had been thoughtful enough to leave a kettle of stew hanging over the fire pit, and Kyle and Nina had eaten every last bite of it. They laughed all through dinner, marveling at the fact that they ran all the way to the lodge under a blanket without falling. Now, they were nestled back onto a buffalo robe in front of the lodge, watching as the stars popped out one by one, aligning themselves into the constellations that were so familiar to them.

    "I still say you were running crooked!" Kyle teased.

    "I was not!" Nina argued, punching him playfully in the arm.

    "Were too!" He grabbed her and they rolled together on the ground laughing harder. Kyle rose above her and smiled down into her face, reaching out to brush a lock of hair from her brow. They looked at each other, their smiles fading simultaneously as Kyle leaned down and kissed her, softly, slowly.

    "Mmm," Nina murmured after he pulled back, "that was nice, Mr. Ghostkiller."

    "Glad you liked it, Mrs. Ghostkiller," he smiled back. "Guess what?"

    "What?"

    "We're married!"

    "I know!" Nina smiled up at him, "and I couldn't be

happier!"

"Are you?" Kyle asked. "Are you really happy, I mean, here in the past?"

Nina didn't have to think twice about it. She knew exactly how she felt about being here.

"I feel so at home here. I can't explain it, but I don't ever wanna go back Kyle," she told him.

"Me, either." He kissed her again. "Let's not talk about this now." He scooped her up and into his arms. "We have other business to attend to." He carried her into the lodge, pausing for a moment to kiss her again. Inside was warm and cozy. The women of the village had set everything up for them before they got here. It was tradition for the family to provide what the newlyweds needed on their wedding night.

Kyle smiled down at Nina and brushed a kiss across her lips, murmuring how much he loved her while he nuzzled her neck. She smiled up into his face as he carried her to the buffalo robes, laying her down gently. "We've waited too long for this."

Kyle stretched out beside her, propping his head up on one hand and dragging a brown finger down her cheek, whispering how beautiful she was. He kissed her slowly, running his tongue over her lips seductively, exacting little moans from her. He ran his hand over her body, taking in the curves and softness of her, teasing her with deft fingertips, lingering on her breasts beneath the soft confines of her dress. The anticipation was its own aphrodisiac, but now she was going insane with desire, begging him to take her, but he just chuckled at that.

"Stay," he ordered, roughly searing her lips with a kiss.

He stood over her then, and never taking his eyes from her, he began to undress slowly. He reached up and unfastened his hair, carefully removing the eagle feathers tied there and wrapping them in red cloth that was bundled in his pouch. He pulled his wedding shirt over his head, revealing his muscular chest and rock solid arms. The glow from the firelight cast shadows on his skin as he removed his moccasins and tossed them aside. It was a simple gesture, but Nina was mesmerized as she watched him. He held out his hand to her and she took it, pulling herself up into his arms. They held onto each other as he slowly pulled her dress over her head. She wore nothing underneath and now stood naked before him.

"Mmm," he breathed into her hair as he took her naked body into his arms.

"Guess that just leaves these," Nina provocatively pulled at the ties to his breechclout.

"Indeed," Kyle smiled at her as the cloth fell to the dirt floor.

They stood together, allowing their excitement to build to new heights as they looked at each other approvingly. They had seen each other naked before, of course, but tonight they were going to consummate their love, and that fact alone was an aphrodisiac in and of itself.

Their lips met in one kiss, then two, and an urgency began to envelop them that was a force all its own. There was nothing between them now, and their desire bubbled up and exploded within both of them. Kyle smothered her in kisses, moving his lips over her face and neck, biting her gently. Their hands moved restlessly over each other, pushing, pulling, and feeling as they explored each other feverishly. Kyle tightened his grip around her waist and lifted her up; he had intended to take her slowly, but in the heat of the moment, neither could wait. She wrapped her legs around his waist, and he took what she offered quickly. Lightning cracked and thunder rumbled as a violent shiver ran through them both and suddenly they were rising above the fire, then the lodge, and finally above the clouds, engulfed in a blue mist that left them suspended in space and time for what seemed an eternity. Their breath came in short, desperate gasps, and Nina screamed his name as they both gave in to a second explosion. Kyle continued to move within her, spilling his seed and sealing their place on this side of the veil forever.

The intensity of the moment lasted well into the night and seemed to suspend them somewhere between the past and the future. When they opened their eyes, Nina felt the warm buffalo robes on her back and Kyle nestled inside of her, joined together as one. They looked at each other and gasped, realizing what they had experienced was something bigger than themselves. They basked in each other's arms until the moon rose high. It shone through the smoke hole of the tipi, casting shadows over them and bathing them in a sacred medicine only the moon could offer. They lay together in front of the fire, an intimate tangled web of arms and legs, and fell into a deep sleep.

The next morning dawned with brilliant reds and pinks mixed in with white cotton ball clouds, all against a backdrop of endless blue sky. Kyle awoke before Nina, stepping outside to relieve himself. The pre-dawn was alive with sights and sounds as he walked to the riverbank. A falcon screeched overhead, and the sweet scents of wildflowers mingled with muddy water filled his nostrils. Leaning down to splash cold water on his face, he smiled at his reflection, knowing he was looking at a happily married man and thought of Nina who lay just a few feet away. He felt complete somehow because of her as if the last piece of the puzzle was in place. He remembered how they had run to the lodge the day before under the blanket and was chuckling about it when a sudden chill ran through him. His gaze was drawn back to the water and was startled to see an image beginning to form in its depths. He watched as a picture of several hundred men, women and children materialized before him. They were running and screaming while cavalry soldiers shot at them, huge explosions erupted and white men were yelling and laughing. Peering closer he saw a man under a wagon lying in a pool of blood. Before he could see the man's face, a frog jumped from the bank near him, scattering the image. It left him with a desperate feeling of foreboding.

Just then, Nina emerged from the lodge wrapped in the wedding blanket. He pulled her close and closed his eyes, willing the images away. He was going to burn this time with her in his mind forever so that whatever happened, he would always remember these moments in the past.

"Red at night, a sailor's delight," Nina murmured, smiling at him.

"Red in the morning, sailors take warning," Kyle finished, looking off in the distance.

They sat down on the bank of the river huddled together inside their wedding blanket. The cold, frosty morning entertained misty ghosts that danced on the gently flowing waters of this quiet bend in the river. As children, they called them water spirits, and they always fascinated Nina.

Kyle tightened his arm around her, determined not to think for the moment. He just wanted to enjoy this time alone with her and didn't want to face the vision in the water. But it was impossible not to face it.

"Where were you?" she asked.

"What do you mean?" Kyle looked at her then.

"When I woke up you weren't where I left you," she smiled.

"Oh, just stepped outside to see a man about a horse,"

he chuckled.

She laughed at that and laid her head on his shoulder, snuggling closer to him. God, how she loved this man!

It couldn't be any more perfect, she thought, and she closed her eyes, taking a deep breath of the fresh, sweet scent of a different time. And it did smell different here, clean and pure, so unlike any modern day city smelled. She wanted to stay here forever, just like this, tucked in her husband's arms. Being in the past reminded her of Sundance, the most sacred ceremony of the Sioux. While at Sundance, they camped primitively in every sense of the word. This wasn't so different, except there was a feeling of *time sensing* that she could not explain. Being in the past was not something that happened every day, yet she felt so at home, it was almost scary. She knew they would have to go back to their own time once the treaty was signed, it was inevitable, but she couldn't begin to imagine what it was going to be like when they did. In this time, the women gathered for their own councils and the decisions that they made were just as important as the men's, even more so in some cases. Often, decisions for everything from battles to moving the camp were based on what the women chose, usually decided while they were on their moon, the time of menses when a woman is most sacred. It had been the Europeans who'd pushed their teachings onto the Indians by not allowing women to be involved in decisions, political or otherwise. Nina knew she was expected to be there for the treaty signing, but for now, she would not allow herself to dwell on anything else. She firmly pushed the thoughts from her mind.

She sighed and turned toward her husband. Kyle leaned in and kissed her gently on the lips, and they pressed their foreheads together lightly. They sat like that for a long time, letting the scene wash over them, each knowing that the other was thinking similar thoughts. The river lapped gently at the bank, a bird chirped in a nearby cottonwood tree, tree frogs croaked, and the smell of muddy water, wet leaves and the scent of autumn flowers enveloped them. They both knew that their coming together was something fated, something that went beyond any reasoning, and it went far beyond their lovemaking from the night before. They were here to change history, and it was already happening all around them. They could feel it. Kyle and Nina turned simultaneously to look out over the water, and as they sat watching the sunrise, clarity changed their focus, and the natural elements played a symphony from another time they knew they might not ever hear again.

51

Chase sat down on a stump in front of a stack of wood just outside Little Crow's tipi. It was still early and the sun was barely showing itself over the horizon. He spotted an old branding iron lying on top of the woodpile and picked it up to stir the still-glowing coals. He wondered if the women would get mad at him for doing so, but dismissed the thought. If he hadn't made them mad before now, they weren't going to get mad. He'd made the mistake of asking some of the women what *squaw wood* was and got a swift kick in the rear-end by one of the girls. Mason had laughed so hard he thought he'd developed a hernia, and then explained to Chase that the word *squaw* was a derogatory term, and he was lucky he hadn't gotten himself shot with another arrow for saying it.

Chase sighed as he picked up a couple of the logs and threw them into the fire, watching it spring to life. The women would probably be grateful that he had gotten the fire going again because he knew they'd be by to start cooking breakfast soon. The past couple of days were becoming routine now, and he was getting used to the way things were done. He was sleeping better than he ever had in his life, and meeting characters he'd only read about in history books.

Getting shot up with arrows, yeah I'm having the time of my life! He sighed at the thought and rubbed his leg absentmindedly. He was getting around all right, but his leg was still a little stiff and sore. As long as he didn't move too quickly, he wasn't in any real pain.

Spotting the coffee pot on top of a wooden box, he stood up and limped over to it. Rummaging through the box, he found a bag of ground coffee, a cloth bag marked 'sugar' and some blue tin cups that looked clean enough. Tucking the box under his arm, he made his way back to the lodge. He reached just inside the flap and quietly unhooked one of the water skins and then hobbled back to his seat. He filled the coffee pot with water and coffee, pushed some of the hot coals to the side and sat the pot on them. When that was done, he sat back, lit a cigarette, and took a long, deep drag. He only had one left out of the pack he had brought when they'd left the future, and he wondered briefly about rolling his own. He chided himself, thinking about how he had been rationing them when he really needed to quit altogether, but right now, that was the least of his concerns. He couldn't quit now if he tried.

His brow furrowed as thoughts turned to his real concern – the meeting with Lincoln. It was weighing heavily on his mind, as it was everyone else's, and he simply couldn't wait for it to be over. Not that he was in any hurry to get back to his own time – hell, there was nothing there for him, really. But here it was different. He was drawn here, to this place and these people, these wonderful, accepting people who were so giving and trusting and refused to judge him, even though they had been through so much with whites. He wanted this to work out for them so badly, even if it meant going back to a future that would be forever changed for him.

He wondered about the people he had read about in the newspapers who had died at the hands of the entity. Would they be alive after they changed the past? Damn, but this was confusing! If Ghostkiller was never hanged, then did that mean the evil that permeated the town would have never come into existence? If that were so, then, of course, the people would have never died and their descendants would now be living. That meant Nina's parents would be alive, too. It suddenly dawned on him why Kyle had been so adamant about fulfilling his destiny. Mason stepped out of the lodge then, interrupting Chase's thoughts.

"Mornin'," he yawned, stretching his arms overhead. "The coffee smells good."

"Um."

Mason made a face. "Um...you sound like a real city Indian," Mason chuckled.

Chase smiled. "Sorry, just thinkin'," he said, taking another drag and blowing the smoke out slowly.

Mason sat down next to him. "Yeah, I spent a better part of the night just thinking," he told him. "Ghostkiller's going to get Kyle this morning."

"I know. They didn't have much of a honeymoon," Chase grinned.

"Yeah," Mason smiled, "but they'll have plenty of time for that later. We're kinda pinched for time right now." He poured himself a cup of coffee and then handed the pot to Chase.

"Thanks. When do you think Lincoln will get here?"

"Well, Little Crow seems to think that it shouldn't take him more than four days, and today makes three, so I don't know. Should be any time now, I would imagine."

Chase nodded, pouring some sugar into his cup.

"Geez, a little coffee with your sugar?" Mason laughed.

"Yeah, a little!" Chase joined in good-naturedly. It seemed he and Mason hadn't really had a chance to talk about how this was going to go down, and he decided to take this opportunity to see what Mason's thoughts were while he had the chance.

"How do you think all this will play out, this treaty signing and all?" Chase asked. "Do you really think Lincoln will give in to their demands?"

"If he doesn't want another full-scale war on his hands, he will," Mason answered. "I mean, he doesn't really have a choice. He doesn't have enough men to go up against the Indians since he's got everybody fighting each other back east. That's why the timing of this is so crucial. The Civil War is raging right now." Mason poured himself more coffee. "That's why we came back now, in this time. 1862 was a big year for a lot of things."

"Yeah. Speaking of Kyle, did Ghostkiller already leave to go get him? I didn't see him in the lodge."

"I don't know," Mason answered. "I never heard him come to bed."

The sound of hoof beats galloping into camp interrupted their conversation.

"Hau," Ghostkiller greeted the two men. "Come ride with me to get my grandson and White Horse." It wasn't a request. Chase thought how odd it was that they had just been talking about that very thing. He looked at Mason quizzically as they both rose to go off in search of their horses.

Neither of the men bothered with any tack, and just picked hackamores hanging on a nearby tree branch. The past few days had really turned Mason and Chase into excellent horsemen. Ghostkiller had been riding Macedone, but now he cut an appaloosa out of the crowd and mounted it before they started out. They wondered why he'd changed horses, but figured he had his reasons. They watched as he leaned in to whisper something in Macedone's ear, and a few minutes later, Macedone trotted ahead, taking the lead.

It was a short distance to the other end of the camp, but

they took the long way around, following the river. They rode silently for a while, each man doing battle with his own thoughts. Ghostkiller wondered how Kyle would react to what he was getting ready to tell him. Chase breathed in the clean air and thought again about quitting smoking. Mason pondered the thought of having a few horses once he was back in their own time. Ghostkiller glanced at the two men riding beside him. Their lives were changed forever just by being here, and their options were wide open as to what their own future held once they returned.

With the wedding lodge in sight, Macedone trotted ahead and reached the lodge before the other three. He gave a loud whinny when he saw Kyle. He and Nina were dressed and sitting next to a small fire when the rest of the group rode up.

"Grandfather," Kyle embraced Ghostkiller as he dropped down from his horse. "I've been expecting you."

Ghostkiller's gaze lingered on Kyle's face as he gauged his words. He smiled lightly.

Nina kissed Ghostkiller's cheek then turned to Mason.

"Hello, Mrs. Ghostkiller," Mason winked as he dismounted and hugged her.

"Hello, Uncle," she smiled, hugging him back.

"It's good to see you looking so damn happy!" he whispered to her.

"I really am!" she whispered back.

"Mr. Riley," she greeted Chase as she stepped back to stand beside Kyle.

"It's about time you called me Chase," he smiled to her.

"Okay, Chase."

"We have come to tell you both something very important," Ghostkiller said solemnly.

"Yes, please, everyone sit down," Kyle invited, and

they all took a seat around the fire. Kyle thought Ghostkiller came to speak about the vision in the water, so the shock of what he told them was way out of left field.

"Tasunke Witko was at our camp last night and brought news of an attack." He looked from Nina to Kyle.

"And?" Kyle asked. He could tell by the look on his grandfather's face that the news was not good.

"He killed Yellow Hair," Ghostkiller replied. Nina sucked in a breath. The Indians only referred to one person as Yellow Hair. It was well documented in the discovery of Black Hills gold and the Battle of Little Bighorn.

"You mean George Custer?" she gasped.

"Yes," Ghostkiller said. "There were twelve men with him who were also killed."

Nina did some quick calculations. Crazy Horse would be little more than a teenager in 1862 and just now coming of age. Of course, he was a visionary and knew full well who he had killed, Nina was sure of that. George Custer was fresh out of West Point, having graduated the year before. He was under the command of General Livingston in Virginia. Lincoln must have sent a detachment out ahead of his party and Custer had just happened to be in it.

"My God," Kyle whispered. "But this means there will be no gold discovered in the Black Hills. Custer won't be alive to tell about it!"

"No Custer's last stand?" Mason added.

"No Battle at the Little Big Horn!" Chase chimed in.

"It's the same thing," Mason chided him.

"I do not know of what you speak, but it also means that the long knives will be out for blood when they hear of it," Ghostkiller added.

The group sat quietly for a few minutes, letting Kyle and Nina absorb what was said.

"So what do we do now?" Nina asked. "And what about the treaty?" They all knew enough about history to know that if no gold was discovered in the Black Hills, there was a good possibility that would mean no white encroachment, which left an excellent chance for the treaty of 1868 to be honored.

"We are not waiting until 1868, of course," Ghostkiller said reading her thoughts, "Our new treat will be ready when Lin-con arrives." He paused. "I am concerned about you all remaining here. When word gets back to Lin-con that these men were killed, it will mean war. I do not want you all to risk your lives by remaining here, and I believe that you should think about going back to your own time as soon as possible."

"What?" Mason and Chase said simultaneously.

"No!" Nina said.

Kyle looked at his grandfather, weighing what he said.

"We can't leave now!" Mason said. "Lincoln will be here at any moment!"

"Yes, we can't have come all this way for nothing!" Chase cried.

"Grandfather, surely you aren't serious?" Nina beseeched. "What about the treaty?"

Ghostkiller didn't answer but turned to Kyle instead. "Speak to them *takoja*. You know what you must do." There was an unmistakable urgency in his voice. He rose and climbed aboard the appaloosa that stood nearby. Kyle and the others stood and gathered around the horse and rider.

"I could not have done any of this without each and every one of you," Ghostkiller told the group. He reached out and grasped Kyle's hand. "*Toksa ake, cinks.*" *I will see you again, son.*

"*Toksa*," Kyle repeated and then watched as Ghostkiller let out a whoop and galloped out of sight, leaving Kyle to face the others.

"What the hell?" Chase asked.

"Yeah, Kyle, what's going on?" Mason asked.

"How can we leave before Lincoln gets here?" This came from Nina.

Kyle's head was swimming with his own questions. Why would his grandfather even suggest they go back now? And why did he run off like that without an explanation? Perhaps he just didn't want to speak in front of the others, but he'd never hidden anything from them before. *No, there is something else*, and Kyle intended to find out what it was. Ghostkiller had just said goodbye — a final goodbye — but there was no way Kyle was leaving. He had to say something to reassure the others.

"Look, let's all sit down," he led Nina back to the fire. "I feel like my grandfather figures it this way: with Custer dead, there is no reason to fear for the people anymore. There will be no gold discovered in the Black Hills, no battles to fight if the whites stay out of the west, and our job here is done..." his voice trailed off. He looked to his friends. He could tell by the expressions on their faces that not one of them was buying this explanation.

Chase lit his last cigarette and took a deep drag. "If you're gonna try to tell me that we went back one hundred and fifty years in the past just to watch you get married, I'm gonna punch you."

"We've accomplished much more than that," Kyle assured him but wasn't prepared to say exactly what he thought that was. He struggled with telling them about his vision in the water this morning. He felt sure it tied in with his grandfather wanting them to leave now.

"What about the treaty?" Nina said, "They won't know what the words mean. They might sign something that they didn't intend. You know how the government tricked them before!"

She started to cry. She didn't quite understand it, but she felt fiercely protective of the treaty and those who now call her family here. Visions of what awaited them in the future danced in her head, as she remembered what had gone on at Rosie's when she'd snuck out.

"I don't wanna go back, Kyle," she whispered through damp eyes.

"It's all right, cupcake," Mason slipped an arm around her shoulders and pulled her to him, resting his chin on her head. "It's your call, nephew," he turned to Kyle.

Kyle squeezed Nina's hand and took in a deep breath. He didn't want to go back, either. This place was like the Garden of Eden compared to the future. The air was pure and sweet, the rivers were clean and clear, he had his family here, not to mention the kindness of all the people. He had never felt so at home anywhere. The only thing missing was Aunt Rosie. What did he have in the future? The FBI waiting for him? That, along with a million other reasons was enough to make him want to stay, but the burning question at the moment was why his grandfather expected him to leave right away. He had to find out the reason.

"Look, my grandfather has visions —"

"We know all about that," Chase interrupted. "We've all had them. Not to take anything away from Ghostkiller, he's a great man, but tell me what you think we have accomplished by coming back here?"

Kyle looked at Chase thoughtfully. Yes, his grandfather had visions, but so did he, and as much as he didn't want to return to the future, that wasn't the real reason for his hesitation.

They were not finished here. Had his grandfather seen

the same vision? Up until now, they had both seen the same things – maybe not the same visions, but the same outcomes. He had no intention of second-guessing what he had seen that morning in the river, and he simply had to find out if his grandfather had seen it, too.

"Okay, spill it, nephew," Mason said. "There's something going on that you're not telling us, I can feel it."

They had stuck with him this far, and Kyle knew the best thing he could do for them was to tell them the truth.

"I'll tell you, but you must be prepared for what I am about to say," Kyle looked around at them, and then his eyes settled on Nina. "It's not good."

52

The train carrying President Lincoln and his entourage chugged slowly into the station and came to an abrupt halt, sputtering steam and black smoke like a smoker clear the lungs. The Pinkerton Agency had a buggy waiting to take the President to a hotel where he would freshen up before boarding the wagon bound for Eagle's Beak at first light.

People began to gather around as rumors about the President being on the train circulated. He was greeted with cheers and a few jeers, but for the most part, had no trouble making his way to the buggy and then the hotel.

The Pinkertons were good at their job and surrounded the President on all sides to ward off any attempts on his life. They had groups stationed all over the town at certain lookout points. A group stood just beyond the train's engine, and it was this group that Herbert Tarkington made his way to after exiting the train.

Four men stood talking, each wearing a black band tied around his upper left arm, a signal that Tarkington had been told to look for. He recognized one of the men as Lee Baldwin, an agent he knew well from his days as a youth and the very person he wanted to speak to. He was tall and well-groomed in a brown pinstriped suit and dark brown hair neatly slicked back. He was stroking his mustache, which Tarkington remembered he always did while deep in thought. They had gone to school together back east and had worked together in his father's law firm before joining the Pinkerton agency. They parted ways shortly thereafter, when Tarkington took a job in Washington and Baldwin moved up to Maryland, but had always stayed in touch. Baldwin smiled and greeted him as he approached the group.

"Herbert, nice to see you again." Tarkington shook his hand as the other men nodded a greeting.

"You too, Lee. Have you secured the provisions we talked about?"

"To be sure, to be sure," Baldwin answered. "Do you have the money?"

Tarkington slipped him a note. "Take this over to the bank and the teller will count it out for you."

"Very good," Baldwin glanced over the banknote before folding it neatly and shoving it into his vest pocket.

"Thank you for all your help," Tarkington told him.

"Anything for our country, my good man," Baldwin said. "You will find everything you need in those three wagons over there." He nodded towards the livery where three wagons waited, their contents hidden beneath large canvas covers. "There are twenty men assigned to go along," Baldwin explained, "drivers, shooters, the whole nine yards, and an army of three hundred men are waiting for you in Omaha."

"Anyone in particular I should be looking for when I get there?" Herbert asked.

"Yes, a young man by the name of Custer was put in charge of the men out there. He's proven himself reliable for such an endeavor." Then leaning forward, Baldwin winked. "He's an aide-de-camp who won't be missed much if it goes bad." This brought a roar of laughter from the group.

They discussed Tarkington's route and Baldwin gave

him a map to follow. It was off the beaten path, so they would not be as easily detected, and ended at the banks of the Missouri River near Omaha. They were to then follow the river and down various tributaries to Eagle's Beak, where the majority of Indians were camped. Tarkington was adamant nothing would stop him from making sure the railroad plans were secure, and that those damnable Indians were wiped out once and for all. Lee Baldwin agreed. Ward Lamon was paying them well to make sure it got done and even promised to make Tarkington a member of the Masonic Lodge when it was all over, a position he'd coveted for quite a few years.

Tarkington was most excited about acquiring a new weapon called a Williams gun. It had been invented just last year, but he was told it had worked very well during the Battle of Seven Pines. It fired sixty-five rounds per minute and was the perfect defensive weapon. Using it along with the three cannons he'd secured for this assignment, he'd wipe those stinking redskins off the face of the planet once and for all and come away a hero. All he had to do was beat Lincoln to the camp, which should be easy enough. Eagle's Beak was only a day away.

Later, as he sat in the back of a bumpy wagon, he couldn't help but be pleased with himself. He had secured the men, the weapons, and all the ammunition he would need to put an end to this ridiculous Indian farce once and for all while making himself the richest man this side of the Mississippi at the same time. The group would travel all night and reach the outskirts of the Indian camp by morning. Sleeping in the wagon was just a hazard of the job, and one he could easily live with, especially with the rewards he would receive. Yes, indeed, life was going to be good for this dirt poor farm boy.

53

The group sat quietly while Kyle told them about the vision he had seen that morning on the water outside of the wedding lodge.

"I'm sure I could find the place if I looked."

They decided to go on a scavenger hunt. If they could go to Ghostkiller with tangible evidence, he might not be so quick to decide on the timing of their trip to the future. Although they knew he would listen to what Kyle had seen in his vision, they still wanted to check things out for themselves. No sense in worrying if there was nothing to worry about yet.

Nina and Kyle rode double on Macedone, with Mason and Chase following behind on their own horses. Kyle had an idea where he had seen the firefight, and they knew it was near the water. Although the Indians had scouts out all over, there was a chance that the group they were seeking just wasn't close enough to be detected yet.

They trailed a path that led further away from the village and then followed the river. They navigated their way easily, passing some of the most beautiful country any of them had ever seen. Nina commented that Nebraska was flat as a pancake, but had to admit that she loved the scenery. Wild flowers of every color dotted the green landscape, and some of the tallest sunflowers she had ever seen grew just off the path they followed. Kyle told them the path was an old Indian trail that the Crow used to use and that Ghostkiller had told him about it when they'd first set up the village.

They rode for a few hours and finally came to rest near a small stream that spilled into the river. They dismounted, and each took a long drink of the cool, clear water before leading the horses to do the same. Macedone stamped restlessly at the water's edge, nodding and shaking his head nervously, refusing to drink from it.

"What's a matter fella?" Kyle asked. He tried to stroke the stallion's neck, but Macedone shrugged off his hand and trotted a few feet away, then came back to stand beside Kyle. He did this four times, the last time bumping Kyle in the shoulder with his nose to make him pay attention.

"Look at that," Mason said. "He ain't playin' around."

"And I don't need a written invitation," Kyle said. "C'mon!"

He lifted Nina onto Macedone's back and then swung up behind her. Macedone took off at a dead run as soon as Kyle was mounted, almost unseating them both. Mason and Chase struggled to mount their horses and then raced to catch up. Macedone didn't stop until they were well down the path, sticking close to the river where they could be hidden in the trees. They came to a stop near a stand of weeping willows, close to an embankment that stood about shoulder height to the horses. Macedone waited patiently for Kyle and Nina to dismount and then nudged them over behind some brush.

"Damn, I wish he could talk," Kyle said as he ducked down.

"Easy boy!" Nina whispered as Macedone pushed her down beside Kyle. He then trotted back behind a pile of thorny briars, effectively hiding himself from sight. Mason and Chase galloped in a few minutes later, and once Kyle motioned them over, they quietly dismounted, leaving their horses a few feet behind Macedone.

"What are we lookin' at?" Mason asked as he and Chase hunkered down behind the bushes.

"This is the place," Kyle answered, "Macedone didn't bring us here for nothing."

A bugle sounded just then and the group scurried up the embankment, carefully peering through the tall grass.

"Confederate soldiers!" Nina gasped. Some were standing around eating; some were tearing down tents and packing wagons. A few stood off to the side, laughing while a man dressed in civilian clothes aimed his rifle at a critter rustling in nearby bushes. They looked rough, thin and dirty for the most part.

"Is it the men from your vision, Kyle?" Nina asked.

"Yes," Kyle answered grimly.

"Damn, if that's all they got to send, then I'd say the Indians are in pretty good shape," Chase muttered.

Several dozen tents were still set up and there were two more wagons loaded down and covered with canvas, making it impossible to see what was underneath, but another one sat uncovered near the edge of the camp, and the contents caught Nina's eye. It held a single piece of artillery and she shuddered at the thought of what it could do.

"See that gun mounted there?" she asked, pointing towards the back of the wagon.

"What is that, a Hotchkiss?" Chase asked.

"No, they haven't been invented yet," Mason answered. "That's a Williams Rapid Fire, a modern day machine gun, at least for this day and age. It was built around 1861 and shoots sixty-five rounds per minute."

Nina looked at them gravely. "What do you think they're planning to do with that?"

Before anyone dared speak of that, a roar of laughter

filled the air. Mason caught a glimpse of the man the others were laughing at. He was trying to shoot a rabbit in the brush and his aim wasn't the greatest.

"Tarkington!" Mason spat out. "You gotta be shittin' me!"

"What is it?" Chase asked, trying to get a look.

"It is Tarkington!" Mason whispered harshly. "What the hell is he doing here?"

"Oh, no!" Chase groaned.

"Not your Tarkington from the future," Kyle told them. "His ancestor, though. Remember, even he had a mother," he said dryly.

"The resemblance is nauseating," Mason sneered.

"C'mon!" Kyle urged. "We gotta get back!" They all backed down the small embankment, running to the horses. He lifted Nina onto Macedone's back as the others mounted up. "We've got to get back to the village and warn Ghostkiller and Little Crow!" Kyle said, "If they make it there with that William's gun…"

"Who goes there?" a voice boomed from the top of the hill. A young man scampered down the embankment, and losing his balance, he fell into the bushes.

"It's Injuns!" his voice slurred, as he tried to shout. "Injuns!"

Kyle turned quickly around in the direction of the voice and then looked back at the others.

"The veil!" Nina whispered to him. Two simple words but they all knew exactly what she meant.

Without another word, Kyle swung onto Macedone's back and the group raced back down the river. Nina took over the reins, and Kyle reached into his medicine bag. Although she had now seen it numerous times, Nina gasped as the beautiful blue aurora cast down its shadow, watched as the leaves kicked up and heard the now familiar sound of the giant vacuum cleaner. She braced herself as they ran headlong into the vortex and allowed it to swallow them up.

The young man in the brush didn't bother explaining what he had just seen to the men who came running. What could he have said anyway? That he saw two Indians holding a white couple hostage disappear into thin air? He knew they would've blamed the liquor or labeled him crazy, but he was still scratching his head when he stumbled into his tent and passed out.

54

The wagon train pulled into Omaha in the early morning hours just as the sun was coming up. Lincoln was never so glad to get out of a buggy in his life.

He'd insisted on traveling through the night; he was running behind schedule and he knew the Indians were him today. A few more hours and they would be at the river. He felt a bit nervous about meeting with Little Crow, and couldn't help but feel a bit guilty for assigning that idiot Sibley to head the team up there in Minnesota. Of course, he knew men were driven by their own minds and hearts and he wasn't responsible for Sibley's botch job. The man's heart was in the right place, but the greed of the traders and Indian agents was the real problem. He probably had started out with the best of intentions, but men like Sibley were empowered by greed and the draw of money had probably been too great for him. It was too easy to take advantage of the Indians, and Sibley and those agents wouldn't be the first or the last, to use the poor savages for their own personal gain. Lincoln couldn't wait to get this over with and had every intention of giving the Indians whatever they wanted just to get back east. There was a war going on and he had responsibilities to attend to, and the sooner he got back to them, the better.

Once in his room, he unpacked a fresh outfit and

waited for the hot water he ordered to be brought up. A good, hot soaking was what he needed, then a bite to eat and back on the road. They were due to meet an escort from Little Crow's camp this evening for the final trek to the Indian camp. He had gotten many reports through the night and his scouts reported "too many Indians to count" along the river. They said they didn't see any near Omaha, but Lincoln knew they were there in the trees and the brush, just out of sight. He knew they weren't stupid. The Sioux, in particular, were fierce fighters and, along with the Cheyenne, were the most feared, if for nothing else than their vast numbers. If the Indians decided to converge and organize a revolt against the United States, Lincoln was afraid there wasn't much he could do to stop them. He had little choice but to give into their demands; however, they deserved to be heard, of this he was sure.

What a mess it would be if the army went against them. The country was already seeing too much bloodshed with the war as it was, and what did the Indians want really? *Only to be left alone,* he thought. Surely, he could give them that.

A quarter of an hour later, he was soaking in a hot tub and planning a briefing for his cabinet. He had brought the key players along but did not ride or share a room with any of them. He didn't want to subject himself to their scrutiny. He had enough dealing with Hill.

No one had better dare to try to talk him out of signing anything or there would be hell to pay.

55

Macedone didn't stop after he leaped through the veil, and Mason and Chase's horses were snorting and lathered when they reached Ghostkiller's lodge. He and Little Crow were sitting outside when they arrived. Kyle dropped down from Macedone and approached his grandfather while the others remained mounted, waiting anxiously.

Ghostkiller stood and greeted his grandson.

"*Cinks*, I thought you were going back —"

"You must listen to me!" Kyle implored. "They are coming! There is a whole army coming with rapid-fire guns that will kill the people very quickly. I saw the vision this morning and then saw the men with my own eyes! They are less than a day's ride from here. You must have seen this, too – our visions have been the same!"

Ghostkiller regarded Kyle thoughtfully. "Tell me what it is you saw exactly."

Kyle took a deep breath, mentally trying to calm himself. That group of soldiers was far too close for comfort, and Ghostkiller might not be moved to act unless Kyle was just as convincing as he'd been when they arrived from the future.

Kyle recounted his vision that morning, what they had just witnessed and how they had to escape through the veil to get here. When he was finished, Little Crow signaled one of his sentries over to where they stood.

"Give the order that the camp is to be moved down river two miles behind the bluff known as Scout Hill. The Great White Father will be here soon and he must be protected, but no one else in the white camp shall have that luxury. All men should prepare to fight!"

Ghostkiller nodded his agreement to Little Crow and then turned to Kyle. "Come, sit with me a while. I have a story to tell you." But how Ghostkiller intended to explain that Kyle's vision he'd had at the river was of Ghostkiller's own death was another question altogether.

56

Lincoln's party was met by an assemblage of Indians far too numerous to count. As the sun began to set on the wagon train, they soon found themselves surrounded on all sides, and any thought of a takeover by the military was laughable at this point. Ward Lamon continued to spout off about how they should never have agreed to such a meeting in the first place, but Lincoln did not waver. Lamon was only doing it for show anyway, as he knew what lay ahead and trusted that Tarkington had everything under control. He couldn't have been more wrong, for on the other side of the Platte River which they traveled beside, a war party was mounting an attack.

Mason and Chase had asked to be a part of the war party, but Ghostkiller made it clear they were not to be involved and could only watch from the top of the hill.

"Only warriors are to go." He told them.

Kyle wasn't even permitted to do that.

"You must stay with your wife, *cinks*."

"I cannot stay back and have you risk your life!" Kyle insisted.

Ghostkiller smiled at him. "You must stay back, *Tokoja*, you cannot join us and run the risk of taking a life in this time. You cannot abuse the medicine in this way. Please try to understand me."

Kyle was not about to stay back with the women. After Ghostkiller and the others left, he settled Nina in Tory's lodge for safe keeping. Nina understood and begged him to stay safe. "I'll handle things here," she assured him.

Now, against Ghostkiller's wishes, Kyle was waiting in the wings, holding Ghostkiller's lance firmly in his hand. He looked just like the other Kit Fox Warriors assembled, all wore little foxes on their heads. They had the task of leading the party, and Kyle had no qualms about doing so. He had promised Nina if things went wrong, he would simply disappear through the veil to safety. Of course, he did not intend to do so. He was more than ready to fight the whites with all the pent up frustration he usually concealed on the surface, determined that the vision of Ghostkiller's death would not come true. It would be an honor to fight alongside him, and by the time Ghostkiller knew Kyle was there, it would be too late for him to do anything but let Kyle save him. He vowed to change it one way or another.

The party of Cavalry was moving along the river at a snail's pace and the war party had a great vantage point from the bluffs above. It would be a great moment when the shocked looks on their faces were replaced with terror at the sheer number of Indians that were getting ready to converge upon them. All at once, the soldiers were on alert and the warriors were racing down the hill towards them. Kyle clutched the lance close to his heart, said a prayer and with a war cry as old as the surrounding hills, was off and running.

Chase and Mason watched from the hilltop as war whoops sounded and the war party moved out, with Kyle following closely behind them. The men below were caught completely by surprise, but as luck would have it, the Williams Rapid Fire was already loaded and waiting. Three young soldiers jumped on it as soon as the fighting began and the sound of sixty-five rounds per minute soon filled the air. The bodies started falling immediately. Kyle rode up quickly behind the wagon, driving Ghostkiller's lance into one soldier's body, killing him instantly. Now with guns blazing, Kyle fired round after round, killing the two remaining soldiers in the wagon, while other warriors took over the machine gun and still others fired their rifles.

Everything was happening so fast, yet it seemed to go in slow motion. Kyle saw a man on another wagon striking matches in an attempt to light the wick of a huge canon. The picture of canon fire raining down on his people filled Kyle's mind, and the vision he'd had that morning began coming to life right in front of him. He aimed one of the pistols at the canon, and before the man could light it up, a bullet ripped through, blowing up the gunpowder beside it, tearing the man's arm off. A flaming arrow shot into one of the wooden barrels in the wagon, igniting the gunpowder inside; the whole thing exploded in a huge fireball with choking black smoke that could be seen for miles. It tore men from their horses, uprooted trees and flattened the surrounding landscape.

Macedone stayed on his feet while Kyle searched frantically through the heavy smoke for his grandfather. He spotted him about fifty feet away in hand-to-hand combat with another soldier. Kyle attempted to ride towards him but was halted by crossfire. In the confusion, he lost sight of him. Kyle dismounted, and when he turned to run in the direction he'd last seen his grandfather, a soldier came at him wielding a bayonet and drove it into the back of his shoulder. Instinctively, Kyle jerked away, turned, and came face to face with a wild-eyed soldier bearing down on him with his bayonet.

"You filthy Injun bastard! I'll kill you!" the man snarled

through gritted, yellow teeth. Time seemed to stand still as Kyle looked at the pure hatred in the man's eyes. Slobber came out of his mouth as he spat out each word. "I'll kill you!"

In that instant, Kyle knew what had created the dark entity, knew why all those innocent people had been killed in Moccasin Flats over the years since the hangings. The hatred that the whites had against the Indians had fed the dark spirits who dwelled upon the earth, bred by greed and prejudice. In that split second, Kyle knew he stood for all Indians who had been wronged. He stood for the ones who had been driven off their lands, all Indian Nations of the past, and the future generations, as well, and as the realization took over, Kyle calmly raised his gun and fired, simultaneously blowing the face of hatred, and the evil smile that inhabited it, into a thousand pieces of fragmented bone, brains, and blood.

As the headless figure fell to the ground, Kyle spit on it and shot it again and again as he let out a whoop for all those who had died before him, and then he shot it again just for good measure. He watched as the figure curled up into a tight, black ball that screamed above the roaring gunfire, that same hideous scream he remembered from the cave; a sanction of dead leaves and dust blew up and encircled it, a million black hands with gnarly fingers reached out, grasped it, and then carried it away in the vortex, disappearing with it into the haze of smoke and dust.

By the time Kyle turned to look for Ghostkiller, the fighting was over. He walked among the stench of gunpowder mingled with fresh blood, dust, and dirty white men's bodies. He never realized how filthy they were, and remembered the time Nina had told him that Europeans rarely bathed in those days and usually only in the month of May. It was the reason June was a popular month for marriage because they still smelled relatively fresh. The tradition of women holding a bouquet of flowers was to cover the smell of their body odor in case they started to reek by the wedding.

A warrior clasped his hand, telling him it was a good fight; the Indians lost only six men and two ponies while the Cavalry lost all three hundred men who were there.

The history books would have a good massacre story now. But this time the Indians were victorious, Kyle thought bitterly.

As he picked his way past the dead bodies, he thought long and hard about each of them, their spirits. He prayed for them as he walked, but was ever mindful of his grandfather. He heard Mason call out to him and walked in that direction, picking up a discarded bandana and wrapping it around his injured shoulder. A few minutes later, he caught up with Chase and Mason.

"Kyle! Are you all right?" Mason asked, examining the bloodied bandana.

"I'm fine," Kyle waved him off. "I've gotta find my grandfather. Let's go!"

They passed warriors gathering guns and horses and helping the injured into wagons, but no one had seen Ghostkiller. They split up to search, but a sudden shout in the distance caused Mason to turn around. It was a familiar voice.

"You filthy bastard!"

Mason whirled around and watched as Tarkington raised his gun in Kyle's direction.

"Kyle!"

Tarkington turned towards Mason before he had the chance to fire, and Mason pulled his 9mm sighting down on the man. Chase pulled his gun, but Mason stayed him.

"Please, allow me. Kiss my ass, Tarkington!" Mason yelled then fired, blowing a hole in Tarkington's chest. He fell to the ground like a sack of potatoes.

Kyle looked up, letting out the breath he'd been

holding. "Thanks."

Just then, Chase spotted a wagon on its side.

"Kyle," he yelled, jutting his chin just a few feet from where they stood.

Ghostkiller lay in a pool of blood a short distance from where the wagon with the machine gun had overturned. The heavy gun lay on top of him and he was bleeding from his mouth. The three men rushed towards Ghostkiller, and Kyle dropped to his knees.

"Oh God!" he cried, taking hold of the heavy machine gun and trying to lift it. "Help me!" Kyle shouted to Mason and Chase, who ran to him and took hold. They tried to lift it, but it was no use.

The three men began calling to the other warriors, and soon a large group gathered to help. In the end, it took eleven of them to haul the heavy firearm off of Ghostkiller. He was barely breathing as Kyle gingerly lifted his head onto his lap.

"Hang on. We will get you help."

"No, *cinks*," Ghostkiller choked out. "You must...let me...go."

"No!" Kyle shook his head and hugged the old man close to him. "I came here to save you!"

Ghostkiller smiled weakly. "You have done your job, son. There are some things...in the past...you cannot change. Some things are...just...meant...to...be. The medicine....it is..."

Ghostkiller heaved one last sigh and his body went limp. Kyle tried frantically to revive him, but it was useless. He gathered Ghostkiller's body into his arms and held him close. "Tunkasila! No! No!" He sobbed, rocking the lifeless body back and forth. His vision had been foretold. Ghostkiller was dead.

57

Lincoln sat beside Little Crow in the designated treaty lodge. Along with the lawmakers of his cabinet, they were the only white men in attendance. He wondered how the Indians knew who to ask for to make sure the decision-makers were included in the signing, wondered how they knew once those men signed this treaty with him it would be set in stone. Half the senate was with him, so there would be no going back to Washington to debate it, as they normally would have. He watched as the young and beautiful white girl, who had been introduced as Nina Ghostkiller, read off the terms of Article 1 of the new treaty. He thought briefly that the name Ghostkiller sounded familiar, but dismissed the notion as he listened to what she was saying.

Nina trembled as she held the papers she had so tediously worked on over the past few hours. With Kyle and the others gone, she'd had to write it by herself. She had gone by memory of what they had discussed before, and Little Crow's interpreter was a big help. Little Crow had offered his input, as did a few of the other chiefs, but details were lost in the language barrier, she was sure. This was so important and she really had to trust in herself as she never had before. These people were counting on her. She was about to rewrite history. She took a deep breath and tried to calm herself.

She stood inside the lodge, surrounded by Abraham

Lincoln and the lawmakers of his cabinet. Her emotions threatened to overtake her and she almost laughed out loud as she looked around at men from the past whom she had only read about in history books. She teared up when she looked at Lincoln, knowing he would be killed in three years by an assassin's bullet. She vowed that if she awoke and found that this was all a dream, she was going to write a book about it. This had to be the longest and most detailed dream she'd ever had.

She had not made many changes to Article One, so it was not much different than the Fort Laramie Treaty of 1868. It included a call for truce between the United States and the Indian Nations in attendance and much to Lincoln's relief, it included all of the so- called 'troublemakers' of the plains, and he found it easy to agree with its terms. Perhaps this wasn't going to be as hard as he'd once thought.

Article Two was much more detailed, however, and thanks to her handy work, it was written in favor of the Indians, as were the other fifteen Articles. Anything referring to the United States benefiting in any way at all had been left out.

She had been excited to get started, but now with Kyle gone to fight, she was lucky to keep from throwing up. Where were her husband and Ghostkiller? What if something had gone wrong? What if Kyle had been killed in that battle? No, if something had happened to him, she would've felt it. She tensed up when Little Crow caught her eye and motioned for her to continue. She hesitated for only an instant longer, hoping that Kyle and the others would duck through the flap at any moment.

She again took a deep breath and began to read Article Two:

"The United States agrees that the following district of

country, to wit, viz: commencing on the east bank of the Missouri River...," she glanced up as she read to watch the faces of the white men in the meeting as she named all lands that encompassed present-day North and South Dakota, Montana, Northern Nebraska, and Wyoming. She had to stifle a grin when one of the senators almost choked as she read the size of the land mass: 4,431,464 square miles.

> All land mentioned herewith is officially set apart for the absolute and undisturbed use and occupation of the Indians herein named, and for such other friendly tribes or individual Indians as from time to time, they may be willing to admit amongst them; and the United States now solemnly agrees that no persons, except those Indians herein designated and authorized to do so, shall ever be permitted to pass over, settle upon, or reside in the territory described in this article and henceforth they will and are hereby entitled to all claims and rights in and to any portion of this Territory, including mineral rights, as is embraced within the writings aforesaid, and except as hereinafter provided by authority of said Indian tribes. These lands hereinto named shall be governed by the Indians aforementioned and the United States government shall have no jurisdiction over any portion of the Territory named hereof.
>
> It is further agreed that any and all annuity payments owed to the Santee Sioux as designated by the United States in any past treaties, and any additional amounts submitted by Indians named in said treaties, shall be paid in full, as specified by said Indians, as soon as possible. It is further agreed that all Indians who were involved with and have survived the

battle hereinafter known as the Great Sioux Uprising shall not be charged with any crime, and those formally charged shall enjoy a full and indisputable pardon by the President of the United States and all attempts at pursuit and prosecution shall henceforth cease and desist immediately.

Nina glanced up when she heard more coughs out of the men from Washington, and that's when she saw Kyle, Mason, and Chase enter and take a seat near the door. Kyle's face was impassive, but she saw the bloody bandages covering his shoulder. When she started to go to him, he held up his hand and managed a weak smile of encouragement, urging her to continue reading. The next half hour passed slowly as she read all seventeen articles, warily keeping an eye on Kyle. Finally, she got to the last paragraph:

> It is hereby expressly understood and agreed by and between the respective parties to this treaty that the execution of this treaty by the United States Senate shall have the effect, and shall be construed as abrogating and annulling all treaties and agreements heretofore entered into between the respective parties hereto. Furthermore, from this day forward, this treaty known as The All Nations Treaty shall be legal and binding for all time and shall remain in effect for all time. No governmental entity, deliberately or otherwise, shall have the authority, under any circumstance, to compromise or waiver this treaty or any part thereof, not even in the case of National Security or Marshall Law. Furthermore, any governmental agency or parties in its employ that attempt to compromise or waiver this treaty in any

way, shape, form or fashion, legally or illegally, shall be held in contempt of this treaty and subject to the punishments as set forth by the Indian Nations hereinto named.

In testimony of all which, we, the said commissioners, and we, the chiefs and headmen of all Indian Nations hereinto named, have hereunto set our hands and seals at Eagle's Beak, Nebraska Territory, this twenty-fifth day of September, in the year one thousand eight hundred and sixty-two.

Lincoln's hand was shaking as he dipped the pen into the inkpot. He felt a great sigh of relief wash over him knowing this would put an end to Indian trouble in Minnesota and prevent any future upheaval in the territories. He had been right; all they wanted was their land, and he knew deep down he was doing the right thing. The Santee wanted their money for the land in Minnesota, and it was rightfully theirs. He wasn't sure how he could pay them with the Civil War raging but vowed to do his best. Indians didn't want money anyway. They just wanted to be left alone to live in peace.

He signed the treaty on the back of Hannibal Hamlin and then passed the quill and paper down the line. As he watched the rest of his cabinet sign their names, he was already thinking of Mary and the sweet smells of home. There were clauses in the treaty he didn't quite understand; things about future Supreme Court rulings and congressional input being null and void when it referred to the Indians, but it didn't matter. It was easy to agree with these terms.

He could now feel good about going back to Washington with a clear conscience. He had freed the slaves and had now given the Indians a place to call home that would never be disturbed by white men. Now he could get back to the war that was exploding all throughout the states.

58

Nina was devastated with the news of Ghostkiller's passing and was having a hard time accepting what the consequences of it might be.

"What the hell are we going back to?" She asked Kyle. "After what the four of us went through to save him, what could the future possibly hold now? Is it different? Did we change anything?"

Kyle took his wife into his arms, and then glanced at Mason and Chase. He didn't know how to answer her.

They sat on the riverbank, their horses grazing on the lush grass behind them. Macedone seemed relaxed and none the worse for wear as he munched on some clover.

"I honestly don't know what we are going back to," he told her. "I can't tell any of you what to expect when we get there."

Chase sighed and lit one of the cigarettes Tory had given to him. She had thoughtfully rolled a dozen of them while he was gone. He thought of what his life might be like if he stayed here with her. It was too bad he hadn't had time to get to know her better. The cigarette didn't taste too bad, and he could tell a big difference between it and the chemical laden ones of the future.

Mason looked out over the river as he chewed on a long piece of grass. His hat rested on his bent knee and he fought the urge to take off his boots and jump into the freezing water. It was probably just what he needed to clear the numbness out of his head. The old man was dead and there was no bringing him back now.

"Hey, wait a minute!" he blurted out. "Why not just go back to the battle and save him? Isn't that what we started out to do anyway? Chase, you were given the lance, I was given the messages, and maybe it is up to us to save him and not you, Kyle."

"No, no!" Kyle shook his head. "No one goes through the veil on Macedone but me. The medicine is much too dangerous."

"Then take us back," Chase said. "This can't be it, Kyle. We can't have lost the old man so soon after coming back to save him!"

"No!" Kyle released Nina and stood. "He told me that some things are just meant to be, and this is what he meant!"

"But he died before his time!" Nina said. "He wasn't supposed to die until December twenty-sixth."

"And you have a wonder horse, Kyle, a veritable time machine that you can use however and whenever you want!" Chase argued.

"No! He'd probably still be alive if I had listened to him and not gone to the battle on Macedone!" Kyle cried. "Now leave it alone!"

"*Hiya!*" A voice said from behind them. They all turned simultaneously to see Little Crow walking towards them at a determined pace. As he approached, they saw an escort filing down the river with Lincoln and his entourage.

"Please, let's all sit down," Little Crow said. He was generally a quiet man and one who would not tolerate shouting. Once they were seated, he spoke softly to the group.

"It is not polite to speak of the dead, but I will tell you

that *Wanagi Kte* knew what his own future held and died honoring his people. He knew the price that had to be paid to secure the future and the lands of our grandfathers. Any warrior would happily lay his life down to protect that. And as keeper of sacred medicine, Kyle knows that medicine must be kept in a delicate balance. He has no right to abuse that." They all turned when Macedone gave a whinny of approval.

"I know this is hard for you to understand," Little Crow sighed, "but you must know that to protect the ways that are sacred to us is the most important thing. That is what Ghostkiller was protecting. These sacred ways have been handed down from generation to generation. The land, the ceremonies, it all has to be protected. There are still things about the medicine you must learn, *Wakinyan Hoksidan*. You all have done a good thing by coming here. Other things that belong in a delicate balance are now so. Things have been changed and it is good. Perhaps it is time that you make the final ride, and then you shall see it also."

Wakinyan Hoksidan -Thunder Boy. No one had said Kyle's name while they had been in the past. He had never told anyone, not even Nina, what his name was. It was told to him years ago by Grandpa James. It was a sacred name and one he had protected through the years. He had received it from his father when he was a baby, just before he died. James said Kyle was named after He Runs With Thunder, Ghostkiller's grandson. Tears stung his eyes.

With their meager belongings packed and their goodbyes said, the group struck out on their journey home, Kyle on Macedone, Nina on Dapple, and Chase and Mason on the two horses Little Crow had gifted to them.

They discussed where they should come out on the other side, but it really didn't matter as long as they stayed on the west side of the Missouri. There would undoubtedly be someone or something there that would let them know whether things had changed or not. Kyle wanted to come out in the vicinity of Mount Rushmore. If the faces were not on the mountain, they would know for sure that things had worked out the way Ghostkiller's vision had foretold, and his loss would not have been in vain. Everyone agreed.

As they rode through the veil and into awareness, a faint drumbeat began to replace the loud swoosh and suction of the vortex. The scattered leaves swirled around them, drawing them gently out and onto the ground at the foot of a mountain. The group stopped their horses and took in their environs. As the veil lifted up into the heavens, they could hear a faint drumbeat

They stood in a valley surrounded by hills of towering pines, and huge rocks holding court with nature. The scents of sagebrush, wild sweetgrass, and pine hung heavily in the air. The pine trees were such a dark green that the distant hills looked black; it wasn't too hard to figure out that they had come out exactly where Kyle had intended.

"Let's ride to the top and see what we can see," Kyle suggested. He took Nina's hand and they rode slowly side by side towards the base of one of the hills, with Mason and Chase riding in single file behind them. They chose a hill with a well-worn path, and as they ascended the long incline, trepidation radiated from the group. All at once, they took note of the drum beat growing louder, until the ground seemed to shake beneath them.

"Where is that coming from?" Mason asked. "The other side of this hill?"

"It sounds almost like it's coming *out* of the hill," Chase said, and the other three looked at him as if he had just grown two heads.

"You amaze me sometimes, Riley," Mason laughed.

"What?" Chase was confused. "What'd I say?"

"Well, for someone who doesn't understand a whole lot, you say the most profound things sometimes," Kyle said, and they all joined in his laughter when Chase finally got it. They sobered quickly, however, as they realized what they were hearing — it was the heartbeat of the *He Sapa*, the Black Hills.

Macedone became restless, as did the other horses, and with a whoop, the riders let them go. They raced past each other, laughing and cheering as they ran, feeling the freedom that they prayed would greet them on the other side. Cresting the top of the hill, they were stunned to see thousands of lodges in the valley below. A sentry was making his way towards them, and as he drew near, Mason recognized Thorn Rivers, dressed in leggings and moccasins, his hair to his waist. Thorn smiled as he shook each of their hands.

"Hau, Koda," he said to each of them, "We've been expecting you."

Mason smiled at Thorn, clapping him on the back. Thorn's hair was the first sign that things were different; it was good to know that the curse had not killed Thorn's niece, who had committed suicide on the other timeline. Kyle noticed Thorn's hair, too. He hoped that this also meant that Mt. Rushmore would not be waiting for them in the distance.

As the group headed up towards the peak of the rise, they could feel the heartbeat of the earth beneath their feet and realized what they were hearing. The sound of all the Sioux Nations playing their drums at the powwow below filled the air, creating a unified heartbeat that had never before been heard in this or in any other time.

At the top of the hill, Kyle looked off in the distance where a huge stone mountain sat with its sheer wall facing east. The heads of Mount Rushmore should have been there, yet it was empty, devoid of all traces of the white men who had become presidents. Kyle grinned and pointed, and they all cheered as realization dawned on each of them. Kyle leaned into Nina, giving her a kiss that seared her from head to toe.

"Welcome home, Mrs. Ghostkiller," he smiled to her.

As their horses pranced towards the village, they heard Aunt Rosie's voice calling the children for fry bread, and the voices of the Sioux Nations began to rise up in celebration of a life they had grown to love, a life they had been free to live, and a grand homecoming that was underway for the time travelers.

In the distance behind them, a rush of wind crept up the side of the hill carrying with it a small, swirling ball of black dust and leaves. It hovered as it watched the horses trot down the other side, then hurled itself over the treetops, scampered behind them, and silently laughed on its way toward the bottom.

The sequel:
Scattered Leaves: Beyond the Legend

CHAPTER ONE

"Last stop, Nebraska Territory!" Father Wilson O'Rourke awoke suddenly to the sound of a loud male voice making its way down the corridor of the Amtrak train. He struggled beneath heavy covers, easing himself up from the bunk in his small compartment and shuffled his elderly frame to the door, opening it quickly.

"Nebraska Territory?" the Father called, "I thought this train was going to Montana?"

The young man stopped short and turned towards O'Rourke, making a face, "Montana? Never heard of the place!" The young man smiled; it was a smile that instantly said he thought O'Rourke was just some nice old man suffering from *some-timers.*

"Montana is north of Wyoming," O'Rourke informed him impatiently. When the young man didn't answer, O'Rourke continued. "Surely you know if this train forges west of Minnesota or not?"

With a look of confused understanding, the young man answered, "Oh, you mean Indian territory? No, sir, trains don't travel into Indian country." He grinned happily, revealing a dimple in each cheek. "'Course, the railroad tried to get permission over the years, but the Indians wanted nothing to do with it. They were always perfectly happy with their paved roads leading to the casinos, though!" With that, the young man tipped his hat and walked onward, shouting that they were approaching their last stop to all who could hear him.

    O'Rourke stood in the corridor, fighting the panic that threatened to overtake him. His heart sank as what the young man said registered in his mind. A picture of Kyle Ghostkiller flashed through his head and he remembered the t-shirt Kyle wore the last day he saw him. *My Heroes Have Always Killed Cowboys.* It was, in and of itself, a prophecy.

    He quickly closed the door of his compartment and hurried to the small window beside the bunk. Throwing up the sash, he noted that the landscape was flat and green, typical of Nebraska, with a vault of blue sky that seemed to go on forever. *This is Nebraska*! He thought. But if he were in Nebraska, what happened to Montana, his sister and everyone in Moccasin Flats?

ABOUT THE AUTHOR

Lynny Prince and her husband are founders of Red Road Awareness, an organization that helps American Indians in crisis, and are members of the Native American Intertribal Alliance.

Her Ghostkiller character is based on a warrior named Caske, (pronounced Chas-Kay) who was pardoned by President Abraham Lincoln after the Great Sioux Uprising of 1862, but perished along with the rest of the "Dakota 38." It is her privilege to honor Caske in this book.

Ms. Prince is a musician who also enjoys horseback riding, genealogy, and gourmet cooking.
Please visit her website: www.lynnyprince.com or write to: lynny@lynnyprince.com

Printed in Poland
by Amazon Fulfillment
Poland Sp. z o.o., Wrocław